A CAMEL

CALLED

SWEETPEA

A CAMEL CALLED SWEETPEA

Wendy Guilfoyle

First published in Great Britain in 2022 by Serenity Creations
Copyright © 2022 by Wendy Guilfoyle
Formatted by The Amethyst Angel
Cover Design by PSG Creative

ISBN: 979-8366-208-34-5

First Edition

To all those who have stepped outside their comfort zone
and found something unexpectedly wonderful.

Acknowledgements

My heartfelt thanks to those who have given me their professional and personal support throughout the long process of 'finding' the story that lay hidden in the unknown farmhouse nestled in the arms of an old volcano in Lanzarote, that I saw on a bus tour of the island.

Sam Hartley, of Red Pen Editing, for her knowledge and expertise in story-telling and for guiding me through the development of a story through to crafting a book. She has been very patient and perceptive with an eagle eye for errors and excellent suggestions for improvement.

My thanks to Patrick Guilfoyle of 'PSG Creat!ve' for the eye-catching and intriguing book cover design.

My special thanks also to Michelle Gordon of The Amethyst Angel for navigating all the intricate stages of bringing the book to print on my behalf. Michelle has been so patient, guiding me through each difficulty calmly and clearly. It has been much appreciated.

On a personal level, I would like to thank my friends from CAP+ - Paul James, Lee Blue-Sky and Peter Smith - whose constant support and encouragement kept me going when I was close to giving up on many occasions.

And of course, my friends and support sisters, Kay, Penny and Julia, for enduring months of me whittering on about camels and Lanzarote without making me feel I was crazy and for giving me the courage and determination to complete the story.

Chapter One

"Are you sure? Are you speaking to the right person?" Sarah's eyes widened with disbelief. "I had no idea I had any relatives there! How do you know? Does anyone in my family know about this person?"

She was speechless, as questions stacked up too quickly in her mind to access, like biscuits in an unopened packet. She was sitting in the office of Selby and Mortimer, a firm of barristers and lawyers, back in her home town where her mother still lived. She had just heard that she was the beneficiary of a farm in the north-west of Lanzarote in the Canary Islands. "I have no Spanish relatives. There must be some mistake!"

Mr. Selby smiled at Sarah's reaction. He wasn't surprised: the news of the legacy was quite out of the blue for him and he had known and worked for the family for three generations. He had known about this 'mysterious' relative in Lanzarote but not what the mystery was about. He was a solicitor of the 'old school'; very formal and always dressed in a dark grey three-piece suit with a neat waistcoat and a watch chain looped across his chest. He wore a smart trilby on his commute to and from the office as well as his leather brief case. He had been a solid, continuous presence in Sarah's life.

"No, Miss Jones, there has been no mistake. Your great-aunt Clara moved there as a young woman. She had read about the island and became fascinated by it, when doing some research on Sir Walter Raleigh – apparently, he used the island as a base for seizing gold from Spanish ships, which were returning home from South America. She went there and saw a plot of land with a house and outbuildings for sale. She fell in love with it straight away. There was something about the house and the area that drew her in, and she immediately felt comfortable. She explained it in a letter to her sister that it was like putting on an old comfortable pair of slippers. She bought it on impulse, came back home to sell her house and surplus belongings and left England. I heard, unofficially, that she did return, briefly, after only a couple of years. There was some difficulty I believe, some mystery, but nothing was conveyed to me. Gossip likes to make scandal of a mystery but none was discovered. She may have been here for a few months, perhaps to spend time with her family after her spontaneous departure, I can only conjecture. After that, she returned to Lanzarote and never came back to England."

Mr Selby continued to explain what older family members seem to remember about her departure, but no-one was quite sure why she left. There had always been some mystery or even a secret surrounding it, to which some of the wider family had referred obliquely. However, there seemed to be no-one alive these days who might shed any light on it; no aunts or uncles from that generation were still alive.

He went on to tell Sarah, "Your mother is unaware of any scandal. At that time, I gather, most of Clara's very conservative family were outraged by her behaviour, especially as she wasn't even married. A single woman going off to an unknown island to become a farmer! On her own; no chaperone or anything. It was unheard of in polite society at that time. It was a very different then, as you know. No one spoke about her or communicated with her after her departure. No one, that is, except one sister, your grandmother. They wrote to each other, regularly, in secret, using this office as the P.O. box, which is how I know about this part of the story."

Sarah was really intrigued to learn all this about her family. It was rather exciting. She was impressed by Clara's spontaneity and courage. Did she have a similar daring streak in her like her great aunt? It had remained latent if she had, especially since she had grown up and taken on a responsible job in finance now.

"Oh, my goodness!" said Sarah. "I don't know what to say. Part of me is thinking there must be some mistake and a part of me is curious to know more; more about this relative, more about the farm and how I fit into all this. I have no experience of gardening let alone farming. We didn't even live near one. Why did she leave it to me of all people? I have been in finance since university."

Mr. Selby silently agreed with her. Sarah looked very much the successful city girl. She was 32, slim and of average height. Today, her black hair was drawn back into a neat side pleat, and she was dressed in black trousers, cut straight legged with pleats at the front. She wore them with a cream silk top and a fashionable taupe jacket, with just slightly padded shoulders. The office was filled with the delicate scent of an expensive perfume. That, the outfit, together with the statement earrings, made her appear the least likely person to want to or make a success of farming.

Sarah was thinking the same thing. She looked down at her elegant, red-soled, high heeled shoes, wondering what she would look like in wellies. There was nothing in her life that gave even a hint of rural activities.

"This all sounds so improbable, Mr. Selby, but I must admit to feeling rather curious. Do you know any more about the farm or this great aunt?"

"I know a little," said Mr. Selby. "Gwen, your grandmother, told me a certain amount, more to explain why they were using this office as their contact address and emphasise the need for secrecy. She never divulged why the secrecy was necessary."

Mr Selby went on to explain that Gwen had told him that as the farm got more productive, Clara regularly sent her money, via this office, keeping the arrangement between them and the solicitor, Mr Selby, so no other family members knew of the arrangement. Gwen said the extra money was to go into an investment but wouldn't say what kind of investment. When it came time to make her will and do something about the farm, Clara decided Gwen was too old to be able to handle the farm and, by then, not at all well. Sarah's mother, Clara's niece, was too attached to her home here in England, so would in no way want to go to

4

Lanzarote to live, let alone run a farm.

Mr Selby continued his story, "However, when you were born, she became very interested. Gwen told me that she was always asking questions about you. It amused her that her sister should show so much interest in her grandniece. Gwen told me that Clara was delighted to learn that you were very independent, adventurous and creative – your grandmother's description of you. Your mother thought you were obstinate, naughty and a constant worry as to what you would get up to next!"

Sarah laughed. "I remember the day mum thought I was stuck up a tall tree in the garden and called the fire brigade to get me down. She remarked I was too daring for my own safety. However, by the time the fire engine arrived, I was more than halfway down. Mum didn't know whether to be relieved or furious. I remember she was very embarrassed to have to tell the men I was alright after all. They were not at all worried. A cup of tea and some cake from mum helped the situation a lot I think."

Sarah smiled at that incident and recalled other times when she had worried her mother a lot. She had always felt quite confident that she would be safe.

Mr. Selby, concerned that Sarah would be offended by such a description, hastened to explain, with an apologetic smile, that these were the words Clara had used in the Will, not his.

He was 67 and already past retiring age really, but continued to work in the firm with great interest and ability, adding a sense of continuity for their more senior clients, as well as having a lot of experience to hand on to young interns, should they ask. He had been Sarah's family's solicitor since he started at the firm and had that particular friendship that can develop with clients over time. He had no children of his own and had been aware of young Sarah's adventurous spirit developing over the years. He had done what he could, within the limits of his position, to encourage her development at every opportunity. He went on to adopt a more paternal, but still professional, relationship with her since the untimely death of her own father when she was quite young.

Encouraged by Sarah's comment he continued, "When your aunt became ill, she made this new Will, leaving her farm to you. She never married nor had any children, as far as anyone knows. She wanted you to have it."

"Did my great aunt give any reason why she decided to leave it to me?" asked Sarah. "It does seem strange considering I didn't know she existed until now. My mother has never mentioned her."

"There is no clue in the wording of the Will except a brief reference to your personality, your ability to respond to novel incidents and a streak of daring and adventure in you. Perhaps she saw a younger version of herself in you? I don't know. However, as you might expect or not there are some conditions for you to comply with before the farm can be signed over to you."

He glanced enquiringly over at Sarah to see if she wanted him to continue. He had been talking for a long time.

"Please go on Mr. Selby. This all so amazing. I need to hear all the details."

He continued with a nod of the head and a smile.

"One is that you have to live there for five years at least. She left a considerable amount of money, being a very astute and hard-working lady. You have a portion of this money when you initially move there, to help you with the cost of getting there and settling in. After living there continuously for two years, you will receive another lump sum. The remaining monies are to be released after living there for a total of five years. Then the farm can be signed over to you. You haven't been left a holiday cottage. The initial sum will be £30,000."

"Do I have a choice?" asked Sarah. "What if I don't want it?"

As she asked these questions, Sarah had a fleeting glimpse in her mind's eye of a woman in her 50s standing by a white, flat-roofed building, smiling, shaking her head and beckoning a happy welcome. Sarah frowned and shook her head; what was that? It had been so quick; she was sure she had imagined it. It was if she had inadvertently tapped into someone else's photos on their mobile phone. That was ridiculous. Her phone was switched off and in her bag. She shook her head. She shook her head again and put the incident down to the shock she felt at the news. "Farming in Lanzarote? Me?" A treacherous, quiet voice at the back of her mind whispered "Why not you?"

"There is no clause in here to clarify that I'm afraid. Perhaps she knew you would accept the challenge?"

The meeting with Mr Selby was over and Sarah was in her favourite coffee shop in an easy chair in a quiet corner with a large latte at her side. She was trying to understand why her great aunt had decided to leave the farm to her, when she had no idea of the existence of this relative. She went over in her mind what the solicitor had said.

Sarah remembered then that there was no mention of what would happen if she refused to take on the farm; it was, indeed, as if her great aunt knew that she would accept the challenge. She wasn't sure whether to feel herself truly recognised by this assumption or outraged by the presumption of it. This was such unexpected and amazing news: it was difficult to take it all in. Living on a farm for five years! Sarah had no idea what that would entail, or even if she was capable of doing it. She needed some time to absorb the news and to work out the implications it would have on her life.

Since Sarah's father had died, Mr. Selby had taken more of a paternal interest in Sarah. He had always been available for Sarah to discuss any decisions she had had to make at different stages of her life. This new development certainly was one of those times when more in depth discussion was necessary.

She had valued the extra time she had had with Mr. Selby earlier that day after he had read through the details of the Will. He put aside his professional hat so they could go over in detail what the implications might be if she accepted the conditions of the Will and went to Lanzarote. They discussed what the fall back would be if it didn't work out and what to do about her apartment; whether to sell it or rent it out.

In the end, they both decided it would be best for Sarah to go home and talk to her mother about it. Before leaving the coffee shop, Sarah checked her phone diary to remind herself of the time they had arranged to meet the next day to discuss it further.

She phoned her mother to see if she was at home and would have the time for a chat; she led a very active life, doing some activity most evenings. She told Sarah that she was at work and had planned to go out to choir practice later in the evening.

"Are you in the area? Rather than chat on the phone, why don't you come round. It would be lovely to see you. I was only thinking yesterday, it is a while since we caught up on the gossip! I'll be home in half an hour or so, come then and we can have something to eat together."

"That would be perfect, Mum," answered Sarah, "I'm not far away as I came down to see Mr. Selby – which is why I want to have a chat. Shall I bring something for pudding?"

Elizabeth said there was no need as she had something there that would be enough for the two of them.

Having got that all set up, Sarah hung up. Even with the time spent over a coffee, going over in her mind her meeting with Mr. Selby, her head was still in a whirl. She decided to go for a walk until it was time to go to her mum's house for tea. She considered this new development as she walked through the small park. In one way it was an answer to the questions she had been asking the Universe for some time. "What do I do now? Where do I go from here?" without having any idea as to what answer could possibly come from the life that she presently knew. She and her husband, David, had just ended their long-term relationship. They had been an item at university and got married soon after graduating.

The demands of living and working in the Finance sector in London had taken its toll on both of them. Over the years, the white-hot passion of student days had cooled. They had been too busy building their own careers, Sarah saw now. Neither had noticed that now there was no passion, there was no bedrock of friendship or love to keep them together. Imperceptibly, their relationship had slowly changed until they were living lives independently of one another. They did sometimes talk to each other, but it had become more and more a monologue as David insisted on talking about his own ideas. If she didn't agree, he argued with her, determined to prove his opinion was the only correct one. To avoid the quarrels, Sarah had got in the habit of shutting down and letting him carry on, without any input or gainsay from her. She began to feel lonely, but unable to express her feelings. If she tried, he would counter it by saying they were both busy, what did she expect – being wined and dined every night? They had a lovely house and good jobs, a manageable mortgage that between them had shrunk down from the original precipitous heights and they had friends. 'This is life in London, babe. Get over yourself.' was what he usually said, making her feel foolish for questioning their lifestyle and his attitude towards her. However, she knew he had become more dismissive and belittling recently. It was very hard.

One evening, quite out of the blue, David had drawn attention to this collapse, saying that to continue as they were seemed a nonsense. He had a new, more fulfilling relationship with someone else and wanted a divorce. That was a shock. He had not admitted to any difficulty between them before. There had been only the quiet swish as her feelings were swept to one side – again. She saw all these subtle changes in retrospect now that he had gone.

Sarah felt numb. She was 32; they had been together for so long. She couldn't imagine life without him, even though it had lost some of the chemistry and spark of Uni days. Nevertheless, they were older now and had demanding jobs to maintain. It was bound to be different from those distant carefree days, wasn't it? David had always countered her questions about their relationship by asking her what did she expect. The question always caught her by surprise. She didn't really know what she had expected. Clearly, she had expected something different from how it was now, for her to begin to question it. However, she couldn't quite pinpoint why it wasn't satisfactory. If she thought about it at all, Sarah put it down to exhaustion. Amongst the turbulent emotions following David's announcement, she realised they had continued more or less out of habit.

The shock following the request for a divorce became anger, then a sense of betrayal, grief, and by the time she was able to accept her new situation sometime later, she found she was relieved. She had often felt tense when David started arguments and shouted at her. She hated it and had no energy for such outbursts after a day's work. Now, she wouldn't always have to do what someone else wanted or tolerate being put down, she had a sense of a door opening to a new future. What that would be, she had no idea. Meanwhile there were the logistics of separation and divorce to attend to. They had had no children, so all they had to do was to divide their belongings and sell the house.

After many delicate but amicable conversations, they had an agreement drawn up about how things would be settled, shook hands on it, signed a few papers and that was it.

All that process had just come to an end. They had a buyer for their house. David had found another one and would soon be moving in. That part of her life was all over.

Sarah had come to a full stop. She had bought a small apartment for the time being, putting the remainder of the money from the divorce settlement into savings until she knew where she would be going. Excess furniture and things she wouldn't need immediately went into storage, but she still had no idea what she would do next. Everything had changed and was changing so rapidly.

The job that she had had for a decade had altered dramatically. It was no longer enjoyable and she didn't like the look of proposed future developments. She was seriously considering handing in her notice. Moving jobs would mean moving to a new area, but she didn't know where she wanted to go. She was even questioning whether or not she would stay in Finance. It had become so high pressured. If she didn't do that, what else could she do? Her mind was full of unanswered questions and unknowns.

Her only other consideration was her mother. Her husband, Sarah's father, had died in an accident some years ago. Her mother, now in her fifties, had rebuilt her life and was happy with her own work as a PA, and perhaps, more importantly, in good health. There was no need really for Sarah's concern in that area. But they had grown closer since her father's death and had supported each other when things got tough for one of them. She wanted to check out how her mother would feel about her moving out to a small island in the Atlantic. Elizabeth had been quite strict when Sarah was young, mainly because she had been such a tomboy and was always somewhere that seemed to Elizabeth to be too risky or dangerous for a girl. Sarah had been unconcerned and knew she would be safe. However, since she had grown up, Sarah had always felt supported by her mother in whatever she had chosen to do, even when it was travelling to the Middle East for work. However, this was a bit different; very different in fact. If it turned out well, given that she would stay there initially, she would be there for a long time, even the rest of her life. Her stomach lurched at the thought – part nerves but also part excitement she noticed.

Sarah felt she was at a major crossroads, with no idea as to which direction she should take. She ran various options through in her mind, but they were either a repeat of what she was doing and would be glad to leave or they were located in places she didn't feel drawn to. This new development could be the answer to all her dilemmas. She had never been reluctant to take on new challenges, nor was she risk averse, which is why she had been so successful in her career. Moving to Lanzarote seemed an intriguing proposition. That evening she told Elizabeth all about the legacy and her mysterious great aunt.

"Gosh! Sarah! That sounds amazing. I didn't know we had any relations there either. Your grandmother never discussed it, saying she didn't know anything about it, even if it came up somehow in conversation. The exchange was always very brief when I asked if we had any more relatives, I remember. It puzzled me at the time, but then I thought no more of it." Elizabeth was as shocked and as excited at the news as Sarah had been.

While they were discussing everything Sarah knew about the legacy, an idea came to her that would perhaps clarify things a bit.

"I was just thinking that it might be a good idea to go and see what it is I have inherited before making a decision," replied Sarah. "Mum, do you think it would be a good idea to go over there to see what this farm is, exactly? Would you be able to come with me? I would be leaving as soon as I can really. I am owed some holidays, so I can put in for a week off."

"That sounds great, love," said Elizabeth. "Thank you for asking me. Sadly, we are in the middle of a tricky transaction so I don't think Mr. Roscoe will give me time off. I have booked a holiday in the summer. I expect that is too much of a delay for you, isn't it?"

"Hmm, it is really. I am wondering what to do at work actually, especially now as David and I are divorced." Saying it out loud, caught at her throat unexpectedly. She had to pause and swallow hard.

"Are you OK, sweetheart? You've gone all quiet. It must be difficult for you to get used to the new situation," said Elizabeth.

"Yes, I'm OK really. It was quite a shock when he said he wanted a divorce, but actually, I think I am relieved. It hadn't been all that wonderful for a while. As I was saying, I don't know what to do with this new development, so I ought to go to Lanzarote sooner rather than later. At least then I would know what I was making a decision about. It

14

might help me get a sense of where to go with my life."

Elizabeth thought that would be a good idea for Sarah to do that as soon as it could be arranged. As she said, if Sarah didn't go, they would both always wonder whether she should have gone.

"When you are there, perhaps you would take lots of photos to send to me. Then we can talk about it when you get back. You'll know what you might be taking on, whereas now you have no idea," concluded her mother.

"That's true. Thanks Mum. I'll get onto Mr Selby in the morning. I'll let you know what's decided."

Sarah helped with the washing up, and set off back to her flat. Now she was living more on the outskirts of London it shouldn't take too long. It had been a long day so she thought she would get to sleep really quickly.

The next morning Sarah phoned Mr Selby and told him that she had had a chat with her mother the previous night and wanted to discuss the outcome with him. She told him that they had decided it might be a good idea for Sarah to go over as soon as possible to see what Lanzarote was like and have a look at the farm. It would be easier to make a decision if she had a clearer idea about the facts.

As it seemed time was of the essence, Mr Selby suggested Sarah come over to his office that afternoon.

Sarah was in the office at 2.00, feeling relieved to have the opportunity to discuss things more logically.

"The trouble is," she laughed as she sat down, "I can't

remember the name – what did you say it was called? Something to do with palms?"

"Mr Selby smiled, "Almost there. It is called *finca Los Palmas*. A small farm is called a *finca*."

"Perhaps it's hopelessly derelict so not such an attractive proposition. However, it is intriguing and has come at a good time for me," she explained.

He agreed. "However, you don't need to be concerned about the state of things over there. As I said, your great aunt was an astute lady so the place would be in reasonable condition, if a little dated. It is a good idea all round. A week away will restore you after the last few very hectic months. Enjoy discovering what Lanzarote is like and finding out more about the farm.

They made an appointment to meet again on her return.

Chapter Two

Sarah arranged to take the time off work and was soon on a flight to Lanzarote. She had pre-booked into a hotel in Arrecife. Her great aunt's house had been uninhabited for two years now and she had no idea what she would find. At least, with a hotel room booked for the week, she would have a shower, good food and a clean and restful bed to return to at the end of each day. When the connection bus dropped her off at her hotel, she felt pleased with her choice. It looked lovely: stylish without being over grand. She paused a few moments to admire the large sculpture of five dolphins leaping through the air. Everywhere looked very comfortable and was reasonably quiet. Apparently, it was pretty chaotic during school holidays. She was shown to her room after checking in.

Looking out through the window at the sunshine and the sea, she felt a knot undo in her insides that had been there for so long she had ceased to be aware of it. She was so relieved to be quiet and in her own room. The flight had been cramped with a young, fretful child in the seat in front of her who cried and grumbled and screamed the whole of the two and half hours. Suddenly, having nothing to do, not even cook supper, the full impact of the previous weeks and months rushed over her. She was soon to have no job, though she had yet to hand in her notice; she was divorced, on her own. The life she had known for so long no longer existed at any level. In the quiet and comfort of a foreign hotel room, she gave in to the feelings of grief and exhaustion she had been fighting off for so long, fell on the bed and cried and cried. She hadn't slept for more than four or five hours for months, perhaps years. That evening, she couldn't face the dining room with red, swollen eyes and a tear-streaked face, so she arranged for a room service dinner after which she slept for 12 hours.

She woke the next day feeling lighter and more refreshed and just a little bit excited. Today she would discover what her great aunt had left her. After an excellent breakfast and getting herself organised for the day, she asked the concierge where to hire a car. He was very kind and arranged it all for her and soon she was setting off to find the town of Haria and the farm. Apparently, a farm was called a *finca* on the island. Mr. Selby had received directions to the farm included in the Will, which he passed onto Sarah. However, for the most part, they were no longer relevant because in the intervening couple of years a new network of wide, well laid highways had been built around the island. She had to ask directions several times. She got a few quizzical looks, but was generally seen as just another lost tourist.

She drove through an amazing landscape on her way to the town in the north of the island. Initially, there were no verdant rolling hills such as she was accustomed to in England, but dark, bare, elemental rock and lava flows, interrupted by the steep slopes of extinct volcanoes. As she went further north, the barren slopes developed a greener tinge from the low scrub, stubby plants and lichens that were colonizing them. 'Hmm. There must be some rainfall up here, however small. Perhaps that is why my great aunt chose a farm this far north in the island,' she thought.

There were no trees, apart from palms and prickly cacti. Here and there, people had planted large succulents and shrubs such as oleanders and bougainvillea in their gardens and in communal gardens of holiday villa complexes, but that was all. Sarah thought it didn't look promising for any kind of productive farming. She drove through Teguise, a pretty market town with white single-story houses, thick walled with small green-shuttered windows. There was a big square in the middle with a large church on one side. Bougainvillea and ivory flowered "temple trees," frangipani, grew in the centre or in residents' balconies, providing welcome pools of fragrant, bright colour in a largely monochrome scene. There were several cafés around the square. Their bright striped awnings and umbrellas also added splashes of colour. They had a market there on a Sunday according to the numerous posters advertising it. They were covered in lots of photos of the stalls and products usually on sale there. It all added to a general air of gaiety.

Eventually she came to Haria settled in a valley between

the arms of two hills. The area was known as The Valley of a Thousand Palms – *el val de las mil palmas*.

She later learned that, in years gone by, people planted two palms if a boy was born in the village, and one palm if a girl was born. Sarah was surprised by such discrimination against women, even that long ago. The practice had long since stopped, but whether there were a thousand palms growing there or not no-one knew. However, Sarah appreciated the greenness of the area and the presence of some tall trees after the barren landscape she had just driven through.

The town wasn't at all what she had expected. All the buildings were neat two storeys, except for the church. This was made law in the late sixties by César Manrique, who saw the tourist potential of the Island. He campaigned successfully for a traditional and environmentally friendly development in order to preserve its attractive unique architecture. Sarah was intrigued to notice that although all the houses and boundary walls were painted white, as one would expect that far south, inland the doors and shutters were green, while those at the coast were blue. She would later discover that this was another of Manrique's stipulations for a beautiful and attractive island.

Mr. Selby had arranged for her to meet someone in the main square who would take her to her aunt's *finca*. She had not stood there for many minutes, when an elegant woman, about Sarah's age, wearing slim black jeans, white T-shirt and a pale grey blazer approached her. Sarah was immediately struck by this stranger's proud bearing: tall, erect with her hair pulled into a bun at the nape of her neck. She struggled to find a word for it, and then realized the woman reminded her of a flamenco dancer.

"¿Senorita Sarah?" greeted the woman. "¡Hola! You look very much like your great aunt when she was younger. There is a photograph of her in my mother's house. Come, I will take you to the farm."

She introduced herself as Inés, and said that Sarah should follow her in her own car as the farm was a few miles away and she may need to take her time looking around after Inés left.

After a mile or so further north, Inés turned left onto a track that was barely visible. It would have been difficult to define but for the tall palms and cacti, that Sarah later learned were Prickly Pear or Opuntia, which lined the old lane. The cacti were everywhere over the island and it looked as if they had taken over the place here. There were remains of small fields and what looked like a better-kept vineyard. There were also some strange constructions set out in rows, obviously man-, or on this case, woman-made. They were rows of hollowed out, round concave depressions with a low wall on the same side for each one. Some had one plant or other growing in the bottom, their presence made known by a few green leaves showing over the rim of the bowl.

Following Inés's car, she rounded a slight bend in the lane and there, just a little way ahead, Sarah could see the house, buildings, fields and vineyards in a u-shaped valley, nestled between the steep slopes of a range of volcanoes – a testament to Lanzarote's fiery history when volcanic eruptions and lava flows went on for eight years, laying waste to a huge area of the island in the south and west. The valley sides got steeper as it narrowed. They were green due to a covering of grasses, and low scrub and it looked as though some slopes had been terraced. This area was blessed with a little rain and sea fog that rolled in from the north coast on a regular basis. The farm and buildings looked safe and protected. 'No wonder my great aunt fell in love with the place,' thought Sarah.

The house was the regulation two storeys high. Large and well designed. It wasn't at all what she had been expecting. She had expected a small, shabby almost-shack, run down with weeds and creepers everywhere and probably with snakes and scorpions under everything. She was later pleased to discover that neither of these creatures were to be found on the island. She had obviously been watching too many movies about old properties in Spain and Greece! She smiled ruefully to herself. Sarah was now eager to look around.

"It looks in a much better state of repair than I had expected," Sarah remarked as they stood outside the house.

"*Si*," replied Inés. She went on to explain that her mother and father, who had worked for many years on the farm, still lived in a house on the property and kept things in as much order as they could.

Inés' mother, Carmen, had worked for Clara since she was a young girl: helping in the house so that the English woman could work on the farm. As she got more settled, established and busier on the farm, Clara employed Carmen's friend José, as well. Carmen continued to work in the house, cooking and cleaning and occasionally helping with some of the things that aunt Clara was doing, like cheese making, while José worked on the farm in the vineyards mainly. Carmen and José got married soon after and he came to live at the farm.

"They live here still and have done for many years," said Inés, again. Her defiant tone and nervous looks took Sarah aback. She realised that the young Spanish woman had been courteous but rather clipped and distant since they had first met. She wondered why that should be.

"Umm... are they afraid they will have to move out if I move here?" Sarah's question was tentative in case she had come to the wrong conclusion.

"*Si*. Since we were told you were coming, they and I have been worried," admitted Inés.

"Well, this time I'm just here on a short visit to find out more about the island and my great aunt's farm. I still have a job in London, though I don't enjoy it very much. Your parents may stay where they are. I'm not sure what I will do: I've not made any definite decision yet. I had no idea I had any relatives here in Lanzarote until last week, let alone a farm. It is all such a surprise."

Inés visibly relaxed, but then looked concerned again. "What would happen if you decide to come here to live?"

Sarah was startled by the question. She realized she had not consciously thought of that option. She could hardly believe she was here at all.

"I don't know to be honest," said Sarah. "I'm sure something could be arranged should I do that. Let's go and have a look around to see what my aunt had here. I haven't thought about whether I would actually come here to live because I have no idea what "here" is."

Inés led the way into the house: the front door had been left open in preparation for her visit. They stepped into a large room, cool and shady due to the deep-set windows, as was the custom in hot countries. Once again, Sarah's expectations were wide of the reality. Rather than smelling of dust and rather musty, it smelled pleasantly of wood with a faint lingering smell of polish. In the middle was a large dark wood refectory table with ten substantial chairs arranged around it. On the wall opposite to the door was a large interesting sideboard. It had two half drawers at the top, then two large doors. It stood on four thick heavily carved legs and there was a carved border on the front down each side. It would have looked too massive and out of place in an English dining room, but here it fitted in perfectly. In the corner to the left was a door which led to the stairs and the bedrooms. On the right was another door.

"This is the sitting room," said Inés as she led Sarah through. Again, it was a large, cool room with two windows, and to Sarah's surprise a big fire place.

"I hadn't expected to see a fire place in here, nor in the dining room," said Sarah. "It is so hot outside."

Inés smiled. "Yes, you would not expect it from today's temperatures. However, at times during the winter when the north wind blows strongly, it feels cold by comparison, so a fire is very welcome. It is very snug in here when the fire is lit."

As they got further into the room, Sarah could see that it was L-shaped, giving a useful looking space almost separated from the rest of the room. The main room was furnished by a large sofa covered in a pattern that was mainly in deep maroon and ochre. It worked really well and added to the air of comfort and ease that the room generated.

"Is there a faint smell of lavender in here?" asked Sarah. "Does it grow here?"

"Hmm… I'm not sure you will have to ask Mama. She is the gardener," said Inés. "I think Clara used to have some dried lavender posted to her from England. She used to put sachets of it in drawers and cupboards. I'm not sure why. Maybe it was the fashion in England at that time?"

They crossed the dining room to a door opposite. Sarah admired the table on her way. Inés thought it had come from Spain together with the sideboard. She remembered her mother saying that Clara used to give parties in her youth so it had been well used.

The opposite door led to the kitchen.

Little had changed much since the 1960s. There was an electric cooker, a top loading washing machine and a large fridge. There was also a very Spanish looking sideboard/dresser. It looked a bit sad and old. Sarah found herself thinking, 'Well that will go straight away.' The thought shocked her. It was the kind of thought one would get when a decision had been made to live there.

There were some colourful plates of Spanish design arranged on the shelves of the dresser and three large tureens set out on the shelf above the cupboards. The floor was tiled in square terracotta tiles set on the diagonal. It made the large sparsely furnished room look welcoming. It would be cool underfoot, thought Sarah. At the back of the kitchen was another door that led to a smaller room. There was a stone slab set into the wall one side of it with cupboards on the other. Inés explained that this had been used as a dairy where they made cheese. It was cool in there so doubled up as a store room and pantry. Then they walked back to the door that led to the stairs. At the top was a small square landing with a door leading off on either side.

Inés opened the one on the left. This was the bathroom. It was not too big but had a washbasin, a lavatory with a high tank and a long chain flush that ended in a blue and white porcelain handle. There was also a large free standing, roll-edged bath standing on claw and ball feet. It was painted aquamarine blue on the outside. It smelled faintly of Pears soap, the old fashioned translucent amber coloured soap. It had been the favourite soaps of another 'aunt' – a friend of her mother's really - back home. It brought back a lot of happy memories of holidays spent with that aunt. Sarah smiled at the recollection. It made the house seem even more homely and inviting.

"What a splendid bath," exclaimed Sarah. "My goodness, that must need a lot of water to get even a decent depth in there. What fun though!"

Inés the led the way across the landing onto a corridor that ran the rest of the length of the house. It was lit by three windows, which looked out of the back of the house towards some of the farm fields and the steep hills of the volcano at the head of the u-shaped valley.

Inés explained about the view as they walked slowly along this narrow space at the back of the house. Sarah kept pausing to admire and take in more of the view. It was contained by the walls of the volcano and she leaned forward in order to see the tops of them. She could see blue sky, also a small bus and even smaller cars travelling along the summit.

"I'm surprised to see cars and a bus going along the top of the ridge" she commented to Inés. "It seems very high up from here."

"*Si*. There is a road there that winds around the island. I have driven up there in the past. The farm seems very small when you look down." She opened the first door on the right of the corridor, explaining,

"All the bedrooms lead off this corridor. There are three, but this one is smaller," she said, as she opened the door. "We call it the box room. Well-named as you can see."

Sarah looked inside and saw piles of boxes neatly stacked up in there and nodded in agreement.

"My mother put Clara's belongings and farm papers in these boxes and put them in here to keep them safe. There are some of the newer pieces of china, pots and pans, books and notebooks and so on."

Walking on they stopped in turn at each door to look inside at the size of the rooms. They were fairly large and with wonderful views over the vineyards and on out to the main road.

The furniture in all the rooms was minimal but it was all solid, real wood – no veneers or flatpacks in sight. Her aunt hadn't seemed interested in stylish surroundings, but the overall effect was pleasing and unfussy – much like Sarah's own approach to her home back in London.

However, the young visitor was relieved that during her stay she would be going back to the more modern and comfortable facilities at the hotel.

Once they had gone around the house, they stepped outside through the door in the kitchen. They were in a spacious yard, with a large building about 10m away in front of them. To Sarah's right and again about 10m away was another house, still two stories and a bit smaller than the farmhouse. It looked square rather than the longer design of the main house.

"My parents live there," said Inés pointing to the building. "I and my two brothers were brought up there. It was a happy time for all of us. There was so much space to run around. Señora Clara was always kind to us and allowed us a lot of freedom. She sometimes showed us how to do whatever she was doing when we met her. Whether that was preparing the figs for drying, or milking the goats – I didn't like those much. They smelled very strong, especially the Billy goat. I think Señora Clara got rid of him. He would get rather aggressive if one the nannies was in…."

Inés paused for a minute struggling to find the word she wanted. "Um… ready to breed again."

By this time Inés's parents had heard her speaking and had come out to greet the heir to the farm. Inés introduced Sarah. They were both shorter than Inés, but still had the proud bearing Sarah associated with the Spanish. José looked kind and strong. He had a broad chest and square set shoulders. His face was square as well but a warm smile softened what could be a hard countenance. His slightly greying hair was neat, not too short, not too long and swept back from around his face. He looked strong and capable. Sarah felt his presence reassuring.

Carmen was a little shorter than her husband, with her black hair pulled back in a bun high up on her crown. She was rounder in build than her daughter, but still slim.

Sarah though she would probably be much stronger than she herself was. Though they were both smiling in greeting, Sarah thought they looked a bit unsure, like Inés had said. However, Sarah liked them immediately and knew, that if she stayed, she would be glad to have them next door. The farm was further away from any town or village than Sarah would have preferred. The place seemed very remote, in fact, after her flat in the middle of London.

Sarah stepped forward to shake their hands. "*Buenos dias,*" she said.

"*¡Buenos dias,* Señora!" they said together. "*¡Bienvenida,* Señora!"

They then went to their daughter and gave her a big hug of welcome and had a quick chat in Spanish that Sarah had no chance of following. She took advantage of the slight pause to take in more of her surroundings.

She could see, now she had had a second look at their house that it was, indeed, two storeys high and though smaller than the farmhouse, still quite big. There was a garden at the side of the house with bright pink oleander and orange and red bougainvillea bushes growing along one side of the house. To the side of this colourful show were lots of rows of vegetables, all looking very healthy and productive. Things seem to grow well here. Pots of red geraniums were arranged along the front of the house, flowering even this early in the year. 'It must be relatively warm here during the winter,' thought Sarah, enjoying the burst of bright scarlet against the white house.

'I can see why they would rather not leave: it looks very nice.'

"Ah Sarah. Apologies. I was just telling my parents that you were here to look around, that it was all so new for you but that they would be able to stay, even if you came here to live. I said you needed time to decide what to do."

"Thank you, Inés. I hope they feel less concerned now?"

"Yes. But I must show you quickly the out buildings, so you have a clearer idea of what is here."

She led the way to a number of buildings and sheds. One, just across the yard from the kitchen side of the house, looked like a stable but was bigger than the ones Sarah had seen back home, though she didn't think to ask why that was so. As well as the stalls to the left of the building there were a number of pieces of machinery and tools and all sorts of unknown (to Sarah anyway) bits and pieces. Other sheds at the side and the rear of this stable were smaller and obviously storerooms, some with more tools and racks in. To Sarah's great surprise, to one side and behind the stable building was an even bigger barn filled with equipment to make wine! A winery! Before she could find out more about it, Inés asked if she would like to see the land now?

"I had forgotten there was land as well!" Surprised, Sarah realized she had focused on the house and what it would be like and had not thought about any land, or, if it had crossed her mind, she had imagined a big, rather derelict garden.

The small amount of rain and the sea mist meant that, as she had noticed on her journey, these slopes were greener than those of volcanoes further south in the island where there was often less rain than fell in the Sahara. The slopes and valleys down there were still almost bare of visible life: the reddish brown and black volcanic ground, creating an almost lunar landscape.

Here on the farm, she could see that the very steep slopes on both sides of the valley had been terraced: narrow strips of land retained by walls of shaped lava rocks. Steps at intervals gave access to the ascending levels. Much of the ground on the terraces had been colonized by that prickly pear cactus she had seen growing everywhere on the island, together with low thick leaved bushes, lichens on the rocks and plants she didn't recognise at all. The bottom of the valley to the front of the house that had been cultivated was covered in black lava "beads" making the ground look desolate and unpromising. There were also rows of the inverted conical shaped hollows with a low wall curving around half of the top. In the base of each was one twiggy plant. Inés explained that the smaller ones were vines, while the larger tree-like plants were figs. They were planted in that way to get protection from the cool, northerly winds that blew most of the time. Also, the black beads naturally captured the moisture from the sea mists, which in the cones filtered down to the bottom to feed the vines and trees that were planted there.

"It is an ingenious use of what's here," commented Sarah, on hearing Inés' explanation.

Closer to and in front of the house, where it was more sheltered, there were the more familiar rows of vines trained on wires. These were planted in long shallow ditches for the same reason. Broken lines of stone forming low walls outlined a few plots of land. Sarah wondered if the ones closer to the house had been gardens rather than part of the farm. It was all so new and strange, and so unexpected,

Sarah felt at a complete loss. There was so much to take in. She couldn't even think of anything to ask Inés about or what comments to make. She became very quiet.

Inés mistook Sarah's silence and her bemused expression as disinterest and abruptly suggested she take the English visitor back to Haria to show her where she could get something to eat before returning to her hotel. Sarah was tired and hot, her mind inundated with all the new images of the strange landscape, unformed questions about how the farm had been run and so much more, so was pleased with the suggestion. They said goodbye to Carmen and José, locked up, got back in their cars and drove to town, without saying anything more. Once at Haria, Inés pointed out a café Sarah could go to and was about to leave, but Sarah, laying a hand on her arm, asked if she would stay and have lunch with her and tell her what she knew about her aunt and "*finca los Palmas*," the farm.

Inés was surprised. "Oh! I thought perhaps you were not interested and were impatient to return to England."

"No! I am rather overwhelmed and, to be honest, speechless. It is so different from what I had imagined. The house is bigger and in better condition. There is more land than I had expected and much of it is so steep! How did my aunt farm it? How did she make a living there? What did she grow? Did she sell what she grew? Was she always on her own? Did she marry? Where are the shops here? I have so many questions. Please stay and have lunch with me, if you have time, and tell me what you know about the farm and my aunt."

Chapter Three

Smiling at this gesture of friendship and interest in the farm, a more relaxed Inés took them to a small restaurant just off the square, set between a kiosk selling ice cream and postcards and a house with all the windows shuttered against the heat of the summer to come. It was still January, but a sunny 20 to 23 degrees in the afternoon, a welcome change from the cold, grey weather she'd left behind in England.

Sarah was glad to step into the cooler room. It was spacious without being big, arranged on two levels, with a set of three wide shallow steps leading up to the large, wooden bar, on the left, where they served wine, beer and coffees. To the right, two more steps descended into a large dining room, set with 6 long tables and several smaller ones. 'If they need to seat those many people at a time, they must be very popular,' thought Sarah. Noticing the direction of Sarah's gaze, Inés told her that the town was popular with tours of the island and sometimes they had two coach loads of tourists at the restaurant for lunch. The mention of coach tours brought back an image from her tour of the farm that had puzzled her but had not had the space to ask about it. "Would that have been one of the tour buses I saw right at the top of the side of the volcano earlier? It looked so tiny up there, I wondered what it could be doing in an area where there seemed to be nothing at all."

"Yes," said Inés. "I saw it too and wondered if it may have been coming here, but it looks as if they have been here already as it is rather late for lunch. The tour takes people around the volcanic National Park, the Timanfaya, then on around the north of the island to other locations of interest. They go on to an underground cave where they hold concerts. It is very beautiful there but always crowded with tourists. It is a good tour. Perhaps you would like to take it sometime. Your hotel can arrange it. You get to see more than if you drove there in a private car."

That sounded interesting, but Sarah shuddered at the thought of the small restaurant full of at least 60 tourists all excitedly chattering, and was very glad there were no tours there then.

Another thing that had caught her eye was that all the houses had blue or green shutters and asked why.

"Ah!" replied Inés, "many years ago Cesar Manriqué came back here to his native island, to make it a modern resort island before such a thing was popular. He said all electric cables must be underground, no building could be more than two stories high at ground level and the houses should be painted white with green shutters if they were inland or marine blue nearer the sea."

"It certainly adds to the charm of the place," commented Sarah. "It gives a unified look, but never seems boring or contrived. I suppose that is because it fits so well with the history of the place and adds to its individuality."

They settled at a small round table between the window and the bar. They ordered some local food- soup, fried chicken served with vegetables and Canarian potatoes. Inés mentioned that the potatoes were cooked in seawater. It was a tradition from way back, when fresh water was in very short supply. The potatoes tasted so good that they were still cooked in that way. The two women relaxed with a glass of wine as they waited for their meal to be cooked; Inés at ease now that she understood Sarah's subdued reaction to the farm tour. It had been due to being introduced to so many new unexpected things all at once rather than from any disinterest. After a few sips of wine and a pause to gather her thoughts, Inés began to tell the story of the strange English woman who came to Haria back in the late 1930s.

"Your great-aunt, Clara Fisher, had arrived with just a couple of small suitcases and a trunk. She bought the farm as soon as she had got all necessary legalities sorted out. The farm was badly run down. The previous owners had worked there for many years but illness and advancing years gradually took their toll until they could no longer farm it effectively. Although the couple worked as hard as they were able, they couldn't do everything as well as they used to. It saddened them to see quite large areas already showing signs of neglect and, of course, as a result the crops were not as bountiful as they had been. After a lot of thought, they decided to follow advice, and reluctantly agreed to put it up for sale.

Sadly, for them, but not for Clara, the land was cheaper

because of this neglect than if it had been sold in its prime.

"I don't know if she had had any previous experience of farming," continued Inés, "but she wasted no time in starting on the considerable task of revival. She started nearer to the house, clearing weeds and stones from the ground. My mother says Clara was keen to use as much as she could of what was there already, so used the stones she cleared to rebuild the low tumbled walls that had separated the plots. Surprisingly, the strange looking black soil proved fertile with some irrigation – soon Clara was eating her home-grown potatoes, carrots, lettuce and sweet corn. She had hoped to keep a cow, but this proved too difficult as there were no meadows and not enough grass. There were lots of weeds and scrub though, so she bought a goat to help clear them. Not long after its arrival, the goat gave birth to twins, to Clara's delight, because this meant she would have some milk as well. Her flock increased and thrived as the weeds gradually disappeared. I think by this time she had been able to see what other farmers were doing. Although they were sceptical at first about this eccentric English woman buying a rundown farm, they had noticed how hard she was working and how determined to improve the farm. They proved to be very helpful and gave her what advice and assistance they could when she asked. She realised she would need grazing for the goats so began developing some meadows for them and for hay for the winter.

I think she used to sow Bermuda grass or something. You had better check with Papa to be sure."

"Goodness," interjected Sarah, "She must have had a lot of energy."

"Yes, I often thought that. It used to amaze me how many hours in the day she worked, even when she was older: she even rigged up lanterns and lights in the evening to get more done." Inés shook her head in amazement as she recalled seeing Clara constantly on the go.

"Over the years, she repaired existing terraces and, as she learned more about the technique, added new ones, gaining more valuable ground. She gathered seaweed from the shore nearby with the help of a donkey that had adopted her. Ha! It was a funny old thing: a bit moth eaten at first and grumpy. We kept well away from it. It was as good as gold with Clara and soon got fatter and fitter and lost its threadbare appearance. The seaweed and the bedding from her expanding flock of goats formed the basis of a compost heap I remember."

At first, ugh, *hedor*!" Inés held her nose and screwed up her face. (Sarah quickly knew that 'hedor' meant 'stink'), "but it soon lost the bad smell and turned into excellent fertiliser for the plants that enriched the soil and helped her grow a wide variety of top-quality vegetables."

"I have heard of people making compost," commented Sarah, "but I have no idea what it is."

Inés smiled. "I don't have much of an idea, either. You don't need too much compost as a 'Privilege Concierge' in a popular hotel. You will have to ask Papa or Momia about it."

Sarah made a note to herself to do just that.

"Oh! Would you like some more wine or a coffee?"

"Um… Coffee please. That would be very welcome," replied Inés. "I seem to be talking rather a lot. I hadn't realised I know so much about Clara."

There was a break in the narrative as Sarah ordered the coffee. It came with glasses of water, which were very welcome.

When the coffee was served, Inés asked if Sarah wanted to learn more about her aunt, she hadn't known she had, not wanting to get too detailed and lose Sarah's interest.

"Oh yes please! Please go on. This is all completely unexpected. What a woman! I am sad I never got to know her myself."

Inés continued with Clara's biography.

"As I said, she began to sell her surplus vegetables at the local markets. Her customers were so impressed by the taste and quality of her produce, they bought everything off her stall. There was always a queue waiting for her on each market day.

"It wasn't all plain sailing of course. I think there were many heartbreaks in the early days. There are problems, particular to the island, that contrived to undo her hard work – the hot sun, strong cold winds, meagre rainfall and the thin sandy soil. However, once her neighbours had shown her this very novel form of cultivation, your great - aunt was able to lessen the effects of these potentially damaging factors and start a productive vineyard: these hollows and low walls," indicated Inés, with a sweep of her arm.

"It must have been such a struggle in the early days," said Sarah. "Do you know if Clara had had any farming experience before she came here?"

"No, I don't think so, but she was eager to learn. She planted vines, almond trees and figs in the circular hollows that you saw on the farm. She used this same principle to grow pumpkins and melons and was soon taking these to market along with all the other things."

She hadn't been here that long when she took on a young girl – my mother - to clean the house and help with making the goats' cheese from the surplus milk. People talked about a fiancé or husband killed in the war, whose loss she had never got over, but she never talked about it, not even to Mother who became a close friend as well as help. Clara never married that we knew of, but devoted her life to the development and care of her farm. She fitted easily into the community and made many friends. She worked until she was 94, when she was taken suddenly very ill and died just a few short weeks later, in the house where she had lived for almost 70 years."

"Goodness what a life," said Sarah. These were the first details she had had heard about her great aunt. What a woman! Taking on a derelict farm and working so hard to make it very profitable. She wondered if she would have such determination to continue in her aunt's footsteps. It seemed a hard act to follow, especially as, to date, she had grown not even a window box or house plant. Black fingers of doubt began to creep in and dim her rising interest, but she had felt such an immediate connection to her previously unknown relative, part of her, underneath the doubt, felt that following in her footsteps was something she had to do.

The afternoon sped by and the sun was going down by the time Sarah and Inés, now firm friends, parted company. They arranged to meet again in a few days to visit the *finca*

once more before Sarah returned to England.

Once back at the hotel, Sarah's brain was swirling with all this new information. It had been so interesting to hear about Clara's life. Sarah was amazed at how much one woman could achieve. She was imagining her aunt on the farm, gradually turning unpromising, neglected land into a productive farm that supported three people and later, Carmen and José's family – Inés and her two brothers. Inés had told her about the donkey and goats and later how a camel had just turned up one day. No-one came to claim it, so Clara kept it. A heaven-sent gift as camels were and still are expensive to buy. All of the animals helped on the farm, pulling small carts, ploughs or carrying loads of stones or grapes. It was the donkey that pulled a cart laden with cheese, vegetables and wine to the market in town every week. It was quite a character, apparently, and was soon as much an attraction as her owner's produce. Sarah thought her great aunt must have been so glad to get the extra support these animals provided.

Sarah spent the next couple of days exploring the island generally, finding out how the local people lived, away from the resorts and holiday villas that were present in ever increasing numbers along the coast. More and more locals and foreign companies were capitalising on the popularity of the island for winter holidays and surfing in the big waves on the northern shores. Hotels and villa complexes were being built all around the coast, especially in the east and south where it was less windy and therefore warmer. She remembered Inés' suggestion to take a tour around the island and Timanfaya and asked Max at the hotel to arrange it for her. In spite of being herded to regular "tourist attractions," such as the fire mountain where people could see how hot the ground was, it gave her a good idea of the nature of the island and some of its history. She was staggered to see just how hot and volcanically active parts of the island were – it is not often you see water poured into the ground erupt moments later as superheated steam. She began to wonder how hot the soil was further north and if it could be harnessed to help with energy supplies at the farm. At the hotel, Max had told her that it could feel relatively chilly in the short winter. A source of heat might be comforting after a long day out in the cold north winds – much the same as Inés had said.

The day before she was due to fly home, Sarah met up with Inés at the farm again, this time going over the house and outbuildings in more detail. They worked together to make an inventory of the furniture in the house, together with what china and other necessities they could find. Then they turned their attention to the farm buildings and to what was outside that could still be used. José was very helpful at this point as he knew what would be important to keep or replace and what could be cleared away. He pointed things out for Sarah to take particular notice of, like the water tank under the ground. There was still no mains water supply and not enough rainfall for springs to form, so a tanker came every two weeks with desalinated water and filled up the ground tank that she had seen at the start of the week. The water was pumped from there, up to a tank on the roof of the house, which was sheltered by a simple shed that looked in need of repair. From there it was piped to the bathroom, kitchen and to an outside tap. Her aunt had designed and set up the whole system. By the end of the day, Sarah knew she would go there to live, in spite of all the challenges, at least for the specified minimum of two years. Like her great- aunt, she experienced that same emotional draw to the place. She felt, deep in her heart, this was the place for her. Before she left, she told Inés, Carmen and José of her decision, explaining that she needed to return to England to hand in her notice at work and make all the necessary arrangements and preparations for her emigration to Lanzarote.

Sarah thoughtfully reassured Inés' parents that they could stay on in their house for as long as they wanted to. She would be glad to have their company and also someone nearby to help, if they were willing to, especially as they knew so much about the history of the farm and how things were run. She explained that she had absolutely no experience of farming. No member of her wider family were farmers. Her only experience of such a life had come from a few, and rather hectic and muddy educational farm visits when she was at school, which wasn't a great base of expertise from which to start! Carmen and José were delighted, and relieved at the prospect. The farm had been their home for so long, it would be hard for them to leave. Although they had only been with Sarah a short space of time, they already felt that they would get on well with her. She reminded them so much of Signora Clara who had been their employer and friend.

Chapter Four

Once back in England, Sarah plunged into a buzz of activity. She handed in her notice – three months, which included two months owed holidays. This meant that she could leave in four to six weeks' time, but with the reassurance of three months' pay during the move. – Perfect!

She visited Mr. Selby to inform him of her intention to go to the island at least for two years, thus honouring the first condition of her mysterious and adventurous aunt's Will. She was puzzled why her mother had not talked about this aunt. When she asked her, her mother knew nothing about it and was as surprised as Sarah by the Will. She could find no information about this great aunt either, but was excited about her daughter's new venture – and also the prospect of going out to visit her. Perhaps the family had been so outraged by her behaviour they cut her out of any part of their lives. What scandal had been so bad as to make them decide on such a drastic action?

'Mind you,' Sarah thought, 'In those days there were very strict social rules, which those aspiring to 'better themselves,' adhered to with a ferocity not observed by those established in the upper echelons of society. Ah well. That will have to remain a mystery,' she concluded.

Both mother, and daughter had recovered themselves after the death of Mr Jones many years before and were well established in their lives – or so they had both assumed. The news of this legacy of Sarah's had thrown many things up in the air – especially for Sarah – even more than the collapse of her marriage had done.

Mrs Jones senior was not surprised by Sarah's plan to "give it a go" as she thought of it. She was excited about a free holiday in the Canary Islands and was very happy for her daughter to go ahead and live over there. Secretly, she knew she would miss Sarah a great deal, but didn't want to say as much. She sensed this new challenge in new surroundings might be just what Sarah needed to find some purpose in life.

Sarah was relieved that her mother had agreed so readily for her to go. They both agreed that Elizabeth must definitely visit. However, that would have to wait until Sarah had settled in. There were only the two of them and Sarah felt responsible for her mother's wellbeing now her father was no longer alive.

Having settled matters with her, Sarah turned her attention to the myriad things that needed sorting out before she could leave for *finca Los Palmas*.

She contacted an estate agent to rent out her apartment. He advised that it would be better to rent it empty, but it would need to look smart. "It attracts a better class of tenant," he said. She had raised her eyebrows when he mentioned what he would charge for the rental. The Agent reassured her that property was in such demand in that part of London there would be no shortage of people who could afford to move in. 'People doing the sort of job I hate I expect,' she thought. When she really looked at it, it did look rather tired and the colours a bit past their time. The agent arranged for some decorators to paint the entire flat. They would use the colours Sarah chose - neutral but modern colours, a soft white that was light bright and washable, maybe a touch of grey – no purple walls! For that level of rent it would need to look sophisticated and elegant.

With that taken care of, she turned her attention to what to take with her, what to sell or throw away and what to store and where to store it. Luckily, she found a company in a nearby town that had huge, climate-controlled sheds housing rows and rows of large wooden crates, stacked three high. 'It looked like something out of the *Raiders of the Lost Ark*,' she thought, smiling to herself.

There followed days of sorting her belongings into those three groups. She was staggered when she saw that she had been holding onto so much "stuff" that she never used or that held sad, anxious or angry memories. No wonder she had got to feel stuck and fed up with her life.

Luckily, in the middle of all this bustle, she made time to check on progress at the flat. She was horrified to find the decorators all sitting around, smoking ('The smell is so hard to get rid of!') with only one room sort of painted. On top of everything else it was the last straw. Sarah exploded. They had been there a week. She had expected to find the flat almost completely decorated not just one room with an uneven coat of paint that hardly covered the old colour. The men scrambled to their feet in a rush, knocking over stools and nearly knocking over a tin of paint that Sarah grabbed just in time. They came up with all sorts of excuses but Sarah was having none of it.

"Pack everything up and leave, now. This is appalling. Not only have you done very little, when you agreed to do it in a week, but it is very bad workmanship. Also, it is some cheaper paint and not the colour I chose at all! If you are the best the agent can come up with, I would do better painting it myself. You will be paid for one days' work only. By the look of the cigarettes and rubbish everywhere you have done little but smoke, eat and drink. How dare you! You know what the situation is and you have taken advantage of everything. Go! Now."

The men fled, spurred on by her very definite and angry reaction to their lack of commitment to the task she had expected of them. She contacted the agent and told him, in no uncertain terms, what she thought of his choice of workmen. Then, after a quick word with Mr Selby, she also relieved the agent of his task of managing the flat rental and set about engaging someone more reliable and honest – a bit tricky in London she was beginning to realise. However, a friend of a friend, who had recently had her house decorated and whose interior design skills Sarah admired, got news of the disaster and was able to recommend the company she used. They had proved excellent, working hard and quickly, even when she had to go away for a few days on business. Perfect! She engaged a new agent also personally recommended to oversee the decorating and the letting procedure and after care.

On reflection, the young woman was surprised at her firm handling of the situation. It had always been very much in her character to make definite decisions. However, since her marriage, she saw now, she had left much of the organising, 'hiring and firing' to David. It was the easier option as he inevitably dismissed her actions and ideas as nonsense.

'Huh! That attitude has not been good for my confidence. Well, it is back now. I feel more like my former determined self. It feels good too, especially now when I might /will be taking up farming. Me, a farmer! Now that is a challenge to take up with both hands.'

She hoped she would still feel like this once in Lanzarote, looking out at the farm.

After a day or two to settle the new agent and herself after all this fiery outburst, Sarah returned to the business of packing and preparing to leave. The list of things to take grew alarmingly. She had to remind herself that she could get most things there. It would also be best not to take gardening or farming tools. She could be duplicating what was there or getting things that were hopelessly unsuitable. However, she wanted the comfort and refuge of having enough familiar items to start with, so she wouldn't have to spend time locating things there and battling with a language that she knew nothing about apart from *gracias*!

She was grateful for her aunt's advance on the inheritance. She expected that she would need a significant sum to repair and modernize the *finca*. As the two retainers got older so some of the maintenance may not have been done. Sarah wondered if they knew that her aunt had planned to leave the farm to her. Maybe they hadn't heard anything for a while. The wheels of legality always turned slowly. Perhaps they thought no one was going to come to claim the farm so had lost some direction and certainty? Perhaps they were wondering what she would be like? Anxious that she would want to change everything or eventually ask them to leave.

A lot of uncertainty on both sides. She smiled ruefully to herself and made a mental note, that on arrival, she would make sure she reassured them and herself of their future together at the farm.

Mr. Selby promised to keep in touch with Sarah after she left, forward any mail and keep an eye on her apartment to make sure the new agent actually did his job. They both had had experience of an agent not fulfilling his side of the contract. The place could end up ruined by misuse or neglect if he didn't – which it nearly did even before she left.

Finally, all the legal matters were finished. *Finca Los Palmas* was now in her name, crates stored or sent on by sea. She would need advice and help getting the crates from the port to the farm when the container ship arrived. Inés had already said she would help with that as she sometimes needed to help hotel guests with import legalities.

There were as many words of encouragement and admiration for such a bold move, as there were warnings of disaster and madness, with mutterings of "midlife crisis" even though she was too young to even think about such a thing. However, a party and promises of potential holidays seemed to silence most of her naysayers.

It was with a huge sigh of relief that Sarah finally boarded the P&O cruise ship to Lanzarote. She was going to fly originally, then Mr. Selby suggested she sail there and enjoy a few days of rest and luxury before she got down to whatever waited for her on the farm. He was as excited by the adventure as Sarah, though her excitement was tempered by doubts and anxieties about her lack of gardening and farming experience.

She had to admit as she stretched out on one of the deck loungers, having had an excellent lunch, that it was indeed an excellent idea to go by sea. She relaxed into her oasis of comfort and luxury.

Ten days passed very comfortably, by which time they had arrived at Portugal. Looking out over the railings of the main deck as they sailed up the Tagus River to Lisbon, she had an amazing view of The Belen Tower. It was where explorers set off on their adventures: an apt place for her to be stopping she thought as she was embarking on her own adventure of discovery and exploration. The thought sent a shiver up her spine, of anticipation mingled with apprehension. She had an enjoyable day here in Alfama district. She bought a pretty wrap for her mother from one of the many small shops amongst the Moorish and medieval buildings.

Next stop was Madeira. She could have come back on board with armfuls of flowers and plants but restrained herself, settling instead for a small sample of their famous lace. It was beautiful there. The fragrance from all the flowers filled the air.

'Perhaps I will be able to grow some perfumed flowers at the farm. That would be good,' she thought as she walked through the gardens.

In between visits ashore, Sarah was more than happy to be left alone to read the books she'd brought with her about farming and gardening in a dry climate. There was a lot more to it than she had supposed, but it looked an interesting challenge – at least from the comfort of the cruise liner.

She began to draw up a plan of what to do in the early days after her arrival. She had already booked the hotel in Arrecife where she had stayed before. She planned to stay for a week or two. Having somewhere comfortable to return to at the end of the day had been a great support on her initial visit. Also, she anticipated some considerable upheaval while the renovation and cleaning were going on at the house. She wasn't sure what she would find at the farm. She couldn't remember clearly what condition the house was in. It was one thing looking at it as a 'visitor,' another thing giving it the really deep scrutiny needed prior to actually living there. She couldn't remember clearly if it would be habitable. Would there be fresh potable water available? Did the 'fridge work? Was the washing machine safe to use? There had been so much to take in, she hadn't particularly noticed these details. She came to the conclusion that if, by the end of two weeks, the house still wasn't ready, she would find a good B&B in the nearby town of Haria. It would be cheaper than the hotel and she could stay there a little longer, without using up too much of her resources.

She thoroughly enjoyed the journey and felt rested by the experience. However, by the time they docked at Arrecife she had tired of the constant presence of so many people and was looking forward to getting on with whatever waited for her at the farm.

Chapter Five

Sarah had planned to spend her first week cleaning the house, but it looked as if Carmen and José had been busy since her last, brief visit. Each room looked swept, washed and freshly polished.

"Thank you so much! *Gracias*! You have worked very hard. Everywhere looks very inviting."

The older couple smiled, pleased that Sarah had noticed their hard work. They shrugged deprecatingly, "*Di nada. Di nada.* (no problem, you are welcome)."

Sarah's mind was a whirl. She was planning to buy her truck, and then she could take out the old, warped cupboards from the kitchen. She could then do any repairs to wall and floor that were needed so the room would be ready to install the new units that were in a container that would be coming by sea, due to arrive in a few weeks. The expected delay gave her time to prepare everything in the house. The rooms could be left as they were for the time being, so they went outside to take a closer look at the outbuildings.

Passing Inés' parents' house, they continued the tour of

the stables, barn, winery and cellar. There was so much to take in, she could hardly think straight. They emerged from the last building on the list, the winery, tired, dusty and a bit cobwebby having pulled out old, rusty bits of equipment and tools from the other sheds. Sarah arranged for them to be left near their original positions so they could be returned once renovated or used as a model from which replacement parts could be made or purchased. Looking around at everyone Sarah realised they were all looking rather fed up. Not so much by the huge scale of renovations to be done because there weren't any like that. It was more the number of little things that needed attention, the tidying to be done, to bring the *finca* back to how Carmen remembered it when Clara was there – busy and purposeful. They had done their best in the time between her death and the arrival of the new owner. However, with the future being very uncertain at that time, things had been just maintained but not moved forward. Sarah hoped she would be able to advance it to a level where it could once again provide Sarah with a good living as it had done for Clara. Maybe their serious faces betrayed their concerns about how effective Sarah would be and how she would compare with her great aunt. She had tried to reassure them that, if she moved there, she would want them to remain to help her.

Seeing them all with wisps of cobweb trailing and dusty smears on their hands and face, she burst out laughing, which set the other three off as well, releasing the tension and anxiety that had built up during the day.

"I don't know about you, but I'm really hungry. It seems a long time since breakfast. I've brought some food. Shall we have a picnic on the terrace?"

The idea was welcomed with enthusiasm. Sarah brought out a bowl of water and soap so they could wash their hands and get some of the dust off their faces. José and Inés pulled the table out from the kitchen onto the terrace, while Sarah went back to the car, bringing back two large cool boxes full of the things to eat that she had bought en-route that morning. Carmen carried out some of her delicious, crusty home-made bread. Inés retrieved a bottle of wine from her car. They found plates and cutlery in the kitchen that Carmen had washed a few days earlier and José, with a flourish, presented Sarah with one of the remaining bottles of wine Aunt Clara had made before she was taken ill.

Over a leisurely lunch, conversation turned to Carmen's house – the one they had lived in since they got married. Sarah asked Carmen if there was anything she needed replacing and updating in their own house. She wondered if everything was working as it should. Perhaps things were getting worn out, so not as effective as they once were. She invited Carmen to have a real good look round and to let her know in a few days' time what changes she would like to happen – maybe a more up to date kitchen altogether.

Although it was half way through February, the sun was hot. Sarah was really enjoying the feel of its warmth on her skin. Sarah thought she could hear a sound of some birds singing that was familiar. Inés said she thought that was a blackcap. Carmen joined in the bird conversation by adding that sometimes she saw a falcon flying over but that was about as far as it went for her. José was quiet on the subject, perhaps thinking what did birds have to do with vines except they could steal the fruit or nibble away the new leaves. Sarah had taken the birds back home for granted – sparrows, pigeons, blue tits… they were just the background to her life. However, here there were so many new kinds of birds which could be helpful – or not – so she thought it would be beneficial to find out more about them, but not at lunch time!

There was a break in the conversation and Sarah leaned back and closed her eyes to enjoy the sun. She became aware of a delicate perfume wafting her way on the sun's rays. When she asked where that was coming from, Carmen pointed to the cascade of deep pink bougainvillea hanging over the nearby wall. Sarah paused a moment to enjoy it, remembering the fragrant flowers she had seen on Madeira. When she looked more closely at the plants Carmen had pointed out to her, Sarah recognised them as some that she had seen and relished in the perfume of when she was there. She smiled. Part of her intention to have a perfumed garden here was already in place. She decided that was a good sign!

Sarah roused herself from her sunbathing dreaming. She was hungry!

There was quite a spread for their picnic: hams and salamis, local cheeses, olives, figs, salad, tomatoes and Carmen's bread. It was accompanied by the island wine and the *Los Palmas* wine. Sarah rather liked the farm wine. It was a smooth red wine, not too dry, just the right amount of tannin. She wasn't sure about all those descriptions of a wine having blackberry or chocolate flavours though. However, as she was now the owner of a vineyard that had produced wines in the past that had been very popular, she thought she should find out more about wine and to learn how to appreciate the different levels of flavour and depth. She would ask José and Hugo about it later.

Lunch was a talkative and leisurely affair. Conversation was mostly about the farm and how it was when Clara was alive, particularly the variety of foods she produced and sold at the markets and from a farm stall. Sarah had been thinking of ways in which the farm could start bringing in an income, no matter how small, so all this information was very useful. Carmen and José were very willing to talk about Señora Clara and life on the farm with her. With Inés acting as translator when their English faltered, the three of them painted a wonderful picture of the farm when it was flourishing. Even allowing for the rosy glow of nostalgia, it sounded as if life here had been abundant, though hard and constant work. Sarah was fascinated: making mental notes of the many enterprises her aunt had developed in the early days to create various sources of income to maintain a steady flow of business. She quickly realized there would be a lot of hard, physical work ahead and a vertical learning curve, as she delved into the mysteries of market gardening and viticulture.

Catching sight of the shadows stretching low across the yard, they all realized how late it was getting. A brisk wind had blown up, creating a chill after the warmth of the sun.

"This wind is the big problem to farming; together with the low rainfall," explained Inés. "It can come from the north and kill the tender buds of the vines."

They hastily gathered up plates, glasses and baskets of food to take them into the kitchen. Carmen had switched on the old refrigerator, which, although noisy, was working. While they were talking about the 'fridge and its effectiveness, Sarah took the chance to talked to Carmen and José about their house, again. Clara had specified that a certain amount of money be made available to modernize their home in order to make it easier for them as they got older. Having watched them through the day, Sarah thought it would be a long time before they would want things to be 'easier' for them. Carmen said she would have a think about it and talk to her husband that evening and discuss it with Sarah the next day.

Sarah sighed. She suddenly felt overwhelmed by 'lack': lack of a utility vehicle, her own comfy bed, a modern kitchen, but mostly lack of any kind of relevant, useful knowledge. She was going to add lack of organizational skills as well, then realised that many of the skills she had developed in her previous job could be transferred to her new situation in some way, particularly the financial side of things. She just needed to approach things more creatively from a wider perspective and remember her innate inner strength and adaptability.

She locked the front door with a certain self-conscious flourish, said "*Adios,*" to her three Spanish friends and left to return to the hotel on her own, as Inés was staying to have supper with her parents. The sun had almost set by this time, even though it was still quite early. The lane to the farm seemed very dark with the towering palms and prickly pear borders. She was glad to reach the lights of Haria. She was not usually nervous of the dark. She put her unease down to so many new tasks ahead of her and tiredness: it had been a long and demanding day.

'The first of many, I suspect,' she thought.

However, once on the main road, she was soon back at Arrecife and in the hotel. After a wonderfully refreshing shower, she dressed in clean clothes, and feeling rested and relaxed, went down to dinner. Was there a shower in the bathroom at the farm? She couldn't remember. It was one more thing she must remember to check out tomorrow. She had, with her, a book written by Eileen Caddy. The author had been responsible, with two colleagues, for developing a different way of gardening on a cold and inhospitable site on the NE coast of Scotland. It was now a well-established community continuing with the original philosophy and known widely as Findhorn. They use an alternative way of growing things. It was a bit 'out there,' very alternative, but they had grown amazing vegetables in what appeared to be harsh, salty gravel. She had heard earlier that day from Inés that north Lanzarote was a difficult place for growing things because of the climate. She hoped Eileen's experience would give her some ideas.

After a short while Sarah realised that her mind was so busy with the events of the day, she wasn't actually taking anything in, though it all sounded intriguing. With a sigh, she closed the book and put it to one side. When she had finished her meal, she took the book back to her room and, picking up her notebook, settled herself in a comfy chair, poured a glass of wine from the fridge and began to write. She began to list all the initial work that she thought needed doing at the farm to enable her to live there rather than in a hotel or B&B - nice as it was to have all her meals prepared for her.

Priority:
- The water tank and water supply
- Electricity
- Drainage/sewage – was there any? If so, what was it?
- Update kitchen
- New large 'fridge
- Painting inside and out
- Flooring – what was there now? She couldn't remember.
- Fixing the stone stairs to the roof.
- Update Carmen and José's house.
- Curtains
- Repairing yard surface where it was very stony, broken up and weedy.

Sarah groaned inwardly. This list was only what she could recall from her visit and was probably just the start. Each task seemed huge and costly in both time and money. She didn't know where to get any of the things she would need. She wasn't even sure if they were available on this island, on one of the other islands or if she would have to order things from mainland Spain. She didn't even want to think of that possibility.

'Oh dear!' thought Sarah, 'this is getting me nowhere other than despondent.'

With that she shut the notebook and went for a short walk. There was a path behind the hotel that ran between the building and the rocky coast. It was so soothing to hear the wash of the waves as they curled in off the Atlantic. It was calm today so no metres of spray to avoid which hotel staff had mentioned seeing during storms in the past.

Today, it was a gentle walk, - no steep inclines or boulders to negotiate. She returned to her room after her stroll along the promenade feeling more relaxed with a clearer mind and went to bed falling asleep immediately.

Chapter Six

The next day was overcast with a brisk chilly wind blowing. Her confusion and heavy heart were still with her when she woke. It was a day when Inés was working at the hotel, so Sarah decided she would get some white paint, brushes, rollers and paint trays on her way to the farm and start painting the rooms inside, maybe her bedroom or the kitchen. She checked with the helpful receptionist, Max, where she could get these things and how to get there. Once loaded up with all the things on her list, including a small pot of blue paint for the doors and shutters, she set off for the farm feeling a bit more optimistic and energetic than when she got up. She stopped at the supermarket to get some more things for lunch – they had eaten so much yesterday. 'It must have been the sense of celebration,' she thought.

Her buoyant mood collapsed when she approached the house. There were three cars there already, but no one around that she could see. She wondered what had gone wrong. Had Carmen or José been taken ill? However, as she drew up in the yard, the couple came out to meet her all smiles and obviously very well. Relief flooded through Sarah. The thought of tackling all this work without their support and local knowledge made it all seem such a huge task as to be almost impossible. She wasn't used to such emotions. Back in London she had taken each challenge and difficulty in her stride, approached it methodically, researched what she didn't know and got on with it. She realised it was because she knew what she was doing. She knew the world of finance and that knowledge gave her confidence and direction. Here, now, all she could think of was how little she knew. She was even questioning her wisdom, taking on this whole thing. Had she been beguiled by the romance of the situation, her common sense clouded by the strong connection she had felt immediately with her deceased great aunt? Before she could tumble further into a black hole of negative thoughts, such doubts were replaced by curiosity when she saw, coming out behind Carmen and José, a procession of six people – 4 men and two women of varying ages.

"*Buenos dias,* Senorita Sarah," they all cried. "*Como estas?* (how are you?)"

"Uh, *Buenos Dias,*" Sarah replied, looking quizzically at Carmen for an explanation. She wasn't in the mood for a party, nor did she have the time.

"Ah, Sarah, meet your helpers for the day," said Carmen. "This is my sister, Valeria. She will help you in the house, cleaning and making fresh curtains, whatever you want. She is retired now but it was her profession for many years."

"*Hola,* Valeria," greeted an amazed Sarah.

61

"*Hola,* Sarah, *encantado de conoceria,* (pleased to meet you)," said Valeria, shaking Sarah's hand.

"This is José's cousin, Daniel. He will fix the steps to the roof and put in new water tank and pipes to bathroom and kitchen. He is, how you say? *El fontanero, el plomero.*"

"A plumber? asked Sarah.

"*Sí!* This is Antonio and Manuel, some friends. They will start by painting the walls of the house. This is Isabella."

"*Hola, encantado de conoceria.* Please call me Bella."

"She will work with Valeria, you and me and this is Hugo, José's nephew. He is a farmer. He will clear the sheds, sort your tools and begin work on the vines. It is time now."

Sarah was speechless, then just as Carmen had finished the introductions, two more vehicles approached in a cloud of dust – a car and a truck. The drivers drew up in front of the gathering of people, climbed out and came over to them.

"*Hola! Buenos Dias!*" Carmen greeted each one with a kiss. "Sarah, meet Manuel and Antonio, Inés's brothers, my sons! They have a truck for you and will stay today to help here," she continued proudly.

Sarah was so taken aback by this sudden development. All these strangers had just turned up: all ready and able to help her with all the tasks she had felt defeated by just a short time earlier. She burst into tears. "Oh, my goodness! *Gracias! Gracias!* Thank you. Thank you."

They all smiled at such a show of emotion, shuffling their feet, a little embarrassed. While Sarah tried to compose herself, José and Carmen began talking to them all in rapid Spanish. It must have been instructions, because everyone became very purposeful and strode off in different directions

– to cars to get out tools, to the shed, to the outside steps. In seconds, Sarah was left standing with the three women, amazed by the rapid and upturning of events. The power of the family pulling together in this way reminded her of an incident her friend had described to her. She had been working in the Maldives with the VSO. A building on the island, where she was working, needed re-thatching. Nothing happened for a week or so, then one evening as the sun went down, people began arriving at the site by twos and fours: lorries laden with thatch rumbled in and people wheeling wheelbarrows with rope in. They all set to on the roof and in a couple of hours the whole thing had been completed and everyone was drifting off back to their homes! This is what seemed to be happening here, much to Sarah's delight and relief.

Carmen explained that she had sent everyone off to the different projects that they had discussed over lunch the day before, but now she was handing over the management to Sarah. Carmen would translate where necessary.

Meanwhile Valeria and Isabella had gone to their car and returned carrying many collections of fabric samples from which Sarah could choose her curtain material. Sarah went to the car to get out the paint and brushes and followed them into the house.

"Aah! ¡Excelente!" said Antonio, examining the tins and relieving Sarah of all of them. He brought in more paint tins, two for the inside and two for the exterior – all bright white, with rollers, trays with other tools Sarah hadn't known you would need for decorating. Before Sarah could say anything, Antonio grinned and went upstairs with the interior paint and Manual took the paint for the outside walls. As he passed Sarah, he winked and said, "Two days, all done. *No hay problema!* (no problem)"

Sarah shook her head in incredulity and went to join the women in the kitchen, where Valeria had laid out some of the samples already. However, Sarah was still emotional from when all these people had arrived to help and who were now very focused and busy. She began worrying that they knew what they were doing. Would it look presentable? The memory of those useless decorators, who had first come to paint her apartment in London, was still fresh in her mind. It was too late to worry now. She would have to relinquish her need to be always in control and let everyone get on with what they were doing. They seemed to have a better idea of how to do things than she would ever have. She drew in a ragged breath to calm herself and draw her mind together.

She had read somewhere that a few slow deep breaths worked wonders in calming an agitated spirit, bringing everything back to centre and calm. However, even if she managed to calm herself, there was no way she was going to be able to make decisions about curtains. She couldn't concentrate on the fabrics: even consider what colours she would like in what room. She had felt so dispirited last night and this morning, wondering if she could actually repair the house or find reliable tradespeople to do some of the work. She had worried whether she could revitalize the farm and make a living here. She hadn't got as far as such niceties as colours in each room. It had all seemed a great adventure when she was back in UK. Here, faced by the reality, it all looked very different.

Carmen was concerned by the younger woman's tears and confused expression, unsure if Sarah agreed with what she had done. She asked if Sarah was all right: why she was upset.

"Carmen," said Sarah, "I am amazed why all these people should turn up this morning to help with everything. I was so worried last night and today. There seemed so much to do and I don't really know how to do any of it. I was worried I wouldn't be able to find reliable workmen, who wouldn't take advantage of a foreign woman on her own. I slept very little, wondering if I could manage to live here after all. Now, suddenly, in no time at all, it seems more possible. It is such a change around. You are all so kind. Why would they come? They don't know me: you don't know me."

"No, we don't yet, but we know your aunt, Signora Powell. These people," Carmen waved her arms in an inclusive gesture, "all knew her or knew of her and of all that she did here. She did a lot for the farm. She did a lot for the town. She taught the farmers the more modern methods she'd learned in Europe so their farms became more productive and prosperous. She was loved and respected by everyone. Even now they speak fondly of her. When I said that her niece had come to take over the farm, word got around, and they all just turned up today. Others may come later to relieve the first ones so they can attend to their own businesses. If you think he will the right one, Hugo will stay on to teach you what he knows about the vines." While she was explaining all this, Carmen had been bustling about preparing coffee for the 4 of them. She handed them round.

Sarah took hers, grateful for the comfort and normality of the familiar drink. It was hot and strong, just as she liked it. Then Carmen disappeared for a few moments and came back carrying a big chocolate cake.

"This will make you feel better: settle you down and give you plenty of energy," she said, laughing in delight at Sarah's surprise.

She smiled at this vigorous older lady who as a young girl had worked for Señora Clara. It was a valuable connection and she looked forward to finding out more about her remarkable ancestor.

She felt better after the coffee and the delicious cake really did the trick. Now she felt ready to look at all the beautiful fabrics, while all around her echoed the sounds of work being done, much laughter, arguments and whistling.

There were so many designs to choose from, Sarah got dazzled. She decided to focus on two rooms at a time starting with the kitchen and maybe her bedroom. She was attracted to the simpler blue and white fabrics. They looked fresh and bright, and would contrast well with the terracotta pots and Spanish plates she had seen in the cupboards. She chose one with a random pattern that was bright but not too 'busy.' That was when she began to look more closely at the furniture that was left in the house. On her visit, it had seemed old, dusty and sad looking, and she had thought she would replace it all and bring in items of her own choosing. However, today, now they were all dusted and people were around, some of it looked really beautiful and very useful. The table was in good condition, nice and solid, just her idea of a country kitchen table, though she wasn't sure, when she reflected on it, what exactly that was. There was also an interesting dresser with shelves and cupboards. She had a look inside. It was very spacious and contained some beautiful old plates and dishes in traditional Spanish designs and colours.

"These are so pretty, Carmen. Did my aunt use these? There are a lot here. Did she like to entertain? Have friends for supper?"

"*Si,*" was the answer to all the questions. There was more than Sarah could ever imagine using for a while, so she chose a few of the more striking designs to put on the wall. They would be enhanced by the simpler colours of the fabric.

Chapter Seven

Sarah had been living in the farmhouse for a few weeks. With all the help from Carmen's family and friends, and Sarah's own hard work and long hours, the painting was all finished. The fresh paint seemed to bring more to each room than just a clean, bright finish. It seemed to release the original beauty and character of the house. She hadn't used all the furniture she had brought from England. It hadn't been the right size, the style looked out of place and sometimes the original furniture was more appropriate once it had been deeply cleaned and oiled. The blue and white curtains were up in the kitchen and the shutters in the bedroom painted blue and re-instated.

Carmen and José's house had been refitted with a new stove and some of her English furniture had ended up there, much to Carmen's delight. Huge paellas and delicious cakes through the week were testament to Carmen's delight in the improvements. Sarah still had her old cooker, but she decided she would prepare a casserole for herself, Carmen and José. She turned on the oven and went out to the scullery to bring in the vegetables she had planned to put in it. It took her longer than she expected, as she couldn't find what she wanted quickly. When she returned to the kitchen she shrieked in horror. The whole of the cooker, front, sides and top, was covered in small scurrying, frantic cockroaches: hundreds of them. She rushed outside calling for Carmen, who came running, wondering what had earth had happened. "Come and see," urged Sarah. "Look!"

"Oh! *Cucarachas*! (cockroaches) The oven hasn't been used for many weeks. *No hay problema*." She went back into her own house and quickly reappeared, carrying a red and green can of insecticide.

"*Ten cuidado*, (be careful)," she said, covering her nose and mouth as she proceeded to cover the cooker with some very strong stuff. Then she waved Sarah outside to allow the spray to do its work and for the fumes to disperse.

"You need to have some of this in the cupboard," she said. "These *cucarachas*, umm… cockroaches… get everywhere."

"Of course," replied Sarah. "I had forgotten they are part of life here. I will get some of that spray tomorrow. I expect it is safe to go back in now?"

They both returned to the kitchen to the sight of dead insects all over the place. "Eeugh! I'll get the vacuum cleaner and clear all this lot up, then wash the cooker off inside and out. I think I'll change my mind about what I was going to do this evening!" she smiled.

Carmen laughed. "*Signorina* Sarah, I will bring some paella I have just made. There is always so much. It is not easy to make a small one."

"Oh Carmen! That would be wonderful and so generous.

I must admit my cooking skills and the shopping required to get the food are both rather lacking just now. My head is so full of other things. That is so kind and very much appreciated. *Te lo ag-ra-desco,* (thank you very much)," said Sarah, struggling with some new Spanish words.

Carmen laughed, shrugged then left to return sometime later with a steaming bowl of the most deliciously fragrant paella. It was perfect, restoring Sarah's energy after the shock of all those cockroaches.

The house was more or less sorted now. Daniel, el plomero, had renovated the water system, put in a new tank on the roof, new pipes to the bathroom and kitchen and added a few extra things like an outside tap and water to the stable and winery. With these extra demands on the water supply, he arranged for a more frequent water delivery. He even fitted the ground tank with an inner screen lid, stopping sand and insects falling in each time the lid was opened. 'Brilliant!' thought Sarah. He had repaired the septic tank as well, so the air was definitely more fragrant.

Sarah was expecting him back in a week or two to upgrade the bathroom when she had had time to choose a new shower and washbasin. Even with it as it was, she was able to have a hot shower with reasonable pressure. It was such a relief after all the hard, physical work she now found herself doing. She realised what a soft and sedentary life she had lived in London. 'And I considered myself to be very fit and energetic. I even went to the gym. Hah! There is no comparison!' The present heating system couldn't quite keep up with the demand when it came to a relaxing hot bath though. Sarah decided she would speak to Daniel about how it could be improved economically, maybe even explore her earlier idea of using ground heat, even fitting solar panels if they were available here.

The various sons, nephews and cousins had gone back to their regular jobs. Only Hugo the farmer stayed on. Sarah worked with him to learn a little about the vines and how to grow them in this arid environment. She learned the basics quickly, and soon a lot of the weeding and clearing of the broken or dead vines closest to the house had been done. Hugo then turned his attention to the barn where the grapes were pressed and the juice fermented and turned into wine, the winery. He and José wanted to assess how much of the original equipment would be serviceable or need replacing.

Sarah had been planning to start up a productive vegetable garden and an ornamental garden of some kind. She read and re-read the Findhorn book, though was still not sure how it was done. She certainly wasn't sure about her ability to contact, let alone converse with, what had Eileen Caddy called them – plant elementals? She was clear about needing to feed the strange granular ground with plant material, so had started a large compost heap behind the stable with the weeds and vine prunings. It was all so different here: she wasn't sure if the same things applied as they did in northeast Scotland. She even began to wonder if the *finca*'s plant elementals would understand English. She sighed and decided until further information was forthcoming, she would stick with what she could see and put the more esoteric things to one side for a while. There was only so much new stuff she could take on board at once she felt.

Two areas in front of the house looked as if they may

have been more of a domestic garden than part of the farm. They were along the side of the end of the drive, as it turned into the yard by the main house. Carmen remembered that Clara had grown some vegetables there in the early days, along with a few flowers along the edges, like geraniums. A few sad, lanky oleanders grew here and there, still. Carmen had said that when they were strong and healthy, they were beautiful and spread a wonderful heady fragrance through the yard.

Sarah had been delighted to discover that now that the telephone line had been restored, the internet was available at the farm. It was a lot slower than the speed she had enjoyed in London, but it was good enough. She got online and began researching what to do to encourage sad oleanders into a more cheerful, healthy disposition. Even being able to do this little bit of research and get some information on the plants, greatly improved her resolve. She hated not knowing about so much. At least she had some means of learning what she needed. This eased the tension of 'not knowing enough' as she was able to research each section as they arose rather than carrying them all in her head at once.

Low walls of lava rock had marked out the area of vegetable garden. Their purpose had also been to break up the almost constant wind, but much of it had fallen over. What weeds were growing there were often blown flat. With what little knowledge Sarah had about growing things, she knew that young plants would struggle to grow to maturity under such constant adversity. Sarah decided to make new walls, a little higher, like the semi-circular walls that were around the vine "pits" further away. It was tough work. The lumps of lava that lay scattered about all over the place were not so heavy but very rough and sharp. She'd invested in a pair of leather gauntlets to stop her hands being shredded, which helped a lot. When she first brought them home, Hugo grinned, and then disappeared into one of the sheds. He came out carrying a similar, but very worn, pair of gauntlets. They were stiff and mouldy now but were undoubtedly a pair her great grandmother had used. Both of them regarded this as a good omen that Sarah was on the right track.

For a couple of weeks Sarah laboured away gathering stones that were scattered around the 'garden' area.' She had used all the ones that were closest and was now looking further away around the buildings and up the side of the track. The wheelbarrow was old, very heavy with one handle shorter than the other. It was difficult to push it when empty but with rocks in, it was almost impossible. The heavy wheelbarrow would sink into the soft lava beads and just stop. She considered using the truck but that would sink into the ground even more. If she was going to build these walls and realise her dream of growing vegetables in the gardens there was nothing for it but to fill the barrow with fewer rocks again and again and again, wheeling it from further and further away. The walls seem to hardly grow at all. She hadn't even finished a new layer all the way round the smaller of the two plots. The wind still blew strongly over the ground bending and breaking the weeds that grew there and drying it all out. She was a long way from making it suitable to plant anything there. Each night she would crawl upstairs, hardly able to straighten up. Sometimes she had no energy left to even prepare a meal for herself.

She would occasionally take a look at the compost heap up by the stable hoping for some inspiration and change, but it sat there looking just the same with no sign of this lovely rich compost she was assured would appear and produce an abundance of crops once spread out on the garden.

After a particularly difficult day when nothing seemed to go right, she hurt and ached everywhere and was getting nowhere. She felt very demoralised. Her motivation, plans, ideas, optimism about being able to make a reasonable living here all drained away. It just felt that she would labour here fruitlessly until all the money her great aunt had left her had been spent and she would have to sell up and return to England, defeated and ashamed. She could hardly think about leaving. She had enjoyed living here mostly, had started to make a few friends and her Spanish was improving all the time. People were friendly, more so than where she had lived in UK, even if they were a little bemused by this young English woman, who had no agricultural experience at all, taking on such a venture. She collapsed into bed and wept.

She slept fitfully. Clara appeared briefly in her dreams along with all sorts of other images none of which made any sense. Her mood was no lighter in the morning. During the night she decided she had been so busy with her "nose to the grindstone," as her mother used to describe hard, constant focused work, she hadn't had a good look at what was actually on the farm. She thought it may be a good idea to look around more closely. Perhaps there would be some signs or clues as to what Clara had done during her time there. She wondered what had changed or been discovered since she was alive. Perhaps she would discover a more productive way of protecting future crops in this area.

Chapter Eight

Still feeling despondent, Sarah took her morning mug of coffee outside. She was standing in the yard between the house and the stables, with the stables and buildings behind her, facing the house and the rising sun. It was her favourite place to stand first thing in the morning; she could enjoy the peace of the early warmth on her face, before the activity of the day started. She could relax a moment in the sun, with the comfort of the warm mug between both hands.

She became vaguely aware of someone or something approaching behind her, and of some rumbling, grunting noises. She turned, half expecting it to be her neighbour's pigs that occasionally wandered over to see what was going on and to check if there was anything to eat. She shrieked and jumped back in alarm, dropping her mug, which smashed to bits, splashing coffee all over her shoes and jeans. It wasn't a pig. It was very much larger. It was a huge, white camel! The camel grunted a bit more, blinked long eyelashes and slowly lay down on the floor in front of her and calmly began to chew the cud.

At her cries and screams, Carmen, José and Hugo came running to see what was the matter and almost skidded to a halt at the sight of this animal sitting in the yard, looking very much at home. After a moments' silence the three of them burst out laughing and talking excitedly in Spanish, too rapidly for Sarah to follow. She made out a few words and the general tone seemed to be positive. Then Carmen noticed how alarmed and confused Sarah looked and came over to soothe her anxieties. They gathered up the broken china. Hugo appeared with a bucket of water and an armful of greenery he'd cleared from the vineyard the day before. The camel was very thin and dirty. On closer inspection it looked exhausted. When the water arrived it took a long, urgent and grateful draught of water and after a few investigative pokes and sniffs, began grazing on the leaves as if this happened every day. Sarah's mouth was still open. Too many questions arrived in her head all at once, so all she could say was, "What? How did? But!"

Her friends gathered her up and led her back to the kitchen. Sarah glanced behind her. The camel was still there: very alive and very big! This was no figment of her imagination.

Carmen made some more coffee and they were soon joined by José and Hugo. When Sarah had first moved in, the three seemed to regard the kitchen as much theirs as hers and often just walked in with barely a tap on the door first. She'd bristled a bit initially, in a very British manner, and then thought that, actually, it was rather nice and friendly: especially as they never took the situation for granted. They settled down with their coffee and large slices of cake that

Carmen brought over from her house. "Good for shock," she explained, pointing to the ground and putting her two feet firmly on the floor. Sarah agreed – very grounding.

José began to explain why they were so pleased and excited by the arrival of the camel. With interjections from Carmen and help from Hugo with some of the English, the story emerged. First of all, it was not just a camel, but a white one. Camels are very expensive to buy. A white one is rare and regarded as good luck so costs even more. If a stray one turns up on your land and no one claims it, it is yours to keep. Señora Clara had had a camel – a white one. It was extremely helpful. With its large feet it didn't sink into the picon, the thick layer of lava granules that was used as mulch all over the farm, nor crush or compact it. Clara had used it to plough land prior to planting and to carry heavy loads.

"There are so many more things you can do with the help of a camel," said Carmen.

From their first sight, all of them had noticed the white camel was very thin and looked as if it had been treated harshly and neglected. Maybe its owner had moved away and it had been left to its own devices or it had escaped and had been wandering alone for some weeks. When they had all eaten their big slices of cake and Sarah felt less shaky, the four of them brought their mugs of coffee to the window, quietly regarding this new arrival. Even from there, they could see there were a few signs of dried blood on the animal's neck from old wounds.

"Hmm," said Carmen. "That blood has come from something like a whiplash. It is too straight for her to have got caught in a thorn tree." She sighed and shook her head. "It could be that she has run away from a camel dealer. They are well-known for ill-treating their uh… *camello hembra*."

Noticing Sarah's puzzled expression and that Sophia was struggling for the English, Hugo quietly translated, "Female camel."

"It looks as if she has been travelling on her own for a few weeks, would you say?" said Sarah, who really didn't know what a white camel should look like at the best of times. However, this one seemed as if she had almost come to the end of her endurance, then arrived, with relief, at the *finca*. She wondered what it was about the place that had somehow indicated to the bone-weary animal that this was a good place to be.

Then a thought struck Sarah.

"Oh! If my great aunt had kept a camel here before, was this odd-looking stable not for a donkey or a horse, as I thought, but for a camel! Might that be why this one has decided to stop here? But I don't know anything about camels. What do they eat? Do they have to be brushed? Do they really spit and bite as soon as look at you as people say?"

"Señora Clara had the stable built specially for the camel, to her own design," said Carmen. "We will look later. One end is for the camel: the other end is for a horse or donkey and to store tools and farm machinery. There were no cars here at first."

"Senorita," continued Hugo, "the farm needs hard work. You are wearing yourself out trying to do everything yourself. Now you have a strong companion to do much of that for you." With that he stood up, stuck out his chest and adopted a theatrical, "strong man" pose, then burst out laughing at Sarah's expression. "Not me! The camel!"

They all laughed, then got down to discussing camels, their care, harnesses, camel-drawn ploughs and carts and all the ways a camel could be useful.

"You mentioned the ploughing before but I didn't think they actually pulled the ploughs!" said Sarah.

"Si," said José. "There is *carro de camellos* in barn, *et sillín* (saddle) et 'arness."

Carmen took up the descriptions to help José who was struggling with the English he hadn't used for a while.

"The camel carts, carro de camellos, are big; they can carry a lot more than one barrowful – 150 – 250 kg. The sillín is the special saddle so you can ride it, if need be, though the ride is rather rough. You sway from side to side quite a lot.

Camels are easy to keep here in the north of Lanzarote. They can eat hay made from the Bermuda grass that grows well here – and browse on the trees and scrub, even the thorn bushes, which they need to eat. Is that right Hugo?"

"Yes," said Hugo. "The thorns are needed to keep their mouth in good condition, though I am not sure how."

"They like apples though!" added Carmen. "Be careful of your apple trees!"

Sarah felt relieved, albeit overwhelmed, by all this information and was beginning to think that the arrival of this camel could be a good thing, now she was getting over the initial shock.

"Well, the camel is still here and looks as if it is going to stay. If it does stay, do you know of anyone who would sell us some hay at this short notice? What bedding do camels need? Can we get some of that?"

The other three knew where they could get all these necessary things quickly.

They all went out of the back door quietly so as not to startle the camel. It was still there where it had lain down when it arrived. Sarah thought it looked smaller, less alarming, now she knew what to expect.

She approached the camel slowly, wondering what to say then the words came to her.

"*Hola! Salaam alaikum. Marhaba!* Hello, welcome," said Sarah softly, having remembered the Arabic greeting from one of her business trips to Saudi in the past. The camel looked at her and blinked at the familiar greeting. It struggled awkwardly to its feet.

"Oh! Sweetie, you're hurt," cried Sarah.

Now that the animal was standing, she could see, more clearly, the bloody wounds and scratches on its shoulder and sides and just how thin she was. Camels are bony creatures at the best of times but this poor creature seemed to be nothing but a bag of skin over her bones. She was now obviously completely exhausted from whatever had been going on in her life for some time before her relieved arrival at *finca Los Palmas*. Without thinking and full of compassion, she walked to the camel and gently touched its shoulder. After a momentary quiver, the animal seemed to relax. Sarah stroked its side, amazed at how soft its coat was, even though it was dusty. Then she noticed more cuts, injuries and localized sores.

"Oh Sweetie! What have they been doing to you?" she exclaimed.

The camel turned its head to look at her. The other three, who had been watching in astonishment, gave a united sharp intake of breath, afraid for her safety in case it bit her. However, the camel just looked at her, blinked and made a low rumbling noise in its throat.

"Please. We can look after you. I'll get a vet to check out your cuts and sores. I can feed you. You look very thin and very tired. *Tati!* (Come!) There is a special space for you here. *Tati!*" She was surprised that these random words from years ago should come her aid now.

She began walking to the stable nearby. She stopped, beckoned the camel and waited for it to join her. It was obvious it was painful for it to walk, but it followed her slowly. Carmen, José and Hugo exchanged glances, open mouthed. Once inside, it gave the space a close inspection, then walked back to the door. "No!" said Sarah, afraid it would walk away. "Stay here!" She wanted very much for it to stay. The camel didn't leave but lay down in the doorway looking out at the house, Carmen and José's house and the land around. It sighed and began to chew the cud – a sign of a relaxed and settled camel. Hugo brought the water and remains of the food to the door, but didn't get too close. He was unsure how the camel would react to him.

"Oh, good girl!" said Sarah, stroking its neck gently. "You wait here and we'll see what we can arrange for you."

She walked over to join her friends, who were standing with amazed expressions.

"Senorita, what happened to you? First you scream in fright, now you have a camel following your command and you are speaking in, what, Arabic?"

Sarah shook her head as if coming out of a dream. "I don't know. One minute I was nervous, the next minute I remembered what to do, how to approach it, stroke it and speak to it. Maybe it was because I could see that it was injured and weak." Her voice trailed off as she shook her head again. She didn't say so, but she had felt her aunt close by, which had calmed her and stirred the words she needed from her memory.

"How did you know to say "*Tati*" to make the camel follow you?" asked Carmen.

"Hmm? I worked in Saudi on and off in my last job and must have learned them there. I suppose I just remembered the words." The young woman shrugged and smiled. The other three looked at each other.

"Why? Why are looking like that?" she added.

"That was the word your aunt used to make the camel come to her!" said Hugo.

"I probably had heard them in that context all that time ago and the word came to my rescue in response to seeing the camel."

Sarah shivered. "Carmen, I think I could with some more of your coffee and cake. This is all a bit strange. Then we'd better get things sorted out for this creature, as it looks as if it is going to stay.

"Senorita," began José, "Why you call her, uh... Sweetpea?"

"Sweetpea? No. I said 'Sweetie,' Sarah chuckled, "but I like the name Sweetpea. You said it was a girl?" José nodded. "Then Sweetpea it is!"

With smiles all round they all returned to the kitchen for coffee and to make lots of phone calls.

Chapter Nine

The vet came over to treat Sweetpea's wounds and give her a general health check. She gave the camel various injections against a number of diseases. Some of the wounds were deep and needed careful attention to encourage them to heal. The vet commented on her poor, emaciated condition. She said that the injuries indicated that she had been very cruelly treated and frequently beaten. The vet continued by making a note of this, saying that should the former owner arrive to claim her, Sarah had evidence sufficient to prevent him taking her away.

Sarah could see that the animal had been traumatised by her previous owners and decided she would put some flower essence remedies in the drinking water. She was used to using them herself in England and had brought a supply with her.

'I had forgotten I'd brought these with me. I could use some of this myself as well,' she thought. She gave Sweetpea the remedy in her water every day for two weeks. Gradually Sweetpea became more settled as the tension and pain eased from her body.

The camel stayed in the stable and occasionally came to the door. However, after a quick look around, seeing or hearing Sarah, she would go back in and lie down with a deep rumbling noise. Gradually, she began staying in the doorway for a little longer each day. Sarah visited her often through the day, checking and treating the wounds, which were healing nicely. She cleaned the stable every day, refreshing the food and water, talking to the animal, stroking her and gently brushing out the dust and stones that had got caught in her coat. One day Sarah was standing outside the house with her back to the stable looking out over the ground trying to figure out what to do next, what she would be able to do. Sweetpea left the confines of the stable, walked across the yard and came to join her there for the first time. Sarah stood close to her, leaned on her shoulder and put her arm under and around the long neck. They stayed like that for a long time: two lonely souls finding solace and friendship in each other's company.

Chapter Ten

Sweetpea's arrival and return to health seemed a turning point at *finca Los Palmas*. Sarah felt more settled and had renewed determination to make things work. The camel followed her everywhere, much like her parents' border collie used to. 'A bit of a difference in the size, though,' mused Sarah. She never put a rein on the camel or tethered her. She just stayed wherever Sarah was.

Slowly Sweetpea's wounds healed. Some of them, especially two on her back were big and deep where saddle supports rested on her, so the vet had said. It must have been so painful with a heavy saddle and whatever the load was on that day, each bearing a heavy weight, pressing down on already bare flesh. If she refused to move, she was whipped by the look of other wounds she bore. With Sarah's care, love and attention, good food and shelter Sweetpea began to look better – 'and hopefully feel better,' thought Sarah.

The camel put on some weight and her coat looked much thicker and felt silkier. Sarah continued to brush it gently where she could, keeping well clear from the healing sores. Sarah was still busy building low shelter walls in her "garden," wheeling heavy barrows backwards and forwards as she gathered lumps of lava from other parts of the farm. The camel walked beside her wherever she went.

On this one day, Sarah put her in the shade of the stable when she went in for lunch as usual. Feeling a bit rested, she went to give Sweetpea a shout to come out for the afternoon.

She called several times but no sign of any camel. Feeling a rush of anxiety, Sarah went right into the stable to see if she was alright. With a little sigh of relief Sarah saw her. She seemed to be alright, but was standing at the other end of the stable away from her usual quarters, where there was old equipment and machinery.

"Come on, Sweetpea. What're you doing there?" As if in answer, Sweetpea growled and shuffled around, looking at Sarah then looking into a corner. This was so intentional that Sarah went to look at where the camel was seemingly pointing with her nose.

She had no idea what she was looking at. Hugo, wondering what was going on, had come to the door.

"Is everything alright, Senorita?" he asked.

"Oh Hugo, what is this? Sweetpea seems to want me to see it."

Hugo walked around Sarah to have a look at whatever it was, as intrigued now as Sarah.

"Ah, Senorita Sarah, Sweetpea is a clever animal. She wants to help you. This is a camel cart. It will hold three to four times the load of your wheel barrow."

"Really? But won't that be heavy to pull?"

"Yes! Si! But this girl is very strong now she is better. She is telling you she will pull it for you. You don't need to fill it full straight away. Gradually increase the load. She will tell you when it is enough. She won't move willingly."

"Oh wow! That sounds great! How do we set this thing up?"

They dragged the cart out between them. Sarah brushed off the dust, dirt and cobwebs, rather hoping there wouldn't be any cockroaches hidden in there. Hugo lubricated the moving parts of the axle and wheels, cleaned and put special oil on the harness and reins to soften them, though they were still amazingly soft after all this time. The old lady certainly looked after her equipment.

As they worked quietly together, with Sweetpea looking on with an air of anticipation, Sarah thought how nice it was to be doing something together with someone. She had never had that feeling with her ex-husband she realised with a jolt. They had never done much together that was practical. It had been mostly going out for a drink or a meal with friends, or sex.

Her reverie was broken by Hugo, who pronounced the cart ready for use. Between them they got Sweetpea hitched up to the cart. She was almost dancing with excitement and impatience.

"She really wants to do this, doesn't she?" remarked Sarah, with surprise. She had put some soft cloth under the harness where it put the most pressure on the camel's body. Sweetpea rumbled and growled when this was done. Sarah had learned that this was her noise for being pleased – like a cat purring.

"Will I need a rein or something to steer her with?"

"No, I don't think so. She follows you. Stays with you. No problem"

"OK, let's do this. Come on Sweetpea. Let's see what kind of team we make!"

Hugo smiled to himself and shook his head in disbelief and wonder. Cart or no cart, this slender woman, fresh from London city life and her refugee camel were already a team he had never seen the like of before. There they were, the woman in working dungarees and working boots walking along with her arm on the shoulder of this strange, very clever camel: the animal keeping pace with her new "owner," looking very purposeful and somehow taller and prouder than she had looked since her bedraggled, exhausted arrival.

When the cart was about one-third full of lava rocks, Sarah thought that would be enough and turned to go back to the house, but Sweetpea shook her head and walked further on as if to say "No, this is fine. I can take more."

"OK, if you're sure." Sarah smiled to herself and shrugged. She realised how quickly and easily she had fallen into the way of chatting to this huge gangly beast, as if it understood what she was saying and funnily, Sarah knew, that at some level, she did.

That afternoon they brought back four loads of lava stones to the garden, where Sarah quickly built them into the wall. Without the exertion of wheeling the heavy barrows, she had more available energy and was able to build the walls more rapidly. She was so relieved to see discernible progress at last. Pictures of a "proper garden" resurfaced in her mind, though she knew it would be a while before that was actually realised. There was more urgent work needing to be done than growing some flowers and a few carrots and potatoes.

She gave her new companion a hug around her neck. In reply Sweetpea lowered her head and rested it along the top of the woman's back.

Wiping away the few tears that sprung to her eyes at this tender expression of friendship (as she felt it to be), she led the camel back to the stable. She undid the harness, checked there were no signs of soreness or chafing. There weren't. This meant that the padding she had put in place had really helped, so was something she could do each time. She rubbed Sweetpea down, something the camel obviously enjoyed, made sure there was fresh water and hay for her, clean bedding and a good flow of air to keep her cool, said "Goodnight," and went in for her supper. Her heart felt lighter than it had for a long time.

'I didn't even know how heavy it had become over the last months, since even before I got here. Perhaps that was why I came here and feel so determined to succeed,' she thought. She didn't feel exhausted like she had done for days and she, no they, had almost finished the first enclosure. She could still feel the weight and warmth of the camel's head on her shoulders and how lovely that had been. She was just about to drift off into sleep when a picture of the older woman, whom she now decided was in fact her great aunt, came into focus in her mind's eye. Clara Powell gave Sarah Jones a smile and a nod of the head then faded as Sarah fell asleep.

Chapter Eleven

The camel had been helping at the farm for a couple of weeks. Sarah, with Sweetpea's help, had been continuing with the work of rebuilding the walls around the small gardens. These were to the side of the main drive from the road, and directly in front of the house and were now almost complete. As the new owner of the farm, Sarah was still unsure what she should be paying attention to. She had no idea what the vineyards should look like at this time of the year; she wouldn't know if they were healthy or not. She worried that there were things she should be noticing but wasn't because of her lack of experience and knowledge. She assumed and hoped that José and Hugo knew what to look for, but she wanted to know as well.

She, with Sweetpea at her side as usual, was standing in the yard between the house and the stables in the late spring sunshine, revelling in the feel of the warmth on her skin. In spite of all the uncertainty about what to do, she loved her life on the farm. It was so different from the pressures of her old life in the cold, wet, polluted London environment. She had hardly thought of David since her arrival. Her true self was emerging from the confines that her ex-husband had woven around her so she would be who he wanted her to be. She felt her younger self, the carefree, adventurous part of her that had got buried deeper than she realised, bubbling up even with the concern she was now aware of. She was standing with José looking over the gardens and vineyards.

"José," began Sarah, "I am concerned that I know so little about the vines, apart from the bit Hugo showed me right at the beginning. There is so much I want to know about growing hay, vegetables, when and how to do it. I hope you and Hugo can help me learn more about the vines. I haven't been to the vineyard since my first few weeks."

Sarah wanted to ask about a lot more. She was bursting with questions and full of the uncomfortable realisation, again, of how little she knew about anything to do with the farm. Having been so competent in her previous job, she was unsettled by this new feeling of ignorance. She didn't like it at all. Her Spanish didn't extend to everything she wanted to know. She wanted to know if it might be possible to grow and dry the hay for Sweetpea themselves? Up till then they had been buying hay because her arrival was unexpected. Was it too late to start? She wanted to know if it was too late to plant seeds in the new front gardens. She had been reading what she could about farming and gardening, but she knew almost nothing about any of it and really, really wanted to learn. It was too much to say in English she knew and too much for her Spanish. It would have to be done by degrees. She knew she needed to relax a bit and be comfortable with not knowing for a while. 'Easier said than done,' she thought ruefully. 'Maybe I could ask Hugo about some of it. He seems to be able to speak English with greater ease.'

José was struggling to understand Sarah. She spoke very quickly in her questioning and frustration. However, he had picked up 'Sweetpea, growing, vines, planting' and a few bits in between so he nodded and smiled encouragingly.

"*Los vides de uva, primero*, (the grape vines first)," he said and set off in that direction. Sarah followed guessing they were going to do something with the vines. Sweetpea went along as well.

The yard closest to the buildings where it was more sheltered, was planted in the traditional way, in rows with the vines trained along wires stretched between sturdy posts. To Sarah's uneducated eye they looked pretty good, though there were a few gaps where vines had died.

Hugo, who was working further along the row looked up and was amused to see the two people, followed by the camel, walking down the row. Sweetpea gave the leaves an experimental sniff and nibble as is a camel's wont. Sarah noticed and shouted "No, Sweetpea! Not these!" Sweetpea quickly lifted her head to look around, affecting an air of innocence. "Me, eating vine leaves? Never! As if…"

José and Sarah laughed affectionately at this. The camel was certainly getting to be quite a character.

"*Hola! Como estas?*" greeted Hugo as he drew close.

"*Bien! Bien! Como estas,*" greeted the other two.

"Ah Senorita Sarah, the vines are growing but some have died. *Ven y mira*. (We walk some more)," said Hugo.

As they walked, José and Hugo pointed out different

93

things: the way the vines had been pruned to concentrate the plant's efforts into growing and ripening the fruit rather than into long leafy shoots: the many bunches of tight green grapes still small and hard: how they were planted in the base of wide furrows so any moisture condensing on the picon would collect at the bottom for the vines to use.

The two men had been working hard to renovate the vines, pruning, thinning, weeding, feeding. The rows looked good to Sarah and she told them so. The two men looked pleased that she had noticed the results of their hard labour.

As they walked out to the more exposed area of the farm, the rows of vines stopped and in their stead was the strange landscape peculiar to this grape growing region of Lanzarote. Here the vines were grown in the base of conical depressions, the depth of which was dictated by the degree of exposure to the strong, north Atlantic winds. Low semi-circular walls on the windward side of the depressions provided additional shelter. The area was completely mulched with the black bead-like lava, the picon that she saw everywhere. At this time of the year the depressions were almost full of green leaves, creating a picturesque contrast to the lava, so Sarah thought.

Hugo had not cleared so much of this area so there were a lot of the prickly pear cacti here and there. There was a still a lot of work to do!

The three of them looked out over the old vineyard and the rest of the flatter land beyond the farm buildings. Sarah thought it looked so barren in comparison to the fields around where her parents lived in England and where she had been brought up. Their garden was always so productive:

full of beautiful flowers and shrubs, fruit trees and sufficient vegetables to provide them with fresh produce just about all year.

Here there was this strange black pebbly stuff, lots of prickly pear cacti, (aptly named as far as Sarah was concerned), some random low scrub, with rather ragged palm trees here and there and lining the track leading to the house.

She gave a deep sigh and plonked down on an upturned bucket, abandoned there since the last grape harvest. Hugo started forward, half-expecting the bucket to collapse. He relaxed when it remained solid. Gazing gloomily out on her apparently unpromising land and lost in negative thoughts, Sarah missed this gesture of concern.

The two men shook their heads. They could see the young woman was down-hearted and dismayed by what lay before them. They had seen the farm when it was flourishing and the potential and more that it could reach. However, they could see that in this mood Sarah wouldn't be able to 'hear' what they had to say.

"How can I ever make a living from this?" Sarah asked, sweeping her arm around in the direction of the cacti and scrub. "Is there any soil here or is it all this weird stuff?" She bent down and scooped up a handful of the picon, the black lava beads. She sighed again and tossed them away. Sweetpea came up behind her and nudged her in the back as if to break her downward spiralling reverie.

Sarah gave a short laugh. "You're right, Sweetpea. Being maudlin and sorry for myself isn't going to change anything." She took a deep breath. "José, Hugo, would you come back to the kitchen and tell me how the farm worked when my aunt was here, while we have some coffee and Carmen's magic cake?" Hugo repeated in Spanish what Sarah had said. Both men nodded and indicated to Sarah to lead the way.

Hugo picked up the old bucket to return to the barn and they all set off back to the house. The two men gave the camel a pat of thanks: they hadn't known, themselves, how to bring Sarah out of her low mood.

Carmen had been watching the scene from her house. She saw Sarah slump down on the bucket and sensed her despair. She was about to call them back to the house for coffee and cake, when she saw the group stir more purposefully and make their way back to the farmhouse. She bustled into Sarah's kitchen, quickly getting the restorative coffee and cake ready, putting out plates and mugs.

"Oh Carmen! Brilliant! Thank you. *Gracias*. Just what we need. Can you stay a while? I would like you all to tell me in detail about the farm so we can decide how best to go on from here. I'll go and get my notebook."

While she was gone the other three began reminiscing about when Señora Clara was alive and well, all the things they grew and sold and the wonderful celebrations she held through the year. Sarah came back, notebook in hand and drank some coffee.

"This is very good Carmen, thank you."

Carmen beamed. It was always encouraging to have someone enjoy what she made. Pen in hand, Sarah looked around the table, "OK, where do we begin? Actually, first of all, why are there so many cactus plants about? Are they the only things that grow well here?"

Carmen seemed to be gathering her thoughts and her memory. "When Señora Clara lived here," she began, "the red dye from a certain beetle was used in a lot of things – was called Carmine, I think. (E102 Sarah discovered later). The beetles we dried in the sun, crushed and put in special solution. Señora has the recipe somewhere, I think. Many, many insects are needed to make this dye. They live on these prickly plants. Mil, mil, mmm… thousand on the plants" She went on to explain, with help from Hugo, that rather than spend time clearing the cacti out of the land, Clara decided to use them as a means of making money for the farm. The plants grew easily and made new plants easily from the strange pad-like leaves. In the early days the dye was a good price. She went on to say that the dye could be used in many things – to dye cloth, to colour lipsticks and in drinks, sweets and to colour food.

"Ah! said Sarah thoughtfully, "I remember my mother saying that my Granny used to make pink cakes with pink colouring. Cochineal they called it. Were they cochineal beetles my aunt harvested?"

Hugo nodded.

Carmen continued, "*Si*. When the Señora learned the method, producing the dye was the farm's first income."

"I wonder if there is still a market for the dye," said Sarah.

"*Si*," this time it was José. "In food?" he made a wobble of a flat hand indicating uncertainty. "Not from *animales. Ciertamente* for *artista* and uh… *material para colorear.*" Sarah felt a bit excited – not so much for food colouring but for artists' paint and dyeing fabric!

"Do you have the recipe for making the dye still, Carmen?

Is it very hard? Take a long time?"

"It is patient work," replied Carmen. "The longest time is gathering the beetles. *Uno momento.*" She disappeared into her house to fetch something. Meanwhile the others finished their coffee. As the men chatted on in Spanish, Sarah logged onto her computer. She still felt overjoyed that they had a connection to the internet; this enabled her to discover if there was still a demand for cochineal. She was thinking that this might be what she had been hoping for – a means of income from the land immediately, without having to wait for something to grow.

Carmen returned carrying a large bucket, a small basin, about 500ml Sarah thought, and some big heavy leather gauntlets. She also had some papers tucked under her arm.

"I have found the… um… *receta* (recipe) and these," she said, waving the papers, bowls and gloves. "This bowl full make 5kg of dye. We wore these," waving the gauntlets, "to gather them. The plants are *viciosa!*"

José remembered he used to collect them for pocket money. "They brushed into bucket *facilmente.* (easily)"

The three of them fell into a Spanish conversation of reminiscing while Sarah continued her search on marketing possibilities for the "*Los Palmas* red" as she was already calling it in her head. They were more limited than in her great aunt's day, but they were still there and the price looked reasonable. It depended on how long it took to make the dye whether it would be worthwhile. There was only one way to find out and that was to make some.

Keeping that possibility in mind for later, Sarah led the conversation on to the grape harvest. The number of grape bunches in the sheltered yard looked promising. The men said they would continue clearing the more exposed vineyards to see what the vines were doing there. Sarah offered to help, if they showed her what to do. This offer was gratefully received. It was a big area and had got rather overgrown with weeds and the vines looked a bit straggly.

"There are some small trees growing there dotted about in no particular order. What are they? I don't recognise them."

"They are um… '*Higos*'," replied Hugo, searching for and failing to find the English word for figs. "*Higos blancos et purpureo.*"

Sarah was mystified by the Spanish names. This time in response to her puzzled expression, José disappeared and returned with some small dried fruit in his hand.

Sarah recognised them. "Oh figs! Of course! Blancos? Ah! white figs and 'purpureo' has to be purple."

"*Si*," José beamed, "*estos son blanca*, um, *secado al sol y al viento*," his English reaching its limits with this new turn in the conversation. Sarah thought for a moment following José's gestures. "Dried in the sun and wind?" she asked.

In reply, they all got up, Hugo grabbing another piece of cake as he left, giving Sarah a conspiratorial wink. She laughed at this sudden relaxed and friendly mischief. They all followed José round to the back of the stable. There were stacks of large, slatted trays piled up against the wall, partly covered by tarpaulin.

"*¡Aqui!* (here)," said José, pointing to the trays.

Carmen continued the explanation. "*Viente, triente*, um… twenty, thirty trays. We used to dry a lot and sell them at the market at Haria. Since Señora Sarah died, we have dried a few for ourselves but have not sold any for a few years."

Sarah began to feel a little bit more excited. Here was another possible source of income that she didn't know about. There was a lot to learn and certainly they needed to check on the trees to discover how healthy they were and what sort of crop they might produce. Also, with the mention of the market at Haria, she remembered how much she had enjoyed looking around there with Inés on her initial visit. She realised she had not been there since, nor had she had any time off since her arrival. She decided she would go back soon. Maybe she could meet up with Inés there on her friend's day off. It had been a long time since they had met up. They had both been too busy.

Bringing her mind back to the reason they were all together, Sarah returned to her idea of making and marketing the red dye, so needed to find out more about its production. It seemed there was still a market for it, but not so many people bothered with it. There were so many of those Prickly Pear things, they may as well be earning something for the farm or get cleared away so they could produce something that would. She shared her findings with the others. After some discussion, they decided they would go on a "beetle hunt" the next day.

Chapter Twelve

The following morning Sarah cleaned out the stable and fed and watered Sweetpea. The camel grunted her thanks and settled down to eat her breakfast. Carmen, José and Hugo were already outside, armed with thick gauntlets, buckets and soft brushes as instructed by Carmen. Sarah gathered her things and all four of them set off. They didn't have far to go: the cacti grew everywhere.

Carmen said to look for cottony blobs: those were the beetles. It was obvious the pads of the cacti were infested with them and with gentle brushing the beetles fell off easily and died straight away. In no time at all the bucket was more than half full. Carmen decided it was enough to make the process worthwhile.

They were just about to make the short walk back to the house, when an old truck came roaring down the farm track in a cloud of dust. It swerved to a halt near them and an obviously irate man leaped out, shouting in rapid Spanish and waving his arms in great agitation and rage. Sarah looked at Carmen, hoping she could make sense of this tirade as the Spanish was too quick for her to follow. Their silence and obvious bewilderment sent the man into even more paroxysms of anger.

"He says you stole his camel, keep her tethered and lock her up to keep her," explained Carmen. Sarah was about to explain that there was a camel here but neither tethered nor locked up. "In fact, there she is, standing in the door of the stable," she said, pointing.

The man's gaze followed the direction of her pointing arm, then began shouting again. "*Si*! Me!" he repeated pointing at the camel then at himself.

Sarah knew that there was no way she was going to let this man take Sweetpea and subject her to the same level of abuse and cruelty she had endured before. She had received so many injuries, many of which had taken a long time to properly heal. She was about to offer him a considerable amount of money to buy her, when there was a loud roar from the stable. Sweetpea came galloping across the yard at full speed, neck and head pointing straight ahead, jaw and teeth thrust forward. Sarah had never seen her looking or heard her sounding so fierce, not even when she was tending the worst of her painful wounds. It became obvious the camel was heading straight for the man, growling, roaring and frothing at the mouth.

Hearing the noise, the man turned from his angry remonstrations. The camel was almost upon him. José held Sarah back as she tried to step forward to stop what was so obviously going to be an attack on the man.

"No! Watch!"

The man shouted at the camel, then his anger turned to

terror as he realised the camel was coming straight for him. She was now very close and looking very dangerous. With loud oaths, he hastily leaped back into the truck, swung it round rapidly, taking out several cacti, and shot back up the drive to the main road, with Sweetpea in hot pursuit.

"NO! Sweetpea. Come back. *Vuelve aqui! Eud iilaa huna!* (Come back. Come back here!)" yelled Sarah running after her, afraid she would chase the man out on to the main road and get run over. However, once she got to the end of the track and the man had disappeared, Sweetpea stopped, breathing heavily, agitated and upset. Sarah thought it best to wait a few moments for the camel to calm down. She had been alarmed by such a show of aggression. She had had no idea camels could be like that. Her self-appointed "guest" had always been so calm and friendly. The other three caught up with her talking excitedly, laughing and laughing.

"Why are you laughing?" asked Sarah shocked. "It looked as if she was going to kill him!"

"Yes!" laughed José. "*Si, si!*"

"She recognised her old owner. Camels have a good memory. She wasn't going back to him to be treated with the same cruelty! No way!" finished Carmen.

Then they explained that the man was well known in the area for his cruel treatment of camels. It was not possible for anyone to get near his farm and stables. It was surrounded by high electrified fences. When the camels were led out to take tourists for rides, they were all decked out in colourful rugs and tassels so no-one could see the wounds and injuries caused by his cruelty.

There was no way he could pursue his claim on Sarah's

camel: the results of his cruel treatment were on the Vet's records for anyone to see.

Meanwhile, Sweetpea's breathing had slowed. She had a good shake and began calmly browsing on the scrub that was growing nearby. Sarah went slowly towards her, talking softly, a little unsure after such behaviour. "*Tati!* Sweetpea. *Tati!*"

The camel turned her head at the sound of her new owner's voice. With a quiet grunt and a rumble, she walked towards Sarah, with a very different expression on her face. It clearly said, "Huh! I showed him!" If a camel could look pleased with itself that is what it would look like!

Sarah hadn't realised how much she wanted this strange creature to stay with her at *finca Los Palmas*. It had become her friend and companion. She turned to walk back to the stable with the camel, stroking its shoulder and talking softly to it. The others followed on behind, smiling but shaking their heads in amazement at this unusual friendship.

Chapter Thirteen

It had been a few days since the disturbing and alarming visit by Sweetpea's previous owner. Sarah's jangled nerves had settled down. She had been very disturbed by the aggression Sweetpea had displayed in the attack. She hadn't realised camels could be so violent. Hugo assured her that it was very rare and that it took a lot to rouse them. Things felt more settled, so Sarah and Carmen decided they would make the red dye that had been so financially important to the history of the island and to the farm when Aunt Clara had moved there. Carmen had found the instructions which seemed straightforward enough. Soon they had a bucket of brilliant red dye. The women were really pleased with the result and wanted to test it straight away. Sarah fetched an old white dress she had had for a few years but it had gone rather grey and tired looking. It was a favourite of hers so she had brought it with her hoping to brighten it up. It hadn't worked, she hadn't worn it, so if the dye didn't take or was blotchy it wouldn't matter. Carefully following her aunt's detailed instructions, they dipped the dress in the dye, then rinsed it in salt and vinegar and hung it out to dry.

"Eeugh! I'll smell like a jar of pickles!" groaned Sarah, when she caught the strong smell of the vinegar.

"No, no," laughed Carmen. "The smell wears off as it dries. That looks a lovely colour. I will try something of my own," and off she went to see what she could find.

The next day the dress and the blouse were dry and ironed. The two women could now see that the dyeing had been a great success and the smell of vinegar had disappeared, thankfully. Sarah now had a gorgeous, vibrant red dress, very different from the sad garment it had been. The shade of red really suited her black hair and tanned skin. Carmen's blouse had been equally successful. She looked years younger. The red suited her Spanish colouring too. The kitchen was filled with gales of laughter as they paraded and posed in their "new," old clothes.

There followed a day of trials using different materials and various coloured fabric apart from the white cotton garments they had used first. They had to restrain themselves from dyeing all their clothes red in their excitement and enthusiasm.

One evening, Inés phoned Sarah. It was her day off on the coming Saturday and she wondered if Sarah would like to meet her in Haria for coffee and they could explore the local market there. Sarah was delighted: it was what she had been planning to do.

Saturday came and with Carmen's encouragement, Sarah wore her newly dyed red dress. If she came back with skin that had turned bright red from the dye, then any plans to develop the cochineal dye further would need a lot more experimentation. However, if she had positive reactions from passers-by or stall holders, and no red skin, the two women could then think more seriously about working with Valeria, the experienced dressmaker, to produce a range of unique, exclusive clothes in "Lanzarotean Red."

Sarah looked beautiful. The style of the dress really suited her and the colour complemented the tan she had acquired from working outside nearly all the time. She admitted to herself that it was rather nice to be in a dress, having been in dungarees for so long, to arrange her hair prettily and to put on some make up.

Not long after Sarah had left, Sweetpea ambled out of the stable, wondering why she hadn't started work yet. She was just in time to see Sarah's truck disappear from the farm track onto the main road. The camel set off purposefully up the track after her. José and Hugo watched anxiously, concerned that she would follow Sarah in to town. Calling her name, they set off to stop her and bring her back. However, just at that moment, the camel stopped by a small grove of palm trees at the end of the drive, lay down in the shade and began to chew the cud. It was obvious she was going to wait there until Sarah returned.

"Well! Look at that!" exclaimed the two men. "Thank goodness for that!" Hugo paused for a moment. He had been surprised by how beautiful Sarah looked: he had got used to seeing her in her dungarees, no make-up and hair just bundled up into a pony tail. She was good looking but it hadn't affected him in the same way as he had been just now.

'No!' he thought. 'I am not going that way again: having my heart broken once was enough.' He shook his head to clear his mind and joined José as they returned to the yard and the work of the day. They both kept an eye on the track to make sure Sweetpea was still there and alright. They wanted her to stay on the farm too: she was very useful.

Unaware of all this activity, Sarah got to town, parked up and walking past brilliant bougainvillea and geraniums, arrived at the restaurant where she and Inés had arranged to meet.

Inés was waiting there, a café in the centre of town, *El Rincon de Quino*, on the side of a tree lined square. Tables and chairs were spread out under the trees. It was very busy with local people for the market and a few tourists. Inés loved the red dress saying how much it suited Sarah. "With your dark hair and tanned skin, you look like a native," she laughed.

After coffee and catching up on events since they last met, they set off for the market, with the aim of seeing what was there and if anything could be produced at *finca Los Palmas*. They discussed the products that were for sale, what seemed to be selling quite quickly – indicating there was more demand for it. Sarah was surprised by the standard of the goods displayed, and how attractive the stalls looked. The owners had obviously gone to a lot of trouble presenting their wares.

It was great fun and involved lots of discussion between them and long conversations with the stall holders. Sarah's Spanish skills had improved rapidly and she was able to talk with them all. Having Inés there to take part and fill in the gaps helped a lot. The conversations generally started slowly as the people assumed Sarah was just another curious tourist so were not interested in divulging much about themselves. However, once they learned that she was the new owner at *finca Los Palmas*, their attitude changed. Many of them remembered Great Aunt Clara with affection and high regard. Soon it was the stall holders who were quizzing Sarah about how she came to be there and telling anecdotes about her aunt. Sarah quickly got the idea that her aunt had been a very active part of the community there.

As the morning went on, they learned more and more about the potential of the farm in terms of what could be produced there. Sarah became curious about how such a barren looking place with formidable looking soil could produce such a wide variety of excellent crops. Everyone who had bought things from there in the past enthused about the taste and the quality. There was something extra about them that wasn't present in food from other farms nearby. When asked if they knew how Señora Clara achieved that difference, the stall holders often shrugged and laughed, some even made the sign of the cross and said it was something to do with the moon. There was talk of some sort of botanical spray. It all seemed rather mysterious and a few older people suspected some kind of magic, but agreed it must have been some sort of good magic! Sarah wondered if her aunt had left any information about the methods she had used to such good effect and resolved to search through the boxes that had been left in the house and were upstairs in the small bedroom.

The two women bought something from each stall because it all looked so appetising and to encourage the conversation further. They bought various artisan breads, carrots, potatoes, peppers, onions, courgettes and melons. There were many varieties of goats' cheese, free range chickens and eggs, dried figs, red and white wine and prickly pear jam.

"Prickly pear jam!" exclaimed Sarah when she was told what the jam was. "The plants are so spiny. What part of the plant can possibly be made into jam? – which is very nice," she added with surprise when the stall holder gave her some to taste.

"You have seen the pretty yellow flowers amongst the spines?" asked Inés. "Each flower produces a plum shaped juicy fruit. As it ripens, it goes a purply red and the spines drop off." Sarah was still doubtful.

"You have to use long handled tongs to pick them so you don't get stabbed," added Inés. The jam maker smiled at Sarah's slightly horrified face. "We use these," she said and brought out a tool that looked like outsized sugar tongs, with loops of metal instead of the little claws. "It is very easy and quick, and we don't get scratched," she added presenting hands free of any injury to back up her point.

"Thank you," said Sarah. "It makes a bit more sense now. There's certainly an abundance of the plants at the farm." The jam was very nice, though very sweet, and not many people sold it. Judging by the level of sales and the speed with which the jars disappeared from the stalls, it was very popular – with the local people as well as the tourists.

It was certainly something to consider, though she had

never made jam in her life. 'Carmen would be sure to know how to make it,' she thought.

Sarah got many admiring comments about her dress and Inés noted the admiring glances of passers-by. Two women stopped them to say what a lovely colour the dress was, wanting to know where Sarah got the dress from. They thought it must have come from mainland Spain or Italy. They would love to have a dress like hers. Inés and Sarah exchanged glances and nodded. This was what they wanted to hear. It certainly seemed like a good plan to speak to Valeria about developing their own range of clothes.

"I have always been interested in making clothes," confided Inés. "I went to a class many years ago. Part of it was how to design and make up a pattern of our own. It caught my attention and I made a few things, but then I needed to make more regular money so that is when I went into the Hospitality industry. I stopped doing the design work then, but it was good fun. Perhaps I could do it again…" she wondered.

They put all their shopping in "cool boxes" to keep everything fresh, had lunch then Inés said she would show Sarah around the town.

For a small town there was a lot to see. They went to the museum of Cesar Manrique, who had been a very successful artist. There were a lot of his paintings there. However, he had had a major influence over the style and future development of the island as a unique holiday destination. He wanted the island to maintain its unique character, even when its tourist industry grew. Therefore, he stipulated that the buildings should be no taller than 2 storeys, always painted white, with only blue or green used to paint doors and window shutters. The islanders saw the wisdom of these ideas and conformed to them, creating picturesque villages and an island identity. There were arts and crafts stalls, clothes shops as well as the usual postcard and ice cream kiosks associated with tourist areas. Haria was more out of the way, more distant from the more popular coastal resorts and hotels of the more sheltered east and south coasts, so there wasn't the overwhelm of coachloads of tourists arriving every day, just a few here and there, enough to keep the market thriving through the year.

Meanwhile, Carmen had decided that the "day off" should be celebrated. She had been pleased to see Sarah going off to town. The young woman had worked at the farm almost all the time since her arrival and knew very few people. Inés was coming back for dinner that evening so Carmen decided to make it a special occasion and set about preparing some of her speciality dishes that she loved to make but had little opportunity these days.

In Haria, Inés and Sarah agreed they were worn out with all the talking and walking and set off back to the *finca*. Sarah was delighted that Inés was coming back too. It had been a long time since they had last met. Sarah had been very involved with the farm and Inés was very busy at the Hotel with all the guests

On the journey home, Sarah's mind was buzzing with ideas to develop the farm. There were the figs. She had seen that there were already quite a lot of trees there, but some had died, some looked unhealthy bearing small hard fruits. How do you propagate fig trees? she wondered. Can you buy them? Do they grow from cuttings? How long do they take to dry? What is the best way to package them for sale? Then there was the jam. There were certainly enough cactus plants there. Did Aunt Clara leave any of her recipes? Does Carmen know how to make the jam? Sarah had never made jam in her life, though she had watched her mother make it. She remembered the blackberry and apple jam and jelly from when she was a child: it tasted so good. They used to toast the bread on special forks in front of an open fire, then sit around the fire, making the fronts of their legs go blotchy red, the crunch of the toast blending in with the crackle and hiss of the fire. She had enjoyed watching the sparks race across the soot at the back of the fire. Sarah smiled at the memory.

Then there were the clothes. The colour obviously had potential, judging by the reactions she had had at the market. How best to develop that potential? What was that about sprays and "magic" the people had referred to when they spoke about the quality and excellent flavour of the vegetables her aunt used to sell?

Chapter Fourteen

As she turned into the drive, her reverie was broken by the sight of Sweetpea walking out of the grove of trees to meet her. Grunting and rumbling, the camel lolloped along beside the car until Sarah reached the yard between the house and stable, got out of the car and was met enthusiastically by an excited camel, who was obviously pleased to see her friend return. Inés was amazed. The arrival of cars, laughter, and camel noises brought Carmen to the door to see what was going on. Sweetpea had calmed down a bit and had laid her head on Sarah's shoulder, making her strange, purring noise and Sarah was stroking her neck and shoulder to calm and reassure her.

"Well, I've never seen a camel so pleased to see a human before!" laughed Inés.

"Nor me," agreed Carmen. "She has been up in the palm trees since you left. José and Hugo have been keeping an eye on her to make sure she was all right."

"I have never seen her like this before," said Sarah, "But I suppose this is the longest I've been away since she arrived

114

here. Even if I go to the supermarket, I am gone less than two hours. You daft, lovely thing," she said turning to the camel. "I'll be with you in a few minutes, Carmen. You go on in Inés. I won't be long. I'll get Sweetpea settled in first. I expect she could do with a drink. That was kind of José and Hugo to look out for her. *Tati! Taeal illaa huna. Meyah lal shereb!* [Come! Come here. Have a drink!] Sweetpea followed her into the stable, where Sarah put fresh water for her and topped up the hay. She stood by while Sweetpea took a long drink much needed after being out by the drive most of the day. Satisfied that Sarah was home safely, Sweetpea went into her stall, lay down and began serenely chewing the cud. Smiling fondly, Sarah gave her a pat on the neck then went indoors.

What a surprise! Carmen and José were there, as well as Carmen's two sons and their wives, who had done so much to help out when Sarah first arrived, and Hugo. After more laughter and shaking of hands and fond greetings, Carmen took Sarah's hand, "*Tati, tati!*" she said, laughing at herself using the Arabic term Sarah spoke to the camel, leading the young woman into the dining room. It had been set up as such soon after Sarah had moved in but no-one had eaten there, least of all Sarah, who ate in the kitchen or out on the veranda.

Sarah hadn't been in the dining room for a few weeks so was reminded about how much of the farm she could see from the window when she had walked in ahead of Carmen. She could see the European style vineyard with the neat green rows of the vines stretching away from the house. Next to them were the smaller plots that Sarah had been working on when she first arrived. They were perfect for growing vegetables and salad things for her and Carmen's family. It was a different view to the one she had from the kitchen, which was mostly of the stable and behind it some of the winery barn. She was lost in thought for a moment, becoming aware yet again, of what still needed to be done but also of what potential there was and how much she had yet to learn.

Cheers from the family brought her back to the room. José had just come in with the glasses of Cava, signalling the start of the meal. It warmed her heart the way in which the whole family had welcomed her to the farm, and been so ready with their help and friendship.

"Carmen, what have you done! It looks beautiful!" Her friend had set the table for all of them with flowers, candles, glasses and pretty plates, with a large vase of flowers on the sideboard. The room was transformed.

"You like it?" asked Carmen nervously, not sure if the English woman would appreciate such a surprise.

"What? Yes! yes! Of course! It looks wonderful. I had forgotten what a pretty room this is. Thank you. But what is the occasion? Is it a birthday or anniversary I didn't know about?" She beamed at her friend. She was so glad Inés' parents had remained at the farm. She really wouldn't have managed without them.

"It's my birthday tomorrow," said Inés. 'Also, this is the first holiday you have had since you arrived here so *Madre* [Mother] decided to make a celebration meal for the both of us and invited my brothers and their wives as well. It is also to celebrate the hard work you have put into the farm so far and your obvious determination to make it a viable concern again, even though there is still much for you to learn."

"Oh! That's so lovely," said Sarah, getting a bit tearful, "Happy birthday for tomorrow. You didn't tell me so I have no card or anything. Thank you for your kind words about the farm, but I wouldn't have been able to do even the bit I have done without all your help right at the start and your continued advice and hard work since then. I was only thinking just now, that without José, Carmen and Hugo I would be back in England by now." There were a few sharp intakes of breath at this, then Sarah continued, "but I have no intention of going back. I love it here and I love all of you. Let's make this farm work for all of us!"

There was much cheering and cries of "*Sigue Adelante,*" "*Bien hecho!*" and "*valdra la pena!*" (Keep going! Well done! It will be worth it!). There more cheers and everyone raised their glasses to Inés, Sarah, themselves and *la finca los Palmas*.

It was the most delicious and happy meal Sarah had enjoyed for a long time, if ever. They had chilled gazpacho, bursting with layers of flavours of sweet ripe tomatoes, red peppers, garlic and basil amongst others. This was followed by an enormous pan of paella and even though everyone was very full by now, they all found room for some thick glistening Spanish hot chocolate with the obligatory churros – crisp on the outside, meltingly soft on the inside all accompanied by local wines.

After they had all finished and had moved out onto the veranda with their brandies, Sarah turned the conversation to the Market at Haria and what she and Inés had seen for sale there in terms of what they could possibly do on the farm.

Inés enthused about the red dress and the admiring glances Sarah had had and the interest shown by many of the stall holders for the possibility of selling clothes in that colour.

Hugo was glad of the darkness at this point. He had also thought how lovely Sarah had looked and was now blushing with the memory.

After a lot of discussion, they decided that Sarah and Carmen would invite Valeria to join them to make a Collection of dresses in "*Lanzaroteno roja*."

Inés said that while Valeria was an excellent dress maker, she needed patterns or at least a detailed drawing of the garment she was to make. Marcella, one of Inés' sisters -in-laws said she knew of someone who designed clothes. She had worked with her from time to time, both women producing very popular outfits for all occasions. She would speak to her and then arrange for herself and her friend to come to the *finca* to discuss the idea and how it could be brought into reality. "Can you design clothes as well then, Marcella?" asked Sarah.

Marcella became very shy and muttered something about it being a while since she had done anything. It was not exceptional. However, Sarah had caught the spark and glint in her eye as she spoke about it, so made a mental note to discover what this young woman's talent really was like.

It was now quite late and after all the good food and wine everyone was getting sleepy. "There are several other ideas Inés and I came back with," said Sarah. "However, I think that is enough for now. Shall we meet next week - for coffee rather than a banquet Carmen - to talk about the other ideas." They all knew about Carmen's tendency to make large meals at every opportunity, especially for her family, and chuckled at the proviso.

"Are you listening, Mama? Just coffee!" teased Inés.

"Well, replied Carmen laughing along with them all, "Coffee by itself is too wet: it needs some cake to go with it. I will make cake whatever you say," she finished defiantly.

Everyone cheered then gradually said their goodbyes and lots of enthusiastic thank you's, and went off home, relaxed and chattering after the enjoyable evening. Hugo was a little more reserved. He was still wrestling with the emotions he was feeling for Sarah. His heart was still aching from the callous treatment he received from his former fiancée. He wasn't willing to fall in love again. He couldn't bear to be hurt again.

'Anyway,' he said to himself briskly, 'who said anything about falling in love? Just because I thought she looked nice is a long way from loving her!' On that encouraging, but rather ambivalent thought, he went home too.

Chapter Fifteen

Once everyone had left and Sarah was tidying up before going to bed, she allowed her thoughts to wander over the events of the evening. It had been such a lovely surprise to see all Carmen's family round the table and the transformation that Carmen had created in the room. It had always seemed rather cold and big; Sarah felt small and alone in there so had got into the habit of eating in the kitchen. Carmen had put a small arrangement of flowers on the table, which added to the celebratory atmosphere. However, she had made a much larger arrangement for the sideboard. The flowers had turned it from an old bit of furniture into something that looked like a classic Dutch master's painting. The candles around the room and on the table created a warm and welcoming atmosphere. It all came together to make her feel absolutely included in this joyful family.

The evening's celebrations, laughter and friendship lifted Sarah's spirits. She began to feel more optimistic about the real potential of the farm to become not only self-sufficient, but to be as profitable as it had been in her aunt's day.

Carmen, José and Hugo had kept the farm ticking over, after her aunt's death but had not known how to continue without learning what the new owner had in mind until she arrived.

She realised how isolated she had become back in UK. When she was still with David, the two of them had enjoyed occasional evenings out with a few friends for a meal or a drink and once or twice a year they went to see a show. However, when their relationship began to deteriorate, these evenings got fewer. When she and David finally separated and got divorced, a few of the women had asked her out for an after-work drink now and again, but it became obvious her singe status did not rest comfortably with them. They all had husbands or boyfriends, there was no room for a single female. These invites gradually got less until they stopped altogether.

She saw then that these people had been David's friends who had included her with him, rather than made her their friend as well. Now they weren't together any more there was nothing there to keep any semblance of friendship alive. She had felt isolated and lost. The chance to come to *Los Palmas* was a blessing.

Here, she knew Carmen, José, all their family and Hugo, and she was getting to know her neighbours to exchange a few words now and again. Since arriving on the island she had been so focussed on understanding about the farm, how things worked, how to do things, she had done nothing but work all day until dark, collapse into bed then do the same again the next day. She had forgotten that she knew all these people here now. She still wasn't sure how to extend this circle of friends, where to go to meet people, but decided something would develop in its own time. She had enjoyed the day out with Inés. That was a start. Her Spanish was improving and with it her confidence to chat to people at the market. That was enough for now. Her heart still ached when she thought of David; she could not even contemplate the thought of having another relationship with someone new.

Now she was in bed, she put all that to one side to consider how to develop the "red dress" idea. She had loved wearing it: it had been so nice to feel a bit feminine again, and she had been delighted by the comments of passers-by. Then there were all the other things she and Inés had discussed like the jam, and drying figs, then there was the wine and even keeping goats for the goats' milk cheese. She fell asleep quickly in spite of all these thoughts whirling around her head.

She woke the next day still feeling happy and buoyant from the night before. After a quick breakfast, she went out to the stable to feed Sweetpea and clean her stall as usual. She stopped at the doorway. The stable was empty!

The camel usually lumbered out to greet her, rumbling and growling her pleasure at seeing her self-elected owner. It was an important part of each day. Sarah had grown very fond of this unlikely ally. Her arrival had made such a difference to life at the *finca*. The camel was loved by everyone. They all enjoyed being with her. She was so willing and worked hard and steadily at whatever task they asked of her.

"Sweetpea! Sweetpea! Tati! Tati!" Sarah called, thinking that the camel had woken early and wandered off to graze on whatever was around. She looked all around the stable, the winery. There was no sign of Sweetpea. Feeling a bit anxious, Sarah began looking out over the fields visible from the house and searching up the drive. The camel was very big, she didn't really blend into the landscape or hide behind anything, bits of her always stuck out. Anxiety turned to panic as Sarah ran all over the place calling and calling. José appeared wondering what was going on.

"I can't find Sweetpea!" wailed Sarah. "I've looked everywhere. I can't see her."

José tried to calm her saying he was sure the camel was nearby, probably dozed off in some corner.

"She's never done that. She always sleeps in her stall in the stable. She really likes it there and always seems happy to stay there." A dreadful thought struck her. "Oh! What if that dreadful man came in the night to steal her back, or even sent someone else?"

"No, no," said José in Spanish. "You saw Sweetpea when he was here: she fought very fiercely. He knows that a camel attack can give you a bad injury, even kill you. He won't be back: he knows it is against the law to hurt camels. The vet was here when Sweetpea first arrived. All injury and other signs of cruelty were carefully noted by the vet. Don't worry, Sweetpea will come back."

This was true but where could she be? They split up. José went to search one larger area of the farm and Sarah another. Sarah even went out onto the main road in case she had wandered there and got run over. Their searched proved fruitless. Sarah was near to tears. Sweetpea had seemed so settled here, had become such a major part of her life, and especially after the excited welcome she had had yesterday when she returned from her visit to Haria.

Sarah would not be comforted, but turned her mind to what needed to be done that day. She had no energy and less interest in her task, which this morning had taken her into the vineyard, where the many large clusters of increasingly ripe grapes should have encouraged her. Her worry overcame her and she sat on the earth and sobbed and sobbed. Carmen and José looked on from their house. They knew she needed to have this release of pent-up emotion and left her alone.

Days passed and still no sign of her beloved camel. Sarah felt terribly alone, bereft. Had she done anything to Sweetpea to cause her to disappear as mysteriously as she had arrived? Had Sweetpea, like some character from a movie, turned up to get Sarah on her feet as it were, and now that she was planning new things for the farm, moved onto to someone else to help? No! That was just silly. Still, she felt so sad and lonely. She hadn't been aware of just how an important part of her life the white camel had become. She began to feel guilty about going to meet Inés in Haria the day before. It was the longest she had been away. Perhaps Sweetpea had got upset by that, felt abandoned and run away? Sarah knew that was nonsense, but the thought sent her into even more of a depressed and anguished state.

It was now five days since Sweetpea's disappearance. Every morning Sarah had gone to the stable hoping to see the camel there. Every morning her heart became heavier. She walked all around the farm searching, but to no avail.

She put notices, with photos, up at the gate and in town, asking for information. None was forthcoming.

Carmen and José looked on, dismayed, unable to bring the young woman out of this state of anxiety. They had no idea that Sweetpea had become such a significant part of Sarah's life. Any suggestion of getting another camel or even a donkey, which would be a cheaper option, brought forth wails of protest and tears.

A week went by. Still no camel. On her early morning visits to the still empty stable, Sarah would sit in the stall on an upturned bucket for an hour at a time. She wasn't sleeping very well nor eating much. Images of Sweetpea languishing somewhere in the inhospitable volcanic wastelands with a broken leg, no water… Oh dear! She knew she should take control of such negative imaginings, get a grip on herself. She, herself, was shocked by her reaction to Sweetpea's disappearance and had had no idea that she had become so attached to this large and rather smelly creature.

With a sigh, she got up went to the kitchen for some coffee and toast then set about cleaning the stable and barn, cleaning the drying racks for when the figs were ripe, which shouldn't be long now: talking to Hugo about the grape harvest and the readiness of the winery for when the grapes were ripe: anything to keep her mind from wandering off into catastrophic trains of thought. She began to take drops of various flower remedies to support herself. She was surprised and relieved to notice that they took the edge off her anxiety, enabling her to do at least a few things around the farm rather than sit disconsolately in the stable for hours. Carmen was relieved to see such activity. She was worried about Sarah, and also surprised by how much she, herself, missed Sweetpea. She had got used to seeing her striding about the place and to using her extra strength for various jobs. Sarah got very tired with all this activity so at least she slept when she went to bed, exhausted.

It had been two weeks since Sweetpea's mysterious disappearance. Sarah had reluctantly accepted that her companion had gone and so set about getting on with the business of running the farm, getting some preparations organised towards the development of the plans for the various activities they had discussed after her visit to Haria market. That lovely day seemed ages ago now.

Even so, she still went to the stable first thing in the morning to sit quietly for a while, before starting the day. This is where she was when she heard noises outside and a large shadow dimmed the doorway. Alarmed, Sarah looked up then went to the entrance to see what was going on.

"Sweetpea! Sweetpea! Oh! your alive! You've come back! Sweetpea." The camel walked slowly towards her, growling and rumbling as she used to do when pleased. Sarah put her arms round the camel's neck, burying her face in the now dusty coat. "Oh! Sweetpea where have you been? I have been so worried. I missed you so much!" Relief swept through her and she burst into tears, releasing all her worry and grief.

"I am so glad you have come back. Oh dear!" she breathed out to calm herself, wiped her eyes and blew her nose.

"How are you? Are you alright? You must be thirsty and hungry. *Tati! Ma'a. Tabana!*" She bustled about filling the bucket with fresh water and bringing hay. Gradually, through all her excited relief, delight and joy, Sarah became aware that Sweetpea wasn't alone: that there were 4 more legs behind the big camel's long legs. Heart beating fast in anticipation, Sarah walked slowly round to the other side of Sweetpea, who was drinking noisily. There tucked up close to its mother's side was a white baby camel.

"Sweetpea! You've had a baby! I didn't even know you were pregnant. Are you alright? Is the baby alright?" Sarah moved towards the baby, then became aware of a sudden tension in Sweetpea. "Ok, ok girl." She patted the camel's neck reassuringly. "You show me your baby when you are ready. You'd better come into your stall and rest. Where have you been? It has been over two weeks. I missed you so much." She cried all over again.

Sweetpea grunted and rumbled, laid her head on Sarah's shoulders, then walked into her stall followed closely by the baby, and sank down gratefully onto the fresh bedding. The baby lay down beside her. They were both asleep in no time.

Sarah could hardly take her eyes off them. It was so wonderful to see Sweetpea there and even more wonderful to see the baby.

She stirred from her reverie, suddenly hungry herself and remembering she had better phone the vet to arrange for her to check over the mother and baby.

She ran to see Carmen and José to tell them the good news. They had heard the noise and had come outside in time to see what was going on.

"She's come back!" shouted Sarah. "Sweetpea has come back! She has had a baby while she was away, all by herself. The baby is white too. They are here in the stable. She's come back!" and then burst into tears again. "Oh! Sorry. It is such a relief. It has been awful with her away. Come and see. They are sleeping now."

The older couple were almost as pleased as Sarah to hear the good news, as they had missed the animal as well. Together, the three of them went quietly to the stable to see the new arrivals. They were sleeping soundly, the little one snuggled up close to her mother.

The three people all sighed together, exchanging glances and smiles of pleasure at the peaceful and very welcome scene, then walked back to Sarah's kitchen for some coffee and a celebratory brandy.

The next morning Sarah went out to the stable, feeling just a bit anxious. When she saw Sweetpea and the calf there, she relaxed and was aware that she had been very apprehensive. The calf was suckling, but when Sweetpea saw Sarah, she moved so she was between the woman and the baby, looking very tense and worried.

Sarah understood that she was being protective and kept a respectful distance. She sat on the old crate that had replaced the upturned bucket on her morning visits over the last two weeks. She stayed there, enjoying spending her quiet time with them. Although it was a forlorn reason originally, Sarah had enjoyed those quiet times sitting in the stable away from the demands of the house and farm. Even though there was no more reason to feel sad and grieving, she decided she would continue the practice anyway: the day seemed to go more smoothly when she did. She was pleased that Sweetpea and Daisy looked so settled – and that was how the calf was named. It just came to Sarah's mind. Daisy? Yes! That was the right name for her.

A few days later as Sarah was enjoying her usual quiet time sitting with the camels before the rush of the day, pictures began to form in her mind of an enclosure full of camels. They looked agitated. Then an image of a man came into focus. Sarah started in shock – it was the man who had arrived in a rage a few weeks ago! He was carrying a whip and a big staff and was beating the animals. It was distressing to see: the animals were so obviously frightened and physically hurt. She glanced up at Sweetpea at this point. Her camel was looking at her very intently, a very different expression than those Sarah had seen before.

'Oh, my goodness! thought Sarah, 'Sweetpea is sending me these images. She wants me to know what went on before she came here to me!' The camel grunted and nodded her head.

Sarah settled herself again. More images flowed into her mind. Sweetpea with a little white calf, a bit older than Daisy. Then a picture of the calf being dragged away. Sarah could feel the anguish, grief and anger of the mother who was trying to jump out of the enclosure to join her baby, who was crying and struggling to join its mother. There was a sharp sensation of pain: Sweetpea was being whipped and beaten back. Tears were flowing down Sarah's cheeks. The scene was heart-wrenching. It continued. The scene was repeated again with a different, darker coloured baby. Again, this baby was dragged away and the mother beaten and whipped.

Then the scene changed. The enclosure and all the

camels had gone. Now the picture was of the desolation and upheaval of the raw volcanic land further south on the island.

'Sweetpea has managed to escape and run away,' Sarah thought.

The picture gradually changed. The landscape was now smoother and greener. Then came the image of the farm – *finca Los Palmas*. With the picture came a feeling of relief and calm. Sarah sighed and wiped her face of the tears that she had not been able to stop. 'She feels safe here. Thank goodness!"

Now Sarah understood why Sweetpea always moved between her and Daisy, becoming very tense, almost defensive. She also understood that images were the means of clear communication of complicated ideas that went beyond simple instructions and calls for food and water. After some thought, Sarah concentrated on forming a picture in her mind of Sweetpea, with an older Daisy sleeping in this stable, then another image of the two camels out on the farm, walking side by side with herself. The came made a strange noise. It reminded Sarah of the sound Chewbacca made when he was pleased with something. A new image came to Sarah's mind, one of herself standing with Daisy and Sweetpea in the stable.

She laughed and said, "Yes, absolutely. I agree! *Nem biallttakid. 'ana muafiq.*"

Now she understood why Sweetpea had attacked her previous owner so angrily when he turned up at the farm. Not only had he beaten and whipped her and treated her so cruelly, ignoring her pressure sores and wounds, but had stolen two of her calves. Taking a few deep breaths to bring her back from the deep concentration of telepathy, Sarah stood up to go back to the house for coffee and something to eat. She had been up ages it seemed. First, she put fresh water and food for the camels and replenished the bowl containing salt, dried alfalfa, multi-vitamins mixed with apple cider vinegar, Vitamin E and selenium the vet had suggested when she had come over to check the two camels after their return. Sweetpea came closer, making her deep rumbling, purring noise, and stood quietly by Sarah as she gently stroked the pale soft hair on this dear animal's neck.

Chapter Sixteen

Now that that plans for the Lanzarotean Red clothes were beginning to take shape, Sarah turned her thoughts to other ideas for developing the farm that she had thought of when still at the hotel. One was how to generate the farm's own electricity from a sustainable source and the other was upgrading the bathroom and possibly the kitchen sink.

When she looked at the potential of a sustainable supply, there were so many things one needed to know, so many variables, so many options, her brain was in a complete fog of confusion. She decided that when the time came, she would contact those who knew about such things and take her lead from them.

When it came to doing something about the house electrics, Sarah reasoned that first she should know how much the farm was using or had used when her aunt was alive. She wasn't sure what the wiring was like: if it needed renewing or not. She had seen some cables that looked rather old. It may be that the old system was not as economical as it might be so that could be a place to start.

With the thought still fresh in her mind, she went to see Carmen, who was outside tending her vegetable garden. It looked very productive to Sarah, who was reminded that sometime soon she would like to have a veg plot of her own, though there seemed to be more urgent things to sort out first. She would think about it later.

"*Hola*, Carmen. You look very busy. Can you spare a moment?"

"Ah Signorina. I have spare moments for you always. What is on your mind?" Carmen stood up slowly to ease her back upright. And massaging it. "Ooh! That is better. *Mi espalda se pone muy rigida ahora.*"

Sarah guessed the flurry of Spanish meant her back ached a lot. "It is good to take a break. Come in for some coffee."

Sarah was about to suggest Carmen come to the farm kitchen, thinking it wouldn't be right to go to Carmen's kitchen somehow, then stopped herself. Carmen would be really pleased to give Sarah a drink in her own kitchen – it would be the first time since her arrival.

"That would be lovely. Thank you."

The two women went into the cool of Carmen's kitchen. It did look so much better now with all the new units and sink. Sarah thought she must see Daniel about doing something about the kitchen in the farmhouse. It was still pretty much as it had been in the 60s, but she had paid it little attention with everything else that was going on.

Carmen indicated for Sarah to take a seat at her table while she bustled about making coffee and finding some cake.

"Oh! This is good," said Sarah. "Thank you, Carmen. I

was getting a bit tired. This is perfect. I wanted to ask you if you knew of a reliable e-electricista? I was looking at some of the wiring and it looks rather old. Also, I want to know how much electricity we are using. Did I sort out paying for it after I arrived, now I think about it?"

"*Si*, you should be getting *la cuenta dentro de poco*, (the account soon)."

"Oh good! That will give me the information I need."

"*Si. Uno electritista*? We have used someone from Haria. He is reliable: a friend of Daniel's. Daniel will make sure he is fair."

"*Gracias*! Would you ask Daniel to ask him to contact me, please? I will be needing Daniel's skills soon as well: I want to improve the bathroom."

"*Mama mia! Que muchas* ideas!" said Carmen smiling. "You feel more at home now to be thinking about making the house better?"

Sarah laughed. "Yes. I guess."

"I will contact Daniel this evening. He is busy working. I don't like to disturb him."

"That will be fine, thank you. Goodness! The day is passing quickly. I had better get back to work. Thank you for the coffee, Carmen. The cake was delicious as always. I have never made a cake. Perhaps you could teach me one day?"

"Of course. *Al gusto es mio*. (the pleasure is mine) Tell me when you are ready to do it."

With that Sarah left the cosy smart kitchen and went out to fetch the camels and go to see what needed to be done outside.

The year was moving on. It was time to think about picking the figs and may be the grapes. The drying racks were all clean and arranged ready for the figs, though Sarah had little idea of how many fig trees the farm had nor what sort of crop of the fruit they could expect. She was shocked to realise how little she knew about the details of the farm, even now. Then there was the grape harvest to consider. How did they do that? She had vague pictures in her mind of happy people, with large baskets of grapes and then all of them sitting around a long table eating together.

'Hmm! That seems more informed by the animation from *Fantasia* by Walt Disney than anything to do with the reality of what was no doubt hard work,' she thought and decided she would speak to Hugo about it when she saw him next.

After lunch, she decided to walk the farm, making a note of the numbers and location of fig trees, the amount of fruit, if any, and whether the trees looked healthy or not. She had done a bit of research about them, but still needed to learn about how best to look after them to maximise their potential, even how to propagate them, to replace any that had died or were diseased. She would ask Hugo about them.

She needed to talk to him about the grapes as well. They were growing quickly as far as she could tell, and would need picking at some stage fairly soon. Then what happened? She had seen the bodega with all the vats but had no idea when they were used last, or even if they were in a useable condition. So many questions sat around her head like a cloud of gnats, she could hardly see straight. She could only deal with one thing at a time, so she brushed it all away, collected the camels and set off on her 'fig safari,' as she had thought of it. It would do her good to get out onto the larger farm to see what was there, particularly in the area behind the house, towards the end of the valley. She had hardly gone that way. Events seem to have always been focussed around the house and the land in front of it.

This largely unexplored area seemed a bit greener than the area up around the drive. 'It must be more sheltered by the arms of the volcano,' she thought. There were lots of scrubby growth but also quite a lot of fig trees – around 50 here – each growing in their own circular depression with a low wall on the windward side and mulched with the black picon. In spite of the neglect, there were a lot of figs as far as she could tell. They were quite small though and still hard. From the photos she had seen on her computer, most of them looked all right – no yellowing leaves or ones with brown spots on them. Some had died and some had broken branches though. She would ask Hugo how best deal with those. She felt quite excited about getting out there and actually doing something that could make a difference to the income of the farm, without too much expense.

There were of course plenty of prickly pear plants. No matter how careful she was to get around them, one always managed to stab her leg or bottom as she went by. She could almost hear them snickering.

What she did notice though, was that many of them were looking very different from those in the front up by the drive where it was windier. Here, the pads were carrying what looked like smaller, pear-shaped red fruits. They were so bright the plants looked as if they had been decorated with Christmas baubles. That was an interesting discovery too. Sarah was glad she had decided to go out to that area.

When they got back to the house, Sweetpea took her baby back to the stable to feed her and let her rest. It was the furthest she had been out since the pair of them had arrived there.

Sarah began searching cupboards and drawers for old notebooks or recipe books that her aunt had left there. If the red baubles were ripe fruit, then now would be the time to make some of that delicious jam she had tasted on her visit to Haria market.

There were no books or recipes anywhere that she looked. She wondered if Carmen had taken them to her house to use them and to keep them dry. However, in a box she did find books on something called Biodynamic Farming.

"Ah! 'Biodynamico.' That was the word some of the stall holders had used when they spoke about the produce from *finca Los Palmas*. She hadn't understood the word when they had said it, but she recognised it in retrospect, as it was almost the same as the written English. There were a lot of printed books and leaflets, as well as notebooks filled with observations in her aunt's own handwriting. That had given her quite a jolt. It was the first time she had held anything so personally connected to her aunt. It made the whole experience of being there, so far from home, dealing with things she had no previous knowledge of, more meaningful. Glancing quickly through them, she saw pages about sprays with strange names like 'cow horn manure' and 'silica.'

That particular universe of enquiry would have to wait. She reluctantly put the books back in the box. Opening the next box, she found some of what she had been looking for – lots of unused jam jars, complete with lids and in an envelope, a lot of labels with a *finca Los Palmas* logo. 'Fantastic!' she thought.

Excitedly, Sarah went in search of Carmen and jam recipes, and to tell her the prickly pears looked ripe. She met Carmen who was on her way to tell Sarah the same thing. She had a large pan in one hand and an old notebook in the other. It was a special jam-making pan, with the top a wider radius than the base, to stop the jam from boiling over. Sarah remembered her mother had a similar but smaller one. The memory brought a wave of nostalgia and homesickness, but Carmen's enthusiastic chatter brought her back to the here and now and the moment passed.

'This jam making could be fun,' she thought.

They both bustled about gathering gauntlets, tongs and buckets. Though the ripe fruits dropped their thorns, the rest of the plant still carried vicious ones. Luckily the fruits were held upright around the top edge of each pad so relatively easily accessible. They fitted Sweetpea with two panniers and set off with Daisy trotting alongside.

Sweetpea waited patiently as the two women gradually filled the panniers. Daisy danced about full of curiosity about everything that was going on: looking in the women's baskets, jumping back when she caught a thorn, exploring, but never going very far away from her mother. If Sweetpea thought it was far enough, a grunt from her brought her daughter lolloping back to her side, usually for a quick drink.

Once back in the kitchen and after some concentrated hard work, the two women had filled 20 jars with the sweet, fragrant jam. Sarah labelled them with her aunt's own labels, that had a sketch of the farm on it. On the back Sarah had designed another label for the ingredients with the outline of a palm tree and a camel. The people in the area would recognise the reference and intrigue tourists there for the day. The white camels of *finca* Las Palms were well-known since Sweetpea had attacked and chased off the premises the camel owner up to the road. The man was well-known in the area and much disliked for his cruel ways. A few people had seen her galloping up the drive after the truck and news like that travels fast.

Sarah took 18 jars of jam to the next market day – she and Carmen had kept a jar each to try. She sold them all very quickly and returned home with her purse bulging with the first real income from the farm. It was very gratifying. She split the money between Carmen and herself, much to Carmen's delighted surprise. It is what Signora Clara always did, she told Sarah.

Chapter Seventeen

Hugo and José had been working in the winery, completing the cleaning and repairs in readiness for the grape harvest, which was due to start sometime the following week. They had been at it for a few days, so Hugo had gone back out to the vineyards, leaving José to finish off the last few things. Sarah was on her way out to start on the morning's tasks, when Carmen came over to the kitchen looking concerned. It was already nine thirty and she had expected José for his breakfast at 8.00. He had always started his working day early before coming in for breakfast. He was sometimes late, but never this late. Sarah caught an edge of panic in the older woman's voice and joined Carmen to look for José.

"I expect he has got involved somewhere and lost track of time," said Sarah, though Carmen looked unconvinced. José was a man of habit and punctuality. He wasn't in the stable. They went to the vineyard; Sweetpea and Daisy thinking it was time to work followed them. Hugo was there checking the state of the grapes. As far as he knew José was in the brewing room finishing the cleaning.

"I expect he is pressing on with a few last-minute things to get it finished," said Sarah, hoping to reassure Carmen. However, as she said it didn't sound like José. He enjoyed his food and was always hungry.

The winery was quiet with no sign of anyone working. They were just about to leave, thinking the man had gone home after Carmen had left, when Sweetpea gave a grunt, pushed past the two women and headed for the two tall tanks at the back of the room. Sarah ran after her to bring her out. It didn't seem hygienic to have a camel wandering about in there. The camel stopped at the back of the tanks making a lot of noise. Sarah caught up with her and was about to grab her halter to lead her out, when she glanced to her left and gasped. There in the dim light behind the tanks was José lying unmoving on the floor. Quickly she checked to see if he was still breathing. She breathed out in relief herself when she saw that he was. However, his leg was lying at an odd angle, obviously broken.

Carmen, hearing the gasp, rushed in behind her, her anxiety already high, now went to panic when she saw her husband on the floor, imaging the worst.

"It is not as bad as it looks," said Sarah, "he is alive." Carmen was full of prayers and entreaties to a multitude of saints for José's safety and life. "It looks as if he has broken his leg or his hip. We'd better not move him. There's no bleeding. It was Sweetpea who found him; I was about to leave."

The two women stroked the camel's neck in thanks. By this time Hugo had arrived hearing the cries and urgent tones of the women's voices. Sarah quickly explained what had happened, then asked him to stay with José to keep him still when he came around, sent Carmen off for blankets to keep José warm, while she ran to the farmhouse to call 112 for the ambulance. She knew her aunt had set up medical insurance. That had all been made clear before she left England; it included the people who worked on the farm as well as herself. Her aunt had made sure it would be really easy for Sarah to take over the farm.

The operator was very helpful. An ambulance was in the area and would be diverted to *finca Los Palmas*. It would be with them in about ten minutes. She gave brief instructions about not moving the patient, keeping him warm, but not to give him anything to drink, not even a sip of brandy, and ended the call.

Sarah ran back to the scene of the accident. An extraordinary sight met her. José was lying on the floor, had recovered consciousness and was talking normally. He was covered with a blanket, warm and unmoving – mainly because Daisy, who had followed her mother into the barn, had carefully lain down right next to José, with her back against his 'good side,' keeping him still and very warm. Sweetpea was nearby rumbling and grumbling, obviously giving careful instructions to her daughter. Carmen had rushed forward to push Daisy away, afraid she would injure her beloved husband further, but quickly saw the great care and gentleness with which the young camel was positioning herself in the confined space and relaxed. She stood close by with Hugo, who put a reassuring arm around her shoulders, talking to José, urging him to keep still and asking what had happened.

Seeing this, Sarah realised how close everyone had become and how much of the family they now were, including the camels. It was a new feeling for her. Her parents had not been able to have any more children after her, so she had been an only child. Her father had worked in a bank and they were always being moved around the country. She would eventually make a friend or two, then they would move again, Sarah would go to a new school and have to start all over again. She had not had this sense of belonging to a group of people or to a place before. It was filling a space inside she hadn't known was there, because it had always been there. She was startled out of here memories by the swirl of gravel and dust thrown up by the ambulance as it arrived on the yard.

The two paramedics were surprised to see a camel next to the patient, but quickly got their equipment out of the van. Sarah called the two camels outside, noting the delicacy and care with which Daisy got up. It was surprising really because she was still young, at that all-legs-and-elbows ungainly stage. She reminded Sarah of a toy she had as a child. It was of a jointed horse on a platform, held together by elastic. If she pressed the bottom of the base, the tension went and the horse collapsed, with its legs all which way under it. When she released the base, it sprang back to its proper shape. It had always made her laugh.

The ambulance man and woman, having made all their basic checks, said that José had broken his leg between the hip and the knee, but apart from that and some shock, he was alright and would make a good recovery – if he did as was told, they had said, laughing.

They stabilised the leg and moved José carefully onto a stretcher then onto the van. Carmen was fluttering about like a worried moth, telling them to be careful, for José to be brave, drying her eyes and sending one prayer after another to whomever came to her mind. They made room for Carmen to go in the ambulance and they set off to the hospital in Arrecife. Luckily, in spite of her worry and haste, Carmen had remembered to pick up her Health Insurance papers when she went to collect a blanket, so their admission to hospital would go smoothly and swiftly. Sarah said she would follow on once things had been secured on the farm. She led the camels back to the stable with a great deal of fussing, patting and congratulations for the part they had played in the discovery and care of poor José. The barn and the two houses were soon locked up and Sarah, with Hugo to show her the way, followed the ambulance to the capital, pausing briefly to phone Inés, to tell her what had happened and where José and Carmen were heading, but reassuring her that it would be all right and not to worry. She would be able to get to the hospital before them as she was already in the capital. She could keep Carmen company and calm while her father was being examined. At the hospital, it was no time at all before José was taken to the operating theatre, had his leg set and put in a cast and was soon in bed and reasonably comfortable in bed in the Orthopaedic ward. They were all amazed that José, apart from the broken leg, was otherwise uninjured. No bleeding, internally or externally, no head or brain damage and no other broken bones. Carmen quietly gave him some Arnica pillules for the bruising and some drops of Rescue Remedy for the shock. Sarah smiled; Aunt Clara's influence was still there, caring for her friends.

Inés' two brothers had arrived by this time. José was still woozy from the anaesthetic but aware of everyone there and pleased to see all his family around him. Sarah let out a big sigh, releasing all the tension she had been holding since discovering her friend on the floor, and seeing that things were more or less settled, she and Hugo set off back to the tranquillity of the farm.

Chapter Eighteen

Back in the farm kitchen over a cup of coffee, she and Hugo chatted about the events of the last few hours, both so glad that José's injuries had not been worse. They laughed at Daisy's understanding of the situation, which prompted her, with guidance from her mother, to lie beside the man on the floor. The ambulance people were surprised that José's markers for shock, cortisol levels and so on, were so low. They attributed it to the warmth and comfort of his unusual "hot water bottle"!

After a lull in the conversation, Hugo said, "What do we do now about the grape harvest and making the wine? I know how to set about picking the grapes, but José has always overseen the fermentation, maturing and bottling side of things. I know the stages of the process but not the essential details."

He had expressed the very same questions that had been going through Sarah's mind.

"Hmm…! I know nothing about any of it," she said. "I was expecting to be led by José and you."

With no answer forthcoming immediately, they decided to get back outside to the farm and pick up on the tasks of the day.

Sarah went to check on the camels, getting fresh water and hay for them. Hugo went to the barn to discover what had happened to make José fall. He was always so sure footed and at ease on the towers. He had cleaned, repaired and monitored them for many years. Hugo took a torch; it was dark behind the tanks and he wanted to see everything as clearly as he could.

He had been shaken by José's accident. It was unlike him. It had all happened in the blink of an eye. José had not even been able to cry out. José had told them that he was making a final check of the pipework and valves at the top of the tank. The next thing he remembers was lying on the floor attributing his inability to get up to that "stupid" camel who, for some reason, had snuggled close to him. It was only when Carmen told him he had fallen and maybe broken something that he knew what had happened.

The ladder was still against the 2nd tank and looked secure enough. Hugo shone the torch there to get a closer look. Ah! Three rungs near the top of the ladder were hanging limply to one side. Of course! The ladder was an old wooden one that had been there when Sarah's Aunt was alive. It was part of the equipment. Familiarity had blinded them to its gradual deterioration. Hugo could see now that some of the rungs had been attacked by woodworm. The top one must have snapped, causing the man to drop suddenly onto the one below, which then also broke, sending José plummeting to the hard, tiled floor. Wanting to take a closer look at the damage, Hugo carefully lowered the broken ladder to the ground. A cursory glance showed that some rungs had snapped, so he left it there to go out to the vineyards and carry on his work.

Sarah was relieved to walk into the shady and quiet stable. The shock and urgency of José's accident gradually subsided as she tended to the needs of her beloved camels. The practical, undemanding actions of clearing out the bedding, putting down fresh straw, filling the manger with Bermuda hay and changing the water were calming and welcome after all the excitement. The camels had such a serene demeanour. Some saw it as haughty, but not Sarah. She saw it as a reflective inward awareness that grazing or browsing animals had, as if they were aware of their digestive processes and were following each mouthful of hay down to their stomach. Cows were like that anyway. She supposed camels weren't too different in that regard.

As her mind relaxed, the question that Hugo had posed on the journey back from the hospital came back to her. Her heart sank. She had no idea what to do. She knew nothing at all about wine making. She'd not even tried to make a demi-john of elderflower or blackberry wine back at home, not even assembled sloes, sugar and gin to make sloe gin. Hugo and José had worked hard rejuvenating the vineyards. Sarah had worked at it as well under Hugo's watchful eye. She had eagerly anticipated their own if small vintage – even designed some labels for the bottles. The grapes were almost ready to harvest. If they weren't picked, they would go mouldy. She knew there were some grapes that were allowed to get mouldy in order to make a special kind of wine, but the grapes here weren't that variety. She had talked about it with Hugo and José, who had told her their grapes mustn't do that. There would be no wine and it could damage the vine itself.

She sighed noisily, said thank you, yet again, to Sweetpea and Daisy, both of whom grumbled a reply, then walked back to the kitchen her mind devoid of any solution or glimmer of hope of their being one.

Hugo arrived at the kitchen at the same time as Sarah. He described what he had found as she made coffee and warmed some croissants and made toast. Neither of them had had any breakfast and it was past lunch time now. The coffee tasted good. It was comforting to cradle the steaming mug between her hands. "Mmm! These croissants are just how I like them. The bakery in Haria makes some great things. I'm glad Inés told me about them."

Having finished the food and poured more coffee, she and Hugo settled down to discuss how they were going to manage now that José was in hospital and unlikely to return to work for many weeks.

"What happened with the grapes when my aunt was alive? Has any wine been made since she died?" asked Sarah.

Hugo had a drink of his coffee, while he gathered his thoughts.

"I was here only a few years before Señora Clara died. I was interested in the system she used, but more or less did as she instructed without learning the details myself. It was different from what I had learned in Austria in some respects. But anyway, there the farm was concerned with growing grain crops and vegetables and ran a dairy selling biodynamic milk, yogurt and cheese. They didn't have a vineyard. The Señora was always very particular about the day we started the harvest. Most of it had to be done in three days. What wasn't done had to wait for a few weeks until the "right time" came around again. I think she had a calendar that she referred to, but I never saw it. Uncle José used to get impatient with it all. We could only work on the vines when Señora said so. It was to do with where the moon was in relation to star constellations, I think. But even José had to admit that the vines were very healthy; they didn't get any diseases even in the years when other yards nearby were having a lot of trouble. The fruit was always excellent and the wine was very good. It was very popular around here. In Austria, when I worked there, people used to talk about a man called Steiner who had taught it in the 1920s and 30s. After he died, it was developed by a woman, Maria Thun. I think she did experiments and took careful notes and photographs of the results. It was very patient work but seemed to prove that the system produced excellent results. I wasn't there long enough really to understand it fully without any books.

"Uncle tried to continue after the Señora died, but without her guidance it wasn't easy. The wine was good but not with that added something her wine had." Hugo looked downcast.

"My aunt must have left the information here," said Sarah. "There are a lot of boxes upstairs I haven't looked through properly. When I was looking for recipes to do with the pear jam, I saw some boxes that may be what we need. I'll bring some down.

Hugo made some more coffee. This could take a long time. He was pleased to be spending this time with Sarah. He had had very little to do with her apart from working on the vines. She intrigued him. He couldn't really understand why a young woman who had had a well-paid job in London should want to even come out to the backwoods of a rather barren island in the Atlantic Ocean when she could have all the glamour and culture in the big city. His fiancée had preferred the big city lights to the peace of Haria. How he wished she could have been more like Sarah. The comparison shocked him. He was in no mood for any more romantic connections. Why would he compare Lucia with Sarah! For goodness' sake!

He came back to earth from his reverie when the young woman came back into the kitchen with two boxes full of papers, files and books. Maybe somewhere amongst it all there would be instructions on what to do with the grapes once they were harvested on the appropriate day.

Silence descended on the kitchen as both of them unpacked the boxes and pored over the information they pulled out, hoping to find inspiration and instruction as to what to do with the grapes.

"Oh! what's this?" exclaimed Sarah. She pulled out a thin, A5 paper back. "The Biodynamic Sowing and Planting Calendar for 1967." She leafed through it. "There's a lot of information in here, with a chart for each month, huh! And an article about looking after bees... Have you ever kept bees, Hugo?"

He laughed, "No, I have thought about it. I like honey. There are bee keepers in the area. One or two sell a few jars of honey at the market."

"There seems to be a book for each year for many years that's about all that is in here. These seem to be specific to each year. I wonder if they are still being published? 'The Biodynamic Sowing and Planting Calendar 1976.' That probably won't apply now, but there are monthly charts in it. It looks a bit complicated. Oh! what's this?" *The Biodynamic Year. Increasing Yield, Quality and Flavour* and *Gardening for Life. The Biodynamic Way.* These two were less specific. Sarah was beginning to feel a bit excited. "I wonder if these are still being produced?" Hugo shrugged, but like Sarah was beginning to feel that maybe they could get the information they needed to carry on with the harvest for maximum results. At least one aspect of their difficulty – when to pick the grapes – might be resolved. She got up to turn on her computer, typed in the title of the book for this and next year. The books came up straight away. She ordered both as well as the two more general ones. They would arrive in 5 to 7 days.

"Will the grapes wait until the books get here, Hugo, so we can work out the "particular days" to harvest them, as my aunt used to insist on? Hmm, maybe not. I can find the section in this year's book and try to photocopy it. Then we will know when to start on the picking

"A good idea. We don't want to miss the optimum window," replied Hugo, looking at all the leaflets, notes and photographs with increasing interest. The techniques seemed strange but the results spoke for themselves. Señora Clara had followed Maria Thun's example and had several comparative studies showing how the timing of sowing or planting and care improved volume and quality of the crops. There was some information on various sprays to use and when, descriptions of experiments on this and that but very little about the actual process of making the wine.

Sarah's excitement was ebbing away as the logistics of the next few weeks hit her.

"Oh dear! How are we going to do this?"

Without José's experience and calm presence, Sarah once again became aware of her complete lack of experience in anything to do with running a successful small farm anywhere, let alone one here in this dry windy island. She'd been really busy, tidying up a lot of areas, organised a few things here and there like the jam making though even then Carmen had provided the know-how. She became aware now that she hadn't started to think about how to actually run the farm as a whole. Even the biodynamic process seemed very complicated and though interesting and something that had made a difference for her aunt, she wasn't sure she would ever understand it enough to implement it to good effect.

Also, now there were only three of them success seemed even more distant. The vines were spread out over a wide area, especially the ones grown in the sunken pits. Those planted in neat rows near the house, like she had seen in France and in parts of UK were a relatively small percentage of the whole vineyard. This system looked as if it would be easier to pick from than wandering way out there and getting the grapes up from the plants at the bottom of the pits. There would be a lot of walking with heavy baskets just to get the grapes harvested. Goodness knows what one did with them next.

She heaved a big shuddering sigh.

Hugo listened to her anxieties and worries. He had been thinking the same. However, he was optimistic by nature and, though not overly religious, had the general attitude that the Virgin Mary or God or something helped those who helped themselves.

"José's injury will certainly have an impact, but he will be here in time to explain to us what we need to do. We can do it Senorita. We have overcome many difficulties since you arrived. We have Sweetpea now and Daisy. They will be able to carry a much bigger quantity of grapes back to the winery from the yards, which will save us a lot of time. It would take us 10 trips to her one. We can pick the grapes much more quickly." He smiled.

He had become fond of the white camel and her daughter and valued the contribution their strength made to his work. Sarah relaxed a bit on hearing these encouraging words and breathed more evenly. She smiled too, thinking about the camels and how much part of the farm they had become. Her mind wandered easily over the happy times they'd had working with them. Having Sweetpea carrying all the ripe fruits of the prickly pear certainly speeded up the whole operation. Into this relaxed flow of memories came a clear and sudden thought;

'There are still two boxes upstairs you haven't opened. Do it now!'

It was so clear and commanding, Sarah woke from her reverie.

"Are you alright, Sarah?" asked Hugo. "You haven't said

anything about my last idea. Wasn't it helpful?"

"Oh! sorry, Hugo. Yes, it was. Of course, I need to remember what we have rather than what is missing. Thank you. I was thinking how useful the camels have been and will be. Also, I remembered that I haven't looked in all auntie's boxes. I'll go and fetch them. Maybe they contain the information we need." She couldn't quite bring herself to acknowledge that she had the clear idea she had been told what to do.

Hugo was pouring the coffee he'd just made, together with two glasses of bottled water, when Sarah appeared carrying two dusty boxes. They were very full.

"Would you search through one while I look through the other?" She took a gulp of coffee. "Ooh! That's good. Thank you for making some more."

Embarrassed, Hugo nodded and carefully opened the box in front of him.

The kitchen was silent apart from the rustle of papers or snap of ring binders being opened. Soon the table was covered in neat piles of paper according to subject matter.

"Wow! This gives such an insight into the kind of person my aunt was. She must have been a force to reckon with! Very clear minded and determined."

"Yes, but very generous," replied Hugo. "Even now, when I mention that I work here, people remember her fondly. They say how she surprised everyone by buying this unpromising valley and over the years turning it into a verdant and productive farm. Many say how good everything tasted. She was very kind and generous, giving talks to anyone, farmers, gardeners, vintners, who wanted to improve their land. She only charged enough to cover the cost of the room hire so no-one would be excluded. She even invited those interested, to visit the farm so they could see what she was doing here. It wasn't just theory."

"She kept meticulous notes," said Sarah. "Look at all this! Conserving water, keeping bees, looking after goats, making cheese, bread and Carmen already has what she wrote about making Prickly Pear jam. Oh look! Here is some information on caring for camels. I wish I'd found this earlier. What else is there? What have you found in your box Hugo?"

"Let's see… growing potatoes, carrots, onions and squash. When to plant sweet pepper seeds, zucchini, beans. Ah! Looking after figs. That will be useful. There used to be a lot of fig trees here, José said. You can tell that from all the drying trays. I haven't attended to them really because I wasn't sure what to do with them. Figs are popular here with Lanzaroteans as well as tourists. Figs and goats' cheese go well together. Nothing on grapes and making wine yet though."

Sarah realized that Hugo was talking in fluent English, saying a lot more than he had ever done the whole time she had been there, even in Spanish.

"What? What have I said?" Hugo stopped reporting his findings, puzzled by Sarah's expression.

"I have never heard you say so much in English all the time I have been here or even so much in any language. I have always struggled to talk with you in my limited Spanish. If you have used English it is very brief. I have just realised that with the shock of José's accident and the anxiety about how we are going to manage now, I have been speaking to

156

you in English and you have been talking to me more than you have ever done before and in English! Why is that?"

Hugo gave a wry smile. "Out of respect and deference to my uncle. He struggles with English. He understands most of what you say, but finds it difficult to find the words he needs to reply. He is very conscious of this so I say very little in his presence. I have a few English friends so I have plenty of practice when I'm not working. I worked in England on a Vineyard in Sussex for two years after I had been in Austria on a vineyard there, learning about biodynamics. I got the idea of it without being able to learn the details. Having the opportunity to work here to continue improving the vines and maybe continue with that style of farming was perfect for me."

"Phew! That's a relief. I can just discuss the farm with you in English instead of expressing myself badly in Spanish, though I will still continue to improve that. I am going to live here so it is important that I do, I guess."

Hugo tensed a little, unsure if Sarah had understood the delicacy of the balance of seniority he maintained with his uncle.

"As long as José is not around – of course" Sarah smiled.

A whole new understanding of how much Hugo actually had done and did, came to Sarah in a rush. He had been working on the farm when she had arrived. He seemed to know what to do, and as Sarah had no idea at all, she had just let him get on with it. He always worked hard and the vines certainly looked healthy and were laden with fruit. She was anxious to get them picked and made into wine. It would be a terrible waste if that didn't happen. It would also be a loss of potential income. She was conscious that she had been relying on her savings and on the money her aunt had made available to use in the first two years there. She knew she would have to make the farm a profitable business as it had been for her aunt. There was a degree of pride in that but also some idea of wanting to do justice to the expectations and trust her aunt had in her, in leaving her the farm in the first place. She often wondered why she did that. Were there no children over here, or colleagues, a friend to whom she could have left the farm to instead of her? She took a deep breath; there were more urgent things to sort out than get to the bottom of that mystery.

"How are you getting on with your box? she asked. "I have got to the bottom of mine. There is a lot of helpful information here but nothing about making the wine."

"A bit like yours, I think. Loads of information about many things but nothing specifically about wine making. Oh! Wait a minute. What's this? I thought I had got to the bottom of the box, but there is still something in here. It is the same colour as the box so I didn't notice it."

He paused as he struggled to pull out a big very full envelope and open it.

"What does it say…? Hey! This is it! 'Wine making at *Los Palmas*.' There is a lot of information here; really useful stuff."

"Oh! thank goodness!" A wave of relief flowed through Sarah. This direct link with her aunt's experience and expertise gave her such a lift. It was like having a personal mentor. A quick thought passed through her mind as she wondered where the message about the two remaining boxes had come from together with a fleeting image of a woman whom she decided was her aunt came to mind. It was all rather beyond her pragmatic mind. But she did breathe a quiet 'thank you.'

She got up to walk around to where Hugo was sitting to see what was in the envelope, when there was a tap on the door. Carmen and Inés were back from hospital and had come to report on José's condition and progress.

Chapter Nineteen

Sarah welcomed them in and sat them at the table covered as it was in unpacked papers. She laughed, waving an arm at the muddle, saying, "I will explain all this later. Now, tell us! How is José? What has happened to him? How are you both? Carmen, how are you? It has been a worrying time for you." She went off to make fresh coffee. Carmen had called in at her house to collect a cake and Inés put a bottle of brandy on the table.

"Inés! Brandy!" Sarah laughed.

"Yes, absolutely! It has been quite a day," said Inés smiling.

The two women sank gratefully into their chairs, clearly exhausted by the anxiety and the long wait at the hospital. The papers were tidied up a bit to make room for plates, mugs and glasses that were quickly laid out. "So, tell us! What has been happening!" demanded Sarah.

After savouring the warmth of the brandy, Inés began the story. The x-ray showed that he has broken his 'femur.' Sarah nodded to show that she understood. Apart from slightly different pronunciation, it was the same as the English word for the thigh bone. Inés continued, "It is broken in two places, but both his hips and his knees are unbroken, thankfully. He may need a plate put in to hold the bone in place until it is healed."

"How long did they think that will take?" asked Hugo.

"He'll be there for about five or six days, to make sure there are no internal injuries."

Carmen gave a little moan, crossed herself and murmured prayers to Mother Mary and lots of other Saints. She was so worried about José. They had been together for such a long time.

"He'll be fine, Mama. You don't need to worry. He is being well looked after in hospital," comforted Inés.

"Will he have to have his leg in traction? asked Sarah, remembering the experience of a friend who had broken her femur.

"Mmm? Maybe for a few days, just to keep it the right length and straight, the doctor said."

"Oh Santa Maria! He won't like that. He is not a good patient," groaned Carmen.

"No, but he is sensible and the doctor did tell him firmly that the outcome for his future comfort and ability to walk and work, depended on what he did over the next few weeks."

"Yes, that is true, Inés. Let's hope he does as he is told," Carmen laughed, knowing how stubborn her husband could be.

"How long will he have to be in the cast, did they say?" asked Hugo, thinking of the imminent grape harvest.

"I think it depends what the tests show about his general

health and how quickly the injury is settling down, "replied Inés. "The operation went well, they said and Papa was coming around from the anaesthetic before we left. He seemed resigned to the situation and relieved he was still alive. Anyway, that is all we know for now; we'll know more tomorrow. Now, what is going on here? What's all this stuff on the table?"

Sarah let out a long sigh. "On a practical level, I have been wondering about the grape harvest and making the wine afterwards. I know nothing and Hugo's experience is more with the growing of the grapes. José is the one with the wine making experience. I remembered there were still some boxes I hadn't opened yet and wondered if there would be any notes from my aunt about harvesting grapes and fermenting them. There were two boxes in fact and all these," indicating the papers on the table, "are the notes my aunt made about all aspects of the farm and right at the bottom were lots of notes about the vines and the wine. We were just going to have a look to see what she had to say when you arrived."

Sarah was about to continue, when there was a knock on the door. Three men were standing outside. She recognised one of them as her neighbours.

"*Hola!* Senorita Sarah. We have heard about José's accident and have come to ask how he is."

"Come in, come in. Inés and Carmen are here. They will tell you all the news." She went to get three more glasses and poured out the brandy. Hugo brought more chairs. It was a meeting of old friends as Carmen, Inés and Hugo knew all of the visitors.

Carmen and Inés brought the three visitors up to date on José's injuries and situation. They listened with much shaking of their heads and drawing in of breath. Such an accident was something they all did their best to avoid because the implications were very difficult. They exchanged glances and the one whom Sarah knew said that they had realised what José's accident would mean for their new neighbour at such a critical time of the year and had called round to offer their help.

Sarah could hardly believe her ears. "Thank you so much. We were just working out how we were going to do the grape harvest and make the wine. I am worried. There are just three of us now and only Hugo is here who knows what to do. The grapes are just about ready he says. We were looking to see if my aunt had left any instructions." Sarah indicated the piles of papers and books.

"*No te preocupes! No te preocupes!*" reassured her neighbour. "*Estudiantes estamos aqui buscando por unas semanas.*" (Don't you worry. Students are here looking for work for a few weeks.) Sarah understood the first few words, but then the conversation continued between the four men, Carmen and Inés, in Spanish too rapid for Sarah to understand. 'Of course,' she thought. 'Students can help us pick the grapes. I didn't even know they did that here. I suppose there must be a lot here at this time of year. I did that in France myself for a couple of summers when I was at university.'

An hour later, and more brandy and translation by Inés, it was all sorted out.

Hugo had been quietly going through more of Aunt Clara's notes and the page from the Biodynamic calendar that Sarah printed. It was Wednesday now. According to the calendar, the "fruit days" when the grapes would be at their best to harvest would be the following Monday, Tuesday and Wednesday. It would be ten or eleven more days before this auspicious time came around again. The grapes would be past their best by then.

"If we can, and if you want to follow your aunt's footsteps, we need to start picking the grapes on Monday and finish by Wednesday!"

It seemed a big challenge, but with enough help and good management, it could be done. The vineyard was not as large as those of some of their neighbours.'

Inés made a few phone calls (Sarah found it difficult to understand Spanish on the phone) and a group of students were all set to arrive on the farm early on Monday morning, with instructions that the grapes needed to be picked in three days.

It was all arranged so quickly; Sarah could hardly believe it. What had appeared to be an insurmountable challenge, now seemed achievable. It would be hard and furious work, but she felt it was worth going for it. Sarah thanked the three men profusely as well as Inés, Hugo and Carmen for their friendship and offers of help. She was amazed and so grateful that, once again, neighbours and their friends had heard of the situation and had come along with real offers of help.

"I have been thinking, said Carmen, "Although José won't be able to actually do anything as he will have to rest, he can still tell us what to do from the house. He will be pleased. He thought he would be unable to be part of it. Now he can. It will lift his spirits. I wonder how he is. It will be very strange for me to be on my own in the house. I can't remember the last time that happened."

The older woman suddenly looked very small and her face showed how vulnerable she felt suddenly without her husband near her. Sarah was about to ask her to come and spend the next few nights in her house, when Inés said, "It will be alright Mama. I will come to stay with you. I have some overnight things in the car. If you wait a moment," she said to the three men, who had stood ready to leave, "I will phone the hospital to find out how José is now."

After a brief conversation with the ward sister, Inés came back with the news that José was comfortable, was recovering from the fall and the operation better than expected and was now comfortable and sleeping. Good news. Carmen was reassured and everyone was thankful that he was not as injured as had been feared.

The three men left with promises to be there on Monday morning. "*No te preocupes, Senorita. No te preocupes*! (Don't worry!)"

Chapter Twenty

By Sunday night everything was ready – food ordered, tables, benches all set out for the pickers, the bins and tanks ready for action, baskets for the pickers to put the grapes in, new panniers for Sweetpea and even two small ones for Daisy. Carmen had been cooking up a storm making cakes, preparations for various dishes. She dug out all the large pans she had used during harvest time in the old days when Aunt Clara was still with them. She was in her element.

There was such an air of anticipation and excitement around the farm, even the camels sensed something different was about to happen and shuffled about restlessly in the stable.

Sarah slept fitfully. Going over all the preparations, checking to make sure she had remembered everything she was supposed to. By 4.30pm Sarah decided she really wasn't going to get any more sleep and got up. As she showered and dressed, she allowed her mind to travel forward through the day – the most important and eventful day since her arrival. In her mind's eye, she saw all the tables set out for the pickers, the camels in their harnesses and panniers. She envisioned the pickers working very quickly, but carefully so as not to damage the grapes. She saw Sweetpea and Daisy going back steadily, repeatedly to the Bodega loaded with grapes, then returning for more. She could hear the chatter and laughter of the students: see how they fussed the camels then held competitions as to how many baskets they could fill before the camels came back. They tried to have enough to fill the panniers almost straight away. In this way she saw the whole three days go smoothly. She even included José who was now home and in a specially modified wheelchair directing activities in the bodega. She saw happy meals around the long tables, Carmen thrilled to be making delicious food for them all. Sarah's reverie ended on the Wednesday evening, with all the grapes safely in, with everyone enjoying a celebratory feast.

With a start, she bumped back to the Monday morning. "If this is all to happen like that, I'd better get things started," she said to herself.

After a quick breakfast and a couple of coffees, Sarah went to the stable to prepare the camels for their hard days' work. She was very surprised to find, instead of their usual working harnesses, there were some very beautiful ones: brightly coloured and decorated with tassels and blankets, as if they were readied for royalty. There was no-one around to ask and as there was no sign of their usual ones, she set about fitting Sweetpea and Daisy in all this new finery. By the time she had finished she was sure that each camel was standing more proudly and taller. They were so obviously aware of their finery. Sarah laughed quietly to herself. She checked each harness carefully to make sure nothing was too tight or too loose. Each one fitted perfectly. Fantastic!

By the time the minibuses arrived with all the pickers, her three neighbours and their regular workmen, everything was ready. Sweetpea and Daisy were fed, brushed and resplendent in their colourful harnesses. Daisy tried to be very composed like her mother but ended up dancing about the yard and Sarah had to catch her to calm her down. Even Sweetpea grumbled at her daughter.

The students were taken aback at the sight of these two camels: a little cautious. Sarah introduced them all to her unusual 'members of staff' and soon they were thrilled to have such splendid helpers. Hugo and Antonio, one of the neighbours, directed the pickers where to start. The other neighbours, Manual and Pablo went to the bodega to get the grapes crushed and the juice into the tank. José joined them on the last day, delighted to be part of the action after all. He had to be encouraged to stay quietly in the chair, under threat of being sent back to the house.

Sarah guided the camels, while Carmen and Inés, who had taken three days off work to be involved, went to the *finca* kitchen to start cooking.

The grape harvest was underway!

Chapter Twenty-One

The students and neighbours were picking amazingly quickly. They were spurred on by the novelty of working with camels in all their festive finery and fuelled by the fantastic cakes, lunches and suppers prepared by Carmen and Inés. The two women had a lovely surprise when the wives of Antonio, Manuel and Pablo came to help them. It was such a happy and positive atmosphere. Everyone said they had never had such delicious food in any of the vineyards they had worked at. The five women beamed with pleasure at all the compliments.

The three days passed in a blur of laughter and activity.

It was now late Wednesday night. The grapes had all been picked and their precious juices were now already fermenting gently in the tanks. All the pickers, neighbours and wives had gone home, as well as Carmen, José and their family, after being reassured by Sarah, that she was fine spending the evening quietly at home on her own. Sarah was in the stable settling her camels down after their hard work. As she carefully brushed the dust, twigs and bits of leaves out of their coats (which they both enjoyed, grumbling and rumbling throughout), her mind travelled over the events of the last, very full, three days.

She recognised the fact that she had a very special relationship with the two camels. Apart from the one exuberant burst of youthful excitement at the beginning when baskets of grapes and vines were in danger of being overturned, Daisy had followed Sarah throughout the three days. There had been no shouting, no long sticks, just quiet guidance. Sweetpea had made her stately way carefully through the rows of vines and especially between the special hollows or pits where more vines were planted. Neither she nor Daisy had caused the sides to collapse and because of their big feet, the picon mulch wasn't crushed or flattened. The calm and colourful presence of these two creatures had certainly added to the festival atmosphere of the busy days.

Sarah had laughed and chatted with everyone, encouraging, complimenting and somehow it all got done very quickly. No-one could have guessed this was all new to her. Occasionally, some of the more experienced pickers made a suggestion for a slight adjustment to something, stopping to discuss it with colleagues and with Sarah. Rather than shout and rant, Sarah would stop and listen to the ideas. Invariably a new way of doing the harvest developed. Cries of "Let's do this/hagamoslo" echoed over the yards many times a day, followed by high fives all round and a lot of laughter.

Sweetpea and Daisy made trips to the bodega as quickly as they could, taking the full panniers to Manuel and Pablo, then returning with the emptied ones for more of the ripe fruit. The grapes just seemed to flow off the vines. People were even competing to see who could pick the most grapes before the camels' return.

Hugo was used to Vintners shouting, complaining and scolding with the work getting slower and slower, with the workforce radiating resentment and negativity. He had never experienced grape picking like this.

The neighbours had complimented Hugo on the quality of the grapes and had been pleasantly surprised by the yield, considering it was the first vintage from *finca Los Palmas* for quite a few years. They had had plenty of advice about how things could be improved though. Hugo listened carefully, filing away what sounded useful. José had come home from hospital on the last day and had spent the day in the Bodega, chatting, laughing and directing things with the two men. It was a real tonic for him and lifted his spirits, even though he was made to stay in his chair – or else!

Sarah brought her mind back to sorting out the camels and finally registered how well the new harnesses had been made. They fitted each camel perfectly, even the smaller one for Daisy. They were so perfect, that in spite of all the heavy loads they had carried throughout the three days, there were no signs of chafing or soreness. She recognised the bright red of cochineal dye, with new ochre and purple. She wondered if Carmen and Hugo had made them; if it was, they had done such a great job in making them.

Hugo had called by at the stable to congratulate Sarah on how smoothly everything had gone and to see if she was all right. He was increasingly aware that he had grown very fond of her. He had respected the way she had engaged with the running of her inherited farm, even though she knew nothing about gardening or agriculture.

Daisy suddenly got up in the middle of her grooming and began heading for the door. Fearing she would set off to the vineyard for more attention and excitement, Sarah got hurriedly to her feet and almost bumped into Hugo standing in the doorway. Daisy had noticed him there and had rushed to meet him.

"Oh, hello Hugo, I thought you had gone home. I didn't hear you coming."

"Hello, Senorita. I wanted to check on things in the Bodega to make sure it was all clean, as it should be and to lock it up. I heard you talking to the camels so came around to say goodnight."

"Lock it up?" Sarah was surprised. "Why would that be necessary?"

"It has been known for someone from a yard, who hadn't had as good a yield as expected, to go somewhere where there had been a bigger and better quality one, and siphon off a whole tank!"

"Really? That's awful. Surely not around here?"

"I suppose it hasn't happened for a few years as people are learning more about growing healthy vines and increasing their own quality and yield, but how do you say, it is better to be safe than sorry."

She finished grooming and bedding down the camels and joined Hugo at the door to walk with him back to where he had parked his car near the house.

"I was just admiring the harnesses. They fitted those two," she waved an arm in the direction of the camels, "perfectly;

not a sore or scratch on them, even after all their hard work. Where did they come from?"

Hugo smiled rather bashfully. "I made them at home over the last few weeks. I found some old harnesses under a …um!… *el lona alquitranada*… at the back of the stable over there."

Sarah looked puzzled. "*El lona?*"

Hugo looked around and pointed at the old tarpaulin. "*Alli.*"

She followed the direction of his arm. "Ah! Tarpaulin!"

"*Si.* There was a set there, complete with tassels, cords and so on. They were not fit for use, so I just copied them. Carmen came up with the idea of using the '*Los Palmas*' dye."

Sarah beamed. "You are a very surprising man, Hugo. Thank you so much for doing all that! I recognised the red dye, so thought Carmen had had something to do with them somehow. I didn't think you would have made them. It must have taken hours! Everyone admired them and said how beautiful and colourful the animals looked. Sweetpea and Daisy certainly seemed to enjoy wearing them. Did you notice how tall and proud they stood? I realised today, how hard you had worked since I arrived, bringing the slightly neglected vineyards back into such great condition. The pickers all commented on them. I really didn't think we would be able to do what we have done in three days. However, here we are with the grapes all picked and crushed and the juice already in the tanks. Amazing! Everyone worked so hard and were so cheerful. It was fantastic!"

"They said they thought the place had a very special

feeling; um… *el ambiente*, very different from other yards they had worked in."

Sarah laughed. "I expect my aunt was here encouraging everyone." Indeed, Sarah had felt Clara's supportive presence throughout the three days. "Oh dear. That sounds a bit fanciful. I must be getting tired." She laughed again, rather embarrassed about sharing her thoughts.

Hugo smiled at her. "Maybe it had as much to do with the hard work her grandniece put into the days. *Felicidades.* (Congratulations!)"

Sarah blushed, suddenly discomfited by the compliment and the gentleness of Hugo's voice. "That's very kind," she said, "But I think it's time you went home. There is still a lot to do tomorrow. Thank you for all your help and hard work."

She went to shake his hand to say goodbye. Hugo took her hand and after a brief moment of hesitation, gave her a very European, very un-British, kiss on each cheek, got in his car and drove off.

Sarah was left, almost shocked, her hand to her cheek, not quite sure what had just happened; something different had just passed between them. An unfamiliar, but pleasant feeling had rippled through her. She wasn't sure she was ready for such feelings, not just yet. After her divorce she had vowed not to be drawn into another relationship. She was in no hurry to risk being involved in an unhappy, unequal one, such as she had recently left behind.

However, the feeling was as pleasant as it was unexpected. Hugo had been so much part of the farm, always out in the vineyards, in the barns, always busy. She had no idea what needed to be done so had relied on José to direct the younger man's work.

'Maybe,' she thought, 'he is more knowledgeable and self-directed than I've given him credit for.' The conversation they had had when searching for any information about the vineyard that may have been left by her great aunt had been a revelation. Her perception of him had come into a clearer focus. In spite of herself, she liked what she now saw. There was certainly more to Hugo than she had first supposed.

Still stroking her cheek thoughtfully, Sarah gave a deep sigh and turned to go into the house, suddenly very, very tired.

Chapter Twenty-Two

Sarah woke with a feeling of relief and gratitude. As she lay in bed still half asleep her mind wandered over the last few days and the months since she had come to live at the *finca*. Less than a week ago she had been very anxious about José's health and future life. She had had a complete collapse of confidence in completing the grape harvest, through lack of knowledge and workforce. It was amazing how it had all been turned around. She discovered all her aunt's farm notes on the subject, in two boxes still unopened in the upstairs room. So much information was in there and the uncovering of it had revealed a completely different Hugo to the one she thought she knew; one who spoke good English and who knew a lot about the biodynamic way of growing vines but not about the wine making. It completely changed her perception of him and had made her actually take proper notice of him. Just as they were beginning to feel concerned about the lack of workers, help arrived from so many neighbours and friends. As a result, after three exhausting but happy days of hard work all the grapes had been gathered in and the juice was now fermenting quietly in the vats, all within the optimum three days. It was amazing. Her mind took her over the last few days, the neighbours, the students, the camels, (who had looked fantastic), Carmen, Inés and friends producing delicious food to keep everyone going, and amongst it all she realised Hugo had worked quietly in a very organised way, directing the pickers, making sure everything was going smoothly but without any fuss or noise. She sent thoughts of gratitude and thanks to all of them as they came to mind. It had all worked out so well. She was determined to treat all those involved to a celebration supper on Saturday.

She wasn't quite sure what to make of the unexpected show of affection from Hugo just as he left. It had disturbed her, but in a pleasant way and had awakened emotions she had not felt for a long time, well before she and her ex-husband had separated and divorced. Her hand went to her cheeks where Hugo had kissed her. She smiled. It was rather nice. However, she had no time or inclination for love and romance. She was still hurting from the collapse of her nine-year relationship back in England. She was in no rush to open that particular door now and risk such hurt again so soon.

Feeling very tired she went to the stables. The camels still looked a bit dusty and tangled; she had been weary the night before and had given them a hasty brushing. This morning feeling more relaxed and having more time, she cleaned out their stall, renewed water and hay and fetched her brushes and combs to do the job properly. She brushed down Daisy first. The young camel loved it and stood quietly for Sarah to get on with the job, then all relaxed and at ease, lay down. Sweetpea came forward for her grooming. When Sarah had combed out the lower part of her body, the large camel lay down for Sarah to reach the top of her back and neck. With the love and attention and good food she had received since her arrival, she had grown to her full size and was too tall for Sarah to reach her back to brush it.

Sarah thought both camels were very beautiful and gentle and told them often, especially when she was grooming them. What with the hard work and excitement of the previous few days, the rhythmic nature of the brushing and the calm, quiet atmosphere of the stable, both animals were soon asleep. Sarah sat down on the clean straw and leaned against Sweetpea's warm side.

Her mind wandered again, but this time over the events of the months since she had moved to *finca Los Palmas*. Her life in England seemed to belong to someone else. She didn't miss the commuting and the stress and rush of her life in the office. She was surprised to realise how little time she had spent outdoors in comparison to now, when she was hardly indoors. The job in London had paid well, she wore smart clothes and knew many people though none that could be regarded as real friends.

However, here, listening to the camels' contented rumbling 'purr,' she realised it had been at considerable cost to herself and to her relationships. Not that her life here wasn't stressful. There had been some really dark times when she had felt desperately lonely, completely at a loss as to how she was going to be successful in making the farm profitable and very homesick. She was mostly aware of how little she knew about farming anywhere, let alone here in the challenging conditions of the northern most, dry, windswept Canary Island. Her mind meandered to the camels, how important they had become to everyone on the farm, but especially to her. Sweetpea had arrived when she was about to give up. Her arrival had given her the energy and determination to continue regardless of her lack of knowledge, assuring herself she could and would learn.

Somehow, Sarah had come through the low times. A kind word from Carmen, a brief conversation and a smile with the stall holders at the market, so many of whom remembered her aunt fondly. The knowledge and hard work of José and his nephew, Hugo, had all helped to encourage her and keep her going. She was also aware that encouragement seemed to come when it was most needed, unbidden and often as a picture in her mind or a gently whispered sentence. She was so sure it was her aunt somehow, though she had never met her, or even knew she existed until a few months ago. It was strange but comforting at the same time. It had all helped to embolden her and strengthen her resolve to keep going and strive to make it all work somehow. The rugged beauty of the valley, so hostile looking when she first arrived, now seemed to be enfolded within the arms of the old volcano, protected, more productive and greener than when she first came.

This is where Hugo found her when he came to discuss the next phase of work on the farm. He wouldn't have known she was there at all if her long black hair hadn't spilled over Sweetpea's neck. He often wondered about that. Most English people had mid brown or blonde hair and a fair complexion, yet Sarah had black hair and had developed a dark tan from being outside so much of the time. She looked more Spanish than many islanders.

The thunder was getting louder and nearer. Lightning forked to the ground. A fig tree, very close to the vines, burst into flames; the fire spread quickly to the nearest row of vines. The sky was blacker than Sarah had ever seen and the wind had risen suddenly and was blowing the flames every which way. More and more vines were burning, the scarlet and orange flames luminous against the black sky. She raced out to the vineyard, trying to phone for the fire brigade; her phone kept slipping from her fingers time and time again. She could feel the heat from the fire on her face. She was feeling desperate, panic-stricken…

"Sarah! Sarah!" someone was shouting her name. "Sarah!"

"Huh?!" She woke with a jolt and for a moment didn't know where she was, just feeling that something urgent and awful was going on. She was aware of a rumbling noise and her face feeling very hot.

"Sarah! Are you alright?"

It was Hugo. He had been too nervous of the protective Sweetpea to go too close to the woman fast asleep, leaning against the camel's side and was calling her to wake her up.

"Hmm?" Still heavy with sleep and exhaustion, Sarah struggled to come to. As she slowly woke up, she realised she had fallen asleep after grooming Sweetpea, leaning against her side. Through the stable door she could see blue sky and warm sunshine. There was a warm, but gentle breeze blowing in and around the stable.

She scrabbled to stand up. Hugo leant forward and offered an arm to help her up. She took it gratefully.

"Oh goodness! I must have dozed off for a moment. I was having a terrible dream. There was a fierce thunderstorm and lightning had set fire to the vineyard. It was the morning of the harvest. It was awful. So real! Oh dear! I could feel the heat from the flames. I still can! What are you doing here so early?"

Hugo smiled. "You must have been very tired. It is eleven o'clock now. You have been asleep for hours. You weren't in the yard or in the house, so I came looking for you. I think the thunder was Sweetpea's rumbling like she does when she is happy. The heat from the fire was the heat from the camel's side that you had fallen asleep leaning on."

Feeling relieved that those awful images weren't real, Sarah stumbled a bit, brushing bits of bedding and camel hair from her clothes.

"Eugh! I smell of camel and straw and am really stiff. Is it really eleven? Drat! There's a lot to do today, I'd better get going, though I think I need a shower and a change of clothes first, then some strong coffee and maybe a slice of Carmen's cake." She was aware she was now babbling, but embarrassed by falling asleep for so long and confused by her vivid dream, she couldn't stop. "The dream was so real. I thought the whole vineyard would go up in flames. I couldn't stop the fire, Oh dear! I feel really sleepy. I must look a fright," she finished lamely, with a wan smile, running her hand through her hair and shaking out the last few bits of straw.

Hugo was just thinking how lovely she looked, in spite of her clothes being crumpled, with her hair tangled and sticking up all over the place. He shook his head. This was ridiculous. It must be the relief from the tension and rush of the last few days and weeks. He had no time or heart space for such thoughts. He was still deeply hurt from when his fiancée broke off their engagement just a week before their wedding. She had said she realised she wanted more than being a 'farmer's' wife, living where that weird old woman had lived. She was moving back to Spain.

Even now the memory made him feel hot with anger and a sense of injustice. She had heaped one insult on top another. Rejecting him as a 'farmer,' rejecting an area he had grown to love and where his friends were, and insulting Clara's memory by referring to her as a 'weird woman.' He wasn't sure which had been the worst, the stab at Clara as she was no longer alive to defend her ideals or dismissing his chosen and much enjoyed profession as a Vintner. He seethed even now at the memory of it and involuntarily clenched his fists.

He had been devastated. He had hidden his heart break in hard work and silence, though he suspected that Carmen had understood the agony he was going through. Now he thought about it, there had been rather a lot of coffee and large slices of chocolate cake that came out to him wherever he was on the farm. Bless her for her silent support.

He had gradually taken over some of the management of the farm as his uncle got older, as Señora Clara had made clear in her Will he should. When she died, neither he, nor Carmen and José, had known if she had left the ownership of the farm to anyone or if the beneficiary would take the challenge on if he or she had.

He loved working there and felt a duty to keep it going, even though it had been a struggle. It was not the most conducive of climates, even with the little rain they had in that part of the island. He hadn't been sure what to think when this young, pale, inexperienced, English, 'city' woman arrived. He was very surprised when she decided to come to live at *finca Los Palmas* and try to make it profitable once more. He had worried at first that she would take on new staff and change everything, even build – horror of horrors – a holiday village, destroying the vines, which were the most profitable part of the farm. He decided he would keep out of her way and get on with the vines and other tasks as best he could and wait to see what happened.

He never expected Sarah to stay, let alone be so determined to learn how everything was run. In spite of her ignorance, she seemed set on learning how best to farm here, so far from her home, in what was a very difficult climate to say the least. He had admired her resolution to keep going regardless of all the challenges, which must have seemed insurmountable at times. He was disturbed to realise his admiration was developing into something deeper and more personal. Better to just get on with the job in hand and keep these new feelings to himself.

Sarah noticed the sudden change in his expression from smiling, open and friendly, dropping back into his habitual closed in, serious one. She mistook the withdrawal for disapproval of her falling asleep in the stable.

Feeling guilty and uncomfortable, she repeated her

apologies. "I'm sorry to have left you alone to move things on from yesterday, Hugo. I hadn't realised I was so tired. Thank you for coming to find me. I was having a horrible dream that the vineyards were being destroyed by thunder and lightning." She smiled then. "As you said, I expect it was my mind making sense of Sweetpea's rumbling body. Thank you for just getting on with things. I appreciate your knowledge and understanding of the farm. You work very hard. You must enjoy working here."

A flare of radiance flickered across Hugo's face, briefly transforming his whole appearance. Reluctantly, Sarah had to admit she rather liked it. It quickly passed though. Hugo stepped back, nodded an acknowledgement to her comments, spun round on his heels and with a "I'll be in the vineyard," strode off, his back rigidly upright.

Sarah sighed, gave Sweetpea and Daisy a pat, checked their water and food and went back to the house to get showered and change her clothes and have something to eat.

Chapter Twenty-Three

It was Saturday morning; the harvest had been completed on the previous Wednesday. Soon the *finca* would be full of people once again. It was today Sarah was holding her "Harvest Celebration" to thank everyone for all their hard work and assistance.

The long tables were back out on the terrace. Sarah had put large pots of bright red geraniums around. In response to their special treatment Sarah had given them after her online research, the oleander bushes were full of carmine pink, white and even a few yellow blooms.

In addition, the bougainvilleas that Sarah had been carefully tending since her arrival, were a riot of colour, cascading over the sides of the roof stairs and wall which sheltered the terrace from the chilly north wind. Strings of fairy lights festooned doors, windows and the roof line of the house.

Between Carmen's enthusiastic skills in the kitchen, the stall holders in the market at Haria, and the owners of the café where Sarah and Inés had first met, a magnificent banquet was all prepared in the kitchens of the two women. They were feeling excited and a little nervous. This was a different from the more casual workday mode of meals during the harvest.

Sarah had bought the wine and cava from most of the Bodega in the area. While she was at one of the larger vineyards, two coach loads of tourists arrived and disgorged into the 'cellar,' where hundreds of bottles were laid out on racks, some already wrapped in bubble wrap to be transported back home by the visitors.

'Ah!' thought Sarah, 'that is why there were so many tasting cups laid out already full of red or white wine on the counter at the rear of the cellar.' She assumed they called the barn a cellar, as this was where so many bottles were stacked, even though it wasn't underground. She wondered if underground would be too warm as they were on the edge of the barren volcanic desert. All the visitors bought at least 1 bottle of wine, some even six or eight, though that would be heavy to carry. 'Perhaps those people were on a cruise so weren't so concerned about space and weight as those who had flown in by charter holiday flights.'

In 30 minutes, everyone had left and coaches moved off onto another tourist destination no doubt.

'Maybe they are moving onto the Jameos del Agua and the underground café and concert hall, just a bit further north?'

Sarah had gone there during the tour of the island she made during her first visit to the island. It was quite a spectacular place she recalled. The cellar was strangely quite after all the rush and scrabble for local wine when all the

186

tourists were there. It needed speed and efficiency on the part of the staff who worked there – and patience Sarah noted. Not all tourists were polite. It was all worth it for the volume of sales made in such a short time. No doubt it wouldn't be the only tour to call in that day. Sarah wondered if they would be able to be part of a tour in this way at *finca Los Palmas*. Hmm. She wasn't sure she could cope with such a cavalcade of eager tourists all at once. She was reminded a bit of a swarm of locusts, in spite of herself.

'Let's just see how this year's vintage turns out before I go that far,' she thought.

She introduced herself to the women behind the counter. They were pleased to meet her. They had heard, from a neighbour, about Sarah's arrival, then the difficulties when José broke his leg. Sarah paid for her 6 bottles.

"One of my daughters came to help with the picking," said one of the women. "She said it was an amazing three days. Often there can be a lot of tension and shouting, but it all went so smoothly. She had a lot of fun. And the camels! She couldn't stop talking about them carrying the grapes from the field. The big one was so careful and patient and quick, Annette told us. What was her name now? Ah yes! Sweetpea and the young one was Daisy. She was a bit of a scamp, wasn't she? She did her best to help, she said. Sarah smiled and nodded. "They looked amazing, all decked out in bright colourful harnesses and drapes. They loved that, especially the red colour. The young people had never seen camels worked like that before. I remember my grandfather talking about them though."

"They are very useful," said Sarah. "Their big hooves

spread out the weight so the Picon is not damaged as they move back and forth. I think the modern machinery may just grind those marble things into a powder. The red colour is a dye we made from the cochineal beetles on the farm. This blouse was coloured with the same dye."

"It is a lovely shade. Just right for the bright sunshine here. Would you dye something for me?"

"Oh yes, why not? Give me a few days to get over the Harvest celebration, which is what this wine is for. I'll be delighted to see you. Carmen and I will make a new batch of dye ready for you, if you let us know when you want to come. Here is a card with my contact details on."

The other woman asked her "Didn't the English Signora who lived there before use the camels?" .'

"Yes" replied Sarah, "She was my great aunt. She left the farm to me. It was a great surprise. I didn't know anything about her or the Island, apart from it being a tourist destination, until January."

"My daughter couldn't believe how helpful the big animals were. She was a bit nervous of them at first. Sweetpea was very tall she said. She loved the young one. What was her name again?"

"Daisy," said Sarah smiling. "Sweetpea is her mother. The wine is for a thank you party I'm holding on Saturday for all the people who helped. I hope your daughter can come along?"

"She has talked about nothing else," said the first assistant. "She and her friends will be there. They knew a lot of the other pickers, my daughter said. The neighbours seemed to have really rallied round. Didn't the man who lived there and had worked there for many years, break his leg in a fall just before the harvest?"

"Yes," replied Sarah, "the neighbours really rallied round. I was so amazed and grateful. I don't know how we'd have managed otherwise."

The women expressed their surprise, said they were pleased to meet her, then carried on chatting to each other recalling days gone by as told by various older relatives as they tidied up the chaos and prepared for the next coach loads.

Sarah smiled and gathered up her purchases. It was a nice surprise to hear about the days of the harvest in such positive terms from strangers. She welcomed the personal contact. The people who lived here were very friendly and helpful. She remembered that the days had run in accordance with the way she had visualised them at 5.00 that morning of the first day of the harvest. She shivered. "Interesting," she thought.

Just as Sarah turned to go, a tall, slim man walked in from a back room.

He approached Sarah; hand extended in greeting.

"Ah! *Buenos dias.* You must be *Señora J*ones. I have heard a lot about you. Maximiliano at your service."

He bowed slightly as he took Sarah's hand, gently. "Please call me Max."

She was taken aback by such profusion and for an awful moment, thought he was going to kiss her hand, like some Spanish courtier of old. Instead, he relieved her of her box of wine, saying, "Let me help you take these to your car."

Sarah felt uneasy; his friendliness reminded her of the

easy manner of her ex-husband back in England; the sense of support that she had mistakenly thought was a part of their relationship, but had quickly become controlling.

Out of the corner of her eye she saw one of the women she had been talking to a moment ago, raise an eye brow, roll her eyes and shake her head. The gesture seemed to indicate the thought – 'Here he goes again.'

"Oh! Um. Thank you, That's very kind."

She turned back to the women who had served her. "*Gracias*!" I hope to see you again," she called, then turned to follow the effusive Max to her car, which was the only one in the car park by that time.

"I have heard a lot about you," said Max as they walked back to the car. "My daughter, with her university friends, went to help with the grape harvest. She was impressed by the organisation, by the quantity and quality of the grapes. But this is your first vintage, no? It is surprising that it was all so good."

"Yes," replied Sarah. "There are some knowledgeable people at the farm and my great aunt left the makings of strong, healthy vines I think."

Something about the man's manner made Sarah hold back on any further information. He seemed very friendly and his attention was flattering. However, the woman's raised eyebrows as she left, seemed to be a warning – but what of? With the wine safely stowed in the car. Sarah turned to him.

"Thank you. Your daughter is coming to the Thanksgiving Harvest Supper. Perhaps you would care to join us as well? It starts at 7.30."

Max smiled, took Sarah's hand and this time raised it to

his lips and kissed it lightly.

"It would be my pleasure, Senorita," he said, looking directly into her eyes.

Sarah smiled weakly at such an intimate gesture from someone she had met only a few moments ago. She quickly withdrew her hand and got into the car. In her rear-view mirror, she could see Max standing in the car park, watching her leave. There was a strange expression on his face, very different from that with which he had accepted her impulsive invitation. She struggled to find a word to describe it exactly, but it set off warning lights in her head. Perhaps his swift acceptance was not really connected to neighbourly interest and support.

'Hmm,' she thought. 'I'd better keep an eye on him.'

When she arrived back at *Los Palmas* the place was a whirl of activity. Hugo, Inés and Carmen had set out the long tables once again, with flowers arranged down the centre. This time there were three extra tables: one for the wine glasses, two for the buffet. The cava was on ice, as was the white wine and the red wine opened to breathe. José, eager to be involved, was carrying things around on his lap in the wheelchair.

By 7.15 the food was all on the buffet table. Sarah had to admit it looked impressive. In the centre was an enormous pan of Carmen's signature paella, then there were the plates of various croquettes, *jamon, bacalao,* (cod), *queso,* (smooth cheese), *moriella* (spiced black sausage), platters of cured meats, *chorizo, salchicon, tortillas,* bowls of *gazpacho, salmorengo, ratatouille,* bowls of crisp salad, sun-ripened tomatoes from a neighbour and baskets of warm crusty bread. On a heated plate at the end were bowls of bean stew, and garlic prawns. It looked amazing and very appetising.

Sarah went upstairs to change. She decided she would wear her favourite dress now dyed bright red. It may give her a little confidence as she was suddenly feeling very nervous. It felt so different from the work day lunches everyone had enjoyed during the days of picking the grapes. She was still harbouring doubts about her impulsive invitation to Max and wished she had thought before opening her mouth. "Ah well! Too late now. What will be, will be." Perhaps her fears were more to do with nerves than the reality of the situation. However, she would be cautious of him and pay him little attention.

Unknown to Sarah, Max had been in the backroom at his bodega when Sarah was buying her wine. He had been about to walk in, to collect the profits from the last coach visit, when he realised who was there. This new English woman who had caused such a stir with her wretched old-fashioned camels. "Camels for goodness' sake. Who uses camels these days? And all that nonsense about lunch and now this Harvest Supper or whatever she called it. Just spending what little profit she will make from her cheap wine."

He decided to stay out of sight but close enough to hear what was being said. He was known to be a mean man, quick of temper and slow to praise. The women stayed there only because they had little to do with him since they had refused his sexual advances in the early days. He usually left them alone because they managed the mayhem of the tourist coaches so efficiently. It was a profitable and oft repeated mayhem. As he listened, he bristled with impatience, and if he had admitted it, jealousy. No-one ever commented on how they had enjoyed picking his grapes. No-one ever volunteered to return to his vineyards the next season. He had to trawl the island for new people to come to help. They had to be new. If they weren't, they would know how he shouted and cursed at everyone for being so slow; criticised how they did everything, gave very few and very short breaks and no refreshments, apart from water. Not even a glass of wine when it was all over. He just paid them their minimum that was due and left, without a word of thanks. He decided he would try to win her over to discover her secrets and take them for his own use and maybe see how he could pierce this golden bubble people had woven around her.

He realised she was leaving. Quickly, he stepped out from where he had been hiding, pretending to be surprised to see her. He was not prepared for how beautiful she was. He had expected either some pale mousey woman or a masculine looking Amazon, possibly in tweeds – though goodness knows where that idea had come from. It was therefore no hardship to be gallant and flattering, even though it was never his true self. It had its desired effect because she had got flustered and had hastily invited him along with his daughter. She wasn't to know he didn't have a daughter. It was the daughter of one of his staff to whom he was referring.

As Sarah drove away, he allowed himself a slight smirk of triumph. He congratulated himself on his acting skills. 'Pretty good, even if I say it myself,' he thought.

Chapter Twenty-Four

It was a fantastic celebration. The people seemed so pleased to be together again. Soon the reminiscences came around to the camels.

"Where are Sweetpea and Daisy?" they were asking. As if on cue, Hugo came around the corner of the house with the two of them. They looked very different. They had on all the colourful harnesses and blankets they had worn for the harvest, but now they were wearing garlands of bougainvillea and geraniums around their necks. They walked very proudly and sedately, even Daisy, obviously aware of their new finery and aware of the special nature of the occasion.

"Oh! They look wonderful, Hugo. Thank you.," said Sarah, delighted and surprised by their appearance, very pleased that Hugo had thought to make this extra effort for the evening. Hugo smiled. He hadn't been certain that the camels would allow him to dress them in their finery nor what Sarah would think of what he had done. The camels had waited calmly while he put on the harnesses and blankets, and seemed pleased to be dressed up again and be part of the celebrations.

"Don't you look wonderful," said Sarah as she patted their necks. Various people clustered around the recent arrivals, petting and fussing them as if they were gentle Labradors. Sweetpea and Daisy loved it. With much contented rumblings, they posed time and time again for people's selfies and larger group photos.

Meanwhile, Max had been sitting a little apart from the group. He was known by many of the people there, but unknown to Sarah, not particularly liked or trusted. Many wondered what he was doing there and why he had been invited. He had proved to be an unhelpful and difficult neighbour, a hard task master in the vineyards and Bodega, wanting maximum loyalty and working them very hard without giving much back in return. He had never given his staff anything over and above their minimum wages, let alone a banquet to show them appreciation for their hard work. He thought such a thing was madness and a waste of money. He had been surprised by the appearance and standard of the farm and vineyards. He had expected them to be ramshackle and "Heath Robinson." He didn't acknowledge it, but he was feeling increasingly jealous and slightly threatened by this unlikely foreign newcomer.

All too soon it was time for the evening to end. Sarah and José brought out some of the bottles from the last vintage her great aunt had made. It was declared a great wine, full-bodied, a complex of delicious flavours, with a pleasing aftertaste and not too much tannin.

(Max had to reluctantly acknowledge that the *Los Palmas*

wine was as good, if not better than his. It hardened his heart even more)

"To Aunt Clara and to more great vintages," said Sarah, raising her glass in a toast to the lady who had made it all possible. She thanked everyone for their hard work and for their willing help. She thanked the stallholders and café owners from the town who had provided many of the tasty dishes for the feast. The guests agreed the food had been delicious and could they have their names along with which dishes they had made. Sarah smiled and waved some papers.

"All the details are here. Please collect a sheet before you go."

The chefs and bakers nodded to each other, pleased that Sarah had thought to recommend them so specifically.

She went on to express her gratitude to Hugo for recovering the vines to full health and productivity so quickly; to José for his experience, guidance and advice since her arrival. She wished him a speedy and complete recovery from his fall. Max shifted his position in his chair very slightly, hoping no-one would notice his momentary discomfort. She particularly thanked Carmen and Inés, for their friendship, support and advice from the moment of her arrival.

"I couldn't have got this far in the time without you all – and of course without Sweetpea and Daisy."

There was much cheering and laughter, but gradually the guests began to drift away back home, all agreeing what a fantastic evening it had been and saying how they would definitely be back next year for the harvest and hopefully another Thanksgiving supper. Hugo led the two camels back to the stables to take of all their harnesses, garlands and blankets. He was pleased that they seemed to accept him as well as they accepted Sarah. He had grown fond of them, in spite of his initial misgivings about having them around.

However, Max hung back and after the guests had left made a point of coming to Sarah to say goodbye. He took hold of both her hands in his. He smiled directly into her eyes again. She was not easy about the strength with which he gripped her hands. She tried to step back to create more space between them, but he held her close, too close. He was smiling, but his eyes were cool. Sarah was already uncomfortable in his presence, because he had flirted with her at every opportunity during the meal. It was definitely not appropriate.

"I am very impressed, Senorita. Your wine is excellent. (This was acknowledged begrudgingly). You have good vines here and of an unusual variety. Would you join me for dinner soon so that I may return your hospitality? I would like to discuss with you the future of *Los Palmas*."

He was overcome by jealousy of Sarah's popularity. beautiful farm and all the good things people were saying about her. No-one ever said anything remotely like that to him, though he never stopped to understand why that should be so. The intensity of it drove him on past the point of politeness, throwing caution to the wind and, as he thought, taking this good opportunity to speak with her on her own.

"It is obviously very hard work for one so inexperienced and used only to city life until recently. You have such a small work force, two of whom are well past their retirement age."

Sarah could imagine Carmen and José's response to such an outrageous idea as retire. Her 'amber light' of earlier in the day now moved rapidly to a flashing red light, possibly with sirens. She remembered why she had been so flattered by his attention. It reminded her of the easy manner of her ex-husband back in England; the friendliness, sense of support that she had thought was a part of their relationship.

It hadn't been long before this 'support' became overbearing and controlling, eventually dictating what she should wear, and how the style of hair would suit her so much better if she changed it to something of his choice. It had taken her a few years but eventually her perception of him and their situation cleared and she had seen him for the controlling person he really was. They separated soon after that and then began divorce proceedings. It had broken her heart because she had believed that she loved him and that he loved her in the same way. However, it had proved to be too stifling, leaving her feeling less than who she knew she had been and could be.

Here, through all the frustrations, difficulties, despair and triumphs, small as they might have been, she knew she had blossomed. She wasn't about to lose all that for a few moments of flattery from a man who wasn't at all what he had seemed to be. During the meal, in general conversation with the two women who had served her at Max's Bodega, she discovered that the man did not have a daughter, was not even married any more. So much for that lie!

Max stepped even closer. Sarah managed to pull her hands free from the strong grip and stepped back from what suddenly felt a very difficult situation. She felt flustered. No-one else was around. The energy now was so very different from the joyous carefree atmosphere of just a few moments ago. People had either gone home or had gone indoors sorting out dishes and the small amount of food that had been left.

"That's very kind of you, but I still have a lot to attend to here. I will be very busy for a few months."

"Oh, I'm sure you could spare an evening. You see, I would like to make you a very attractive offer. It would make your life so much easier and less problematic for you."

"I don't find being here a problem thank you and I relish the hard work. It is kind of you to consider such things." As she said this, she heard her Aunt Clara's voice clear as anything 'He plans to buy the farm, destroy the biodynamic energy of the place, introduce chemicals and more modern varieties of grapes and make it a part of his estate.'

Sarah stiffened, knowing her aunt was correct. Max sensed his charm was not working and was now anxious that the moments of opportunity were slipping away.

"Señora," his voice was hard and business-like. "I want to buy *finca Los Palmas*. It is foolish to think that you can continue in this manner. Do you think these people will be so keen to help you every year? You are a novelty. They are curious about you. They will see you are just playing at being a farmer, they suspect you will soon flee back to England and abandon the place to its fate. Do you think you can buy their friendship with one brief meal? They will soon dismiss you for a well-intentioned but impractical foreigner. I will buy the farm from you then you will have no more worries; you can retire; enjoy life. I can make you an excellent offer!"

Sarah was incensed by this man's judgement of her, a complete stranger. She drew herself up tall. "Signor, I see you for who and what you are. I do not agree with your judgement of my neighbours. They are good people and know the code of farmers the world around – everyone helps out where they can, when needed, but only then. I plan to offer my services to them next year when I have more experience. They are all good, kind honest people." She emphasised the word 'Honest.' Max twitched sightly.

"I have no intention of selling this farm and every intention of honouring the trust my great aunt placed in me by leaving it to me. It is hard work, but I love it. I love living here. My 'staff,' as you insist on calling them, are my friends and are very knowledgeable about the farm and how my aunt ran it. I owe them a great deal for all that they have done for me since the moment I arrived. The farm is not for sale. I intend to continue living here and to make it as successful as my aunt had done. I am not leaving here!"

Max smiled. He knew women could always be persuaded to come around to his plans. He leaned even closer and made to kiss her on the lips, planning to seduce her into submission. It had always worked in his favour before. Suddenly he stiffened, a noise just around the corner caught his attention. Someone was there. He stood to attention and clicked his heels.

"Very well. You may regret your decision. The best of luck!" His eyes narrowed and a cruel smile flickered over his mouth. "As the daughter of an illegitimate child you'll need all the luck you can get. Folk here don't like that sort of thing."

With a curt bow, he turned on his heels and strode off. Soon she heard the roar of his powerful car racing up the track.

Chapter Twenty-Five

Sarah was hardly breathing, shocked and frightened by this man's temerity in making such an unasked for offer and in such a derogatory manner, dismissing her friends and neighbours as just curious on-lookers or too old to be of any use. And what was that parting comment all about? She was reeling, searching for a chair to sit down.

She felt a light touch on her shoulder and jumped, afraid who it might be, even though she had heard Max drive away a moment ago.

"Sarah, are you alright?"

It was Hugo.

"Oh Hugo!" Sarah was so relieved to see him, a friend she trusted (she didn't want her thoughts to stray too far from that idea). She laid her head on his shoulder and sobbed.

Hugo was a bit taken aback but not surprised by Sarah's emotional state. He had heard most of what Max had said to her. He had also realised that his approach had caught Max by surprise and had brought his "persuasion" to a sudden end.

Hugo put his arms around her and stroked her hair. 'To calm her,' he qualified to himself. He tried to ignore the feelings that he really felt, but already he knew that he loved her, loved working on the farm and didn't want to leave the farm or Sarah. He had been so relieved and pleased to hear her say very adamantly. "I am not leaving here."

Sarah's mind was all confusion. How dare that man come here to join in her celebration, then offer to buy the farm, insult her 'staff' (she had never regarded any of them in those terms), friends and neighbours; to call her beloved camels, foolish and antiquated and to judge her by saying she would never be successful here; and what was that parting shot he flung at her? The daughter of an illegitimate child – her mother illegitimate!? What?!

She was about to step away from Hugo, then realised how comforting it felt to be held in his arms, to feel him tenderly stroking her hair and listen to his murmurs of comfort. With a shuddering sigh, she stopped crying and relaxed against his chest.

After a while Hugo said, "Sit down here. I think some brandy would be a good idea, don't you?"

With some reluctance, which surprised her, Sarah went to sit at the nearby table. Hugo soon returned with two glasses and a bottle of brandy. He had also found a few slices of cake which he brought out as well. Sarah gratefully ate a little of the cake; she had eaten hardly anything throughout the evening, being very busy making sure everyone else was eating their fill.

"You did well to stand up against that man," he said, as he poured out generous amounts of brandy into each glass.

"He is regarded with suspicion and dislike in the area. The guests were surprised to see him here."

Sarah felt the brandy warm the chill that had swept through her when Max had grabbed hold of her hands so tightly and wouldn't let go.

"I invited him on impulse. I got some of the wine from his place for this evening. The women who work there were lovely; so friendly and helpful. We chatted about this evening and the harvest for a while. The daughter of one of them had been here with her friends helping with the picking. They were intrigued by her tales of the camels helping out. She remembered her grandfather using camels in that way when she was a child. I suppose I dropped my guard as a result. Max came out to join us all smiles and friendliness. He said he had a daughter who had helped at the harvest and she would be here this evening. I didn't know then that he had no family, was not even married anymore. I was rushing, tired, flustered and flattered by his... hmmm... rather intimate behaviour, so said he could join us and come along. Yuk!"

"Yes. That is what he is like; all smiles and courtesy until he doesn't get his own way. He doesn't like to thwarted. He is a bully. We must be on our guard."

"He is certainly a bully. He really showed his true nature there at the end. I'm glad you appeared when you did. But why should we be on our guard and what was that that about me being the child of an illegitimate mother? Carmen has never talked much about Aunt Clara or her younger personal life. I suppose I have been so focussed on learning what she did on the farm and how much I could learn from

Aunt Clara and Carmen, I never got that far in my thinking … and anyway, how could he know anything about my family in England. My mother's mother was married when mum was born. I've seen the photographs!"

"I don't know. Perhaps it was just to insult you. In some areas around here still, especially amongst the older people, being born out of marriage is regarded as shameful"

"I don't think so. He had a strange expression on his face when he said it; an arrogant smirk almost - I didn't like it at all." She shivered at the memory of it.

Hugo reached out for her free hand and held it gently. "Perhaps there is some mystery here. Maybe Carmen will know, or there may be something about it in the papers your great aunt left. It is late now. We could look more into it in the morning if you would like."

"I would like that." Sarah finished her brandy, the cake had long ago disappeared, and breathed out long and slow.

"Well, until he came along at the end with his 'excellent offer,' it was a brilliant evening. I'm so glad we did it."

Hugo noted the 'we,' not 'I,' with some pleasure.

"Thank you for all your hard work with the vineyard and helping with the preparations for the evening," continued Sarah. "What a great surprise bringing Sweetpea and Daisy to join us, especially all dressed up in their fancy harnesses and garlands. They loved it, didn't they? Revelling in the attention and celebratory atmosphere. They looked very regal. Talking of camels, will you come with me to settle them down? That man has spooked me. His manner was very threatening and harsh at the end. As you said, he obviously likes to get his way and has a tantrum when he doesn't."

The camels greeted the both of them with a sleepy grunt. Sweetpea was almost as fond of Hugo as she was of Sarah. Daisy was now definitely Hugo's camel and had taken to trailing after him as he went about the farm. He was surprised at first, then irritated by the attention, as she often got in the way. However, as she got older and Hugo learned how to encourage her, she got a better understanding of what was expected of her. She became more useful to him, but still full of fun. Hugo looked forward to her following him around and most days found more and more things she could do to lighten his load.

With the camels settled for the night, the two people stood side by side in the stable doorway. The moon was low in the western sky and already the sky was getting lighter in the east. It was very still and calm after all the hustle and bustle of the last few days and weeks. Sarah shivered in the pre-dawn chill.

"Here, have my jacket,' said Hugo. He put it around her shoulders. She turned to look at him and smiled lifting her face to give him a quick kiss on the cheek in thanks and for a 'goodnight.' Instead, Hugo held her face gently in his hands and kissed her lips. All their months of hurt, reservations about falling in love again and thoughts of 'I'm ok on my own thanks; better in fact,' fell away in that moment. Sarah kissed him back.

After a long time, Hugo stepped back, unsure about what this meant. Was it just a reaction to the intensity of Max's bullying and spiteful energy or was something more going on, unrecognised by either of them until now? Sarah's thoughts were wandering along the same lines. She smiled, uncertainly, but didn't let go of Hugo's hands.

Hugo took a deep breath and came to a decision.

"Sarah! I had made up my mind that I would never love again when my fiancée moved back to Spain just a few days before we were supposed to get married, here in Haria. Now I find my heart has other ideas. When I heard an inexperienced English woman, used to city life was coming here to take over the farm, I had serious reservations about you. I thought you would be like Lucia and soon leave to go back to the bright lights of London. When I saw how determined you were about learning what to do here and how everything fitted together and how hard you have been working to create new streams of income, my reservations have given way to friendship. I overheard Max telling you that you would never be any good here and therefore you should sell the farm to him. My heart stopped. I knew then that I didn't want you to leave; that I wanted to stay here and work with you to make it a success like it was before. It feels a risk to tell you, but I don't want you to go."

He sighed. He felt so apprehensive, uncertain how such a revelation would be received. After all, she was nominally his boss.

Sarah laughed quietly. "I, too, had decided love was not for me. I had been married to David for five years, but had been together since university days. We were both in stressful jobs and worked long hours, hardly talking in the short evenings we were at home, though mostly we were at business events or entertaining future clients, so that wasn't very often. Inevitably we drifted apart. I thought we would

207

continue as we were and just rub along together getting on with our lives. However, he had other ideas and came home one evening and told me he had found someone else and was leaving. He packed a suitcase and left, just like that, saying he would be back later to collect the rest of his things. I was so shocked. I had been so wrapped up in my work I had not noticed how bad things had got. I thought then that maybe a lot of his late meetings were not business at all. Huh! How blind can we be? I discovered then that he had had several affairs over the years, one even when we were planning our wedding. He was texting at least two other women at that time. We got divorced and I was living, temporarily, in a small flat, with most of my things in storage. I realised I actually hated my job and wanted to leave but didn't know where to go or what to do differently. When Mr. Selby called me to his office to tell me about my aunt, whom I had never heard of before and how she had left this farm to me, it seemed too good an offer to turn down. I fell in love with the farm on my first visit here and knew then that I wanted to make a go of it, even though I had no idea of how to grow anything. When Max said I should sell the farm to him, it strengthened my resolve and intention to remain and make it a success. Carmen and José have been such good friends and advisors, but you being here, your experience, the quiet confidence with which you go about the, sometimes, overwhelming list of things to do, and your friendship have become a big part of that resolve. I can't imagine being here without you."

They kissed again, with more passion now they each knew how the other felt. Sarah became aware of some warmth on her cheek. It was the first rays of the rising sun.

"Goodness! It is morning already. I could do with a drink – water and coffee this time I mean," she added laughing. "Would you join me?"

Hugo laughed. "Yes please. I could really do with a strong coffee and a lot of water! "

As they walked to the kitchen together, he felt a great weight fall away from him. His heart felt lighter and more open than it had ever been before. The future looked very different now, though it was still all a mystery. Unusually for him, who liked to have everything carefully planned out a long way ahead, that was just fine.

Chapter Twenty-Six

A week had gone by since the Harvest Thank you Supper. Hugo and José, who was now, very occasionally, walking carefully with crutches, were in the winery frequently, checking on the fermenting process. Hugo was busy bringing empty barrels up from the cellar. José thought all the wine that had been made during Signora Clara's time had been bottled and apart from 4 remaining bottles had all been sold or drunk. Hugo was surprised to discover, right at the back of the empty barrels there were three barrels that were still full. He thought they may be vinegar by now, but took a sample from one of the barrels to check. It smelled wonderful. He carefully took it up to José in the main bodega. He was sitting, resting after his exertion of getting to the barn.

"What do think? There are two more barrels apart from the one that I took this sample from."

José went through the rituals of an experienced wine taster, which is what, in fact, he was. Hugo was surprised by this new view of his uncle. It was even more of a surprise to

Sarah when she was told. The wine was declared superior, which could demand a premium price. It showed that the methods Clara had used were worth understanding and introducing them not just to the vineyards and winemaking, but to the farm as a whole.

In spite of Sarah's intentions to develop the rest of the farm, beyond the vineyards and giving a nod to the fig trees, she had made no progress at all.

As an afterthought, thinking of Max's reaction to Sarah's refusal to sell the farm a week ago, Hugo went back and securely locked the cellar door.

Sarah called a farm meeting with Carmen, José and Hugo to discuss the implications of the day's surprising discovery; what to do with the barrels and to discuss the biodynamic method that Clara had used and the future of the farm generally.

The recent development of the relationship between Sarah and Hugo – even though they were tip-toeing around it – created more confidence in the future of the farm and their combined determination to realise its potential.

Suddenly they heard a clatter of hasty camel hooves in the yard and the throaty growling of an angry camel.

"Goodness! What on earth is going on? I hope it is not that awful man that abused Sweetpea so cruelly who has come back to try to take her again!"

She and Hugo ran out of the house. Shouts and growls were coming from the winery.

What a sight met their eyes when they got there! Max was backed up against one of the tanks with a large heavy wrench in his hand, with which he was trying to fend off the two camels, only making them worse.

The camels looked very threatening and Max looked terrified; so terrified that a tell-tale wet patch was spreading down the front of his trousers. Hugo grabbed his phone and took a photo of the man where he stood, brandishing the wrench, the like of which did not belong to the farm. "*Ahda!* Sweetpea, *tahda!* Daisy! *Tahdia, tahdia.* Calm down; quiet!" Sarah called to them. They stopped roaring but didn't move and stayed very close to the interloper, with teeth bared.

Hugo phoned the police and quickly explained the situation. He photographed the scene and sent that as well. Max clearly understood what was going on and in spite of the closeness of the camels, decided to make a break for it.

Sarah gasped, anxious that he shouldn't get away. Hugo ran towards him, hoping to cut off his escape, pin him to the floor and keep him there until the police arrived. However, Carmen and José, hearing all the noise arrived to see what was going on, José in his wheelchair for speed. They were at the door. Max was prepared to push the older man to the floor, recently broken bone notwithstanding, to get past until he saw that he was holding his shot gun, now raised and pointing it directly at the desperate man. More quickly than any of them, Daisy dodged under Sweetpea's neck and reaching out with her long neck, knocked Max to the floor. He shouted in alarm and pain, waving the wrench in the camel's direction. Daisy was joined by Sweetpea and they both towered over the fallen man, hemming him in like two enormous sheepdogs.

"He must have broken the lock to get in," said Hugo. "I'm sure I locked it up before the meeting."

This was the scene the Police saw as they ran to the winery from their parked car. They had arrived very quickly. They suppressed their smiles.

"Ah! Mr. Lopez. In someone else's winery waving a wrench! Senorita," He turned to Sarah, "I believe you are the owner of the *finca*. Did you invite Mr Lopez here?

"Definitely not," said Sarah.

"I hear you make very good wine here."

"The wine we are drinking now was made by my great aunt, Signora Phillips. We have just finished our first harvest since my arrival at the beginning of the year. I inherited it from her."

Max began spluttering and shouting, "It is not anywhere near the quality of wine I produce. This bastard granddaughter has never made wine. How dare she come here with her fancy ideas; Thanksgiving suppers for the pickers and camels!" -Sweetpea moved just a bit closer as Max spat out the word, growling – "Thinking she can move in on my market."

"Has this been your intention, Senorita?" asked the Guardia.

"No. I just want the farm to be revived and made productive, in honour of my great aunt whom I never knew, to support myself and the people who work with me, so I can stay here."

Max spluttered impotent protestations.

"Please call off the camels, Senorita. Mr. Lopez, you are under arrest for breaking and entry, I noticed the damaged lock before I came in, and with trespassing with intent. You have been implicated in other incidents of vandalism in

213

nearby vineyards. This is the first time we have caught you in the act. Anything you say will be taken down and used against you."

"No, no! You have it all wrong. I came here to help. She is a novice and knows nothing. I came to check the valves on the tanks," he said desperately, waving the wrench as evidence of his altruistic intentions.

José was familiar with Max Lopez and his aggressive methods of dealing with potential competitors – burn them out or destroy their wine. He had heard of neighbours going to their cellars to discover barrels broken and a year's vintage on the floor or their vines mysteriously dying. José spoke for the first time.

"We have not invited anyone to help with the fermenting of the wine, only to help with the picking. I was admitted to hospital when I broke my leg, just before we were due to start. I have many years' experience with the wine, working for Signora Clara since a boy. I would definitely not ask this man for his assistance. Oh! And the wrench does not belong here."

By this time, Max was restrained and in handcuffs. At the mention of the accident, Hugo had a thought and went to examine the ladder that José had fallen from. With all the other activities, it was still lying on the floor where he had left it. He gestured for one of the Guardia to follow him. Max saw where they were heading and increased his struggles to free himself.

"No, no! It was an accident. An old man climbing a ladder, what would you expect? It is an old ladder, wood, of course the rungs are going to weaken over time."

They all looked at him puzzled. No-one had mentioned wooden ladders or how José had broken his leg. The policeman looked at Max, then bent over to have a closer look at the ladder and rungs lying on the floor, asking Hugo not to touch anything. At these close quarters he could see that the rungs hadn't snapped but had been partly sawn through; not enough to be visible but enough to break if it was trodden on. There was a small pruning saw almost hidden under the tank. The ladder had knocked it out of its hiding place.

"Does this belong to the *finca*, Signor?

Hugo looked closely. "No, we don't use that type of saw here."

Turning to the prisoner, the policeman said, "You seem to know a lot about the accident, Mr Lopez?"

Max realised what he had blurted out. "Common knowledge," he stuttered. "Gossip and all that," he laughed weakly.

"Signor Hugo, please do not disturb these things; touch nothing. I will send a forensic officer to investigate this matter further."

In a quieter voice he added, just for Hugo to hear, "Please check you tanks and cellars carefully. There are too many rumours about this man and his underhand activities. Call us immediately should you discover something suspicious."

"Mr Lopez," he said more loudly, turning to the spluttering, struggling prisoner. "Please come quietly with us." He nodded to Sarah and the others. "Thank you for your quick actions. We will contact you later."

He glanced towards the camels, now standing calmly

behind Sarah and Hugo and shook his head.

"I have heard of guard dogs, but never seen guard camels before."

Seizing his moment, still not giving up or believing he had been caught in the act, Max yelled, "They are dangerous. I wasn't doing anything. They attacked me. I could have been killed. They should be destroyed."

Still protesting and throwing accusations all around, he was led away to the police car and taken away for questioning.

Chapter Twenty-Seven

As the dust from the departing car settled down over the yard and track, all four people let out a deep sigh then all began talking at once.

"I always knew he wasn't to be trusted."

"Why didn't we think to check the ladder before?"

"Good old Sweetpea and Daisy."

"Has he done any damage?"

Then Carmen noticed that Sarah had hardly moved, had said nothing and was standing pale and very upset.

"Sarah! What is the matter? Are you alright?

Sarah couldn't say anything for a moment. She wasn't sure if she would shout in outrage or burst into tears.

Carmen took an executive decision. "Hugo, would you take the camels back to the stables please and settle them down," indicating with a nod at Sarah's frozen and distressed state.

José, make your gun safe and go with Sarah to her kitchen and give her some brandy. I will fetch some cake then join you to make some coffee. I think we could all do with a break after all that. Sarah, you go with José and help him to your kitchen. I will join you there."

"Hmm? Oh yes, of course! Come on, José." Sarah tried to smile, but it was taut and nervous. Carmen noticed Hugo's concerned expression when he saw Sarah's condition. She nodded to herself and smiled. The deepening relationship between the two of them had not escaped her notice. She was pleased. She loved them both and wanted them to be happy and what a better partnership to carry the farm forward?

Carmen was thoughtful as she went about gathering up the cake and the necessary for coffee. She had heard the spiteful remark Max had spat at Sarah earlier. She had heard similar rumours, of course, but regarded them as just rumours. She was new to the farm in those days, so hadn't been that close to Señora Clara. Her initial reaction to what Max had said was that he was just being vindictive. She was reluctant to believe the rumours might be true. But how could all that come about and Carmen not notice that Clara was pregnant? Why did Sarah refer to Clara as her great aunt and not her grandmother, which she would be if the rumours were true? She obviously knew nothing about Clara's past, so was not at all sure of the truth of the situation. Carmen sighed as she walked to the farmhouse carrying her restorative food. She knew she would have to tread carefully around the issue. Nobody really knew what had gone on 60 years ago.

Sarah managed the tricky business of negotiating the wheelchair through the kitchen door ('Thank goodness there are no steps') and helped him into a chair at the table.

He was still meant to be keeping all weight off his injured leg. 'At least I remembered about that,' thought Sarah.

"Carmen will be here with some cake and to make some coffee, Senorita. I would like some brandy in mine. Will you get the bottle out?"

"Yes, of course. I wouldn't mind some brandy now. I am rather shaky."

She busied herself getting glasses, pouring some brandy out for each of them and gratefully sat down. Her hand was trembling as she raised her glass to her lips and took a mouthful of the liquid. She sighed and revelled in the warming and steadying effect of the brandy. It was really very good.

Carmen bustled in then, pleased to see Sarah sitting down, with a bit more colour in her cheeks. Sarah's feelings were sorting themselves out after being hurt by such rudeness, and was now curious as to whether such accusations could be true. She was wondering how that could be determined, when Carmen bustled in closely followed by Hugo. He gathered up the coffee things and set to work. Carmen was about to protest when she saw how confidently he was getting things organised so left him to it and concentrated on getting brandy for herself and Hugo, topping up the glasses of the other two people and cutting big pieces of cake for everyone. An air of hesitancy and expectancy hung over the usually comforting kitchen.

Sarah took a big bite of her cake. She was really hungry she realised. The cake was delicious and her mouth filled with the flavours of warm vanilla, sweet fruits and spices. Carmen really was an excellent baker as well as a good cook.

She noticed the others were looking at her with concern and curiosity and took a deep breath.

"I was very shocked by the fact that someone, who was already successful, could be so jealous and vindictive as to seek to do something that could have killed my good friend José and then return to ruin our first vintage. I guess that had been his intention, to let out all the grape juice onto the floor or to add something to the tanks to spoil the fermentation? If the camels hadn't heard him, they are clever, and gone to the barn, he would have done that and more, wouldn't he?"

She shook her head in disbelief and took another sip of brandy.

"However, that was not what made me speechless. It was not knowing whether to scream in rage or cry at his parting remark about me being illegitimate. He had said as much before, when he left the thanksgiving supper, just as Hugo arrived and interrupted his demands to buy the farm. Do you remember Hugo; I think you heard it as you approached?"

Hugo nodded. The two older people waited, not sure what to say.

"I don't know what to do. Carmen and José, do you have any idea why he should say that?"

José shook his head, turning to Carmen, who had already been here a few years when he arrived on the farm.

Carmen had a sip of her brandy then tipped the remainder into her coffee.

"No, not really. Signora Clara was never pregnant while I have been here. As far as I know, she had been engaged to a young man who had come from Spain with his family to the Island for work. They were a couple for a while and they got engaged. They planned to get married when he returned from Spain. He went back there to fight for his country's freedom against Franco. Sadly, he never returned. He was killed on his way to battle; blown up by a mine. They collected what seemed to be recognisable as his belongings. I was shown them, but really, they could have been any poor souls. There were not many things. She was distraught, could hardly function. That was when she took on José to help look after the farm. She had been writing to her sister in England who sent her the fare to sail home to recover for a while. Signora reluctantly agreed, after asking us if we could manage for a few weeks. Of course, we agreed, though knew we could only keep things ticking over. She was so upset. I think she must have cried all the way across the Atlantic."

Sarah and Hugo nodded their understanding. They knew what a broken heart felt like – though not through such violent means.

Carmen continued, "The Signora must have had a complete breakdown, because it was almost a year before she returned, still pale, but somehow even more, how do you say, '*resuelta*,' determined to carry on here in spite of her loss."

José took up the tale in Spanish.

"She was um… '*incesante*,' never stopping. It was sometimes hard to work with her. She worked so hard and fast." He paused then spoke in more rapid Spanish to his nephew asking him to say in English what he was struggling to express.

221

Hugo took up the story, feeling confident about speaking in English now he had been asked to.

"After being away for so long there was quite a lot to do, but none of it so urgent as she made it. It was her way of dealing with her feelings I suppose. She never spoke about her time in England and it wasn't for us to ask. She did once say, "I am glad I was able to settle everything when I was with my sister in England," and that was all she ever said."

Carmen nodded in agreement.

The kitchen was silent for a while; each person lost in their own thoughts.

"Of course," continued Carmen, "there were lots of rumours flying about when she was away for so long. People love to make things up about mysterious circumstances, putting two and two together and making eight. There was talk of an illegitimate child, even 'aborto' – ('abortion,' Hugo translated quietly, although Sarah had guessed) both as great a sin as there could be. A few people enjoyed such gossip. I expect it was revived when you arrived and that was what Max heard and used it to be even nastier."

"That is what I thought," said Hugo.

"Yes, but there is still a mystery there without a doubt," said Sarah. "Hmm! Maybe my solicitor might know what went on. He has been working with the family all my life and before. He is very 'old-school' and correctly professional, even slightly Edwardian in his attitude, so would not have disclosed any family secrets unasked. However, as I am here and a grown woman, and I obviously need to know what went on, he may be able to shed some light on the year my great aunt was in England. Whatever happened with my aunt at that time, I would totally understand without any judgement at all." The others nodded their agreement to this attitude. "I will write to him tomorrow."

Chapter Twenty-Eight

They all stood, the meeting over.

"It is dark already," said Sarah. "Thank you for your concern and support after the incident in the winery. It was all such a shock, especially the vindictive nature of that man's comments. Thank you for the cake and the drinks; you are all so kind." A wave of emotion swept through her. She busied herself gathering mugs, plates and glasses to hide the tears in her eyes.

Pretending not to notice, Carmen and José went home, José managing the door in his wheelchair very easily Sarah noticed. She suspected a ruse on Carmen's part earlier, telling her to take him and the wheelchair to the kitchen in order to distract her out of her funk. Hugo said he would go and settle the camels for the night, kissing Sarah lightly on the forehead. He was shy of being overtly demonstrative in company. With the dishes sorted quickly, Sarah went to join him in the stable. The camels needed some fussing for their role in the arrest of Max.

Sweetpea and Daisy were lying clean, comfortable and

relaxed in their stall, after Hugo had settled them in after all the excitement. The space was cool and airy, designed to catch any breeze blowing in from the sea, but it could be made warm if it should get too windy and chill. Clara had done a good job, for it was she who had designed the building. There seemed to be more to this biodynamic business than rushing to get the grapes picked in three days. All these thoughts passed quickly through her mind until everything came to rest, here, with the two camels and with Hugo.

Hugo turned to go. "It is getting late. There will be a lot to check over in the morning and I expect the forensic people will be here too."

Sarah put a finger over his lips. "Don't go yet Hugo. Stay a bit longer." It felt so good to be close to him; she couldn't bear the thought of him leaving her on her own. She was holding his hand already. Hugo didn't want to leave either so hand in hand they walked back to the house, smiling and glancing at each other now and again as if checking the other was still there.

The kitchen door shut. The light went out. A softer light went on in one of the upstairs windows… eventually, that went out as well.

The next morning Hugo was awake first, showered and dressed and sitting on the edge of the bed, afraid to wake her, unsure of what her initial reaction would be. Would her face betray a feeling of regret or be void of any emotion at all? The whole night had felt so natural, so passionate and connected. He had never experienced anything like that in all the time he was with his fiancée. Sarah opened her eyes and smiled. It felt the most natural thing in the world to see Hugo sitting there. She pulled him towards her for a morning kiss. He smelled of lavender shower gel and toothpaste, it was the most wonderful combination; sensuous, comforting, desirable. It was sometime later when Hugo eventually set off to town to get fresh bread, milk and cream. Sarah got up showered and dressed. She had not experienced love-making like that before. It was how she had thought it should be – passionate, sensitive, tender, truly connected, truly wonderful. She could hardly wait for his return so she could experience it all over again. The feeling surprised her. She couldn't remember feeling like this with David, not even when they were first together at Uni. She smiled with the realisation that that was 'lust at first sight'; this was love that had grown out of friendship and respect. So different.

For Sarah it was the best breakfast ever. She was ravenous. Hugo had gathered croissants, pain au chocolat, a short crusty loaf, soft mild goat's cheese and Strawberry jam – St. Dalfour's, her favourite brand. It was all delicious and coffee with cream topped it all off.

They were finishing the last of the coffee when Carmen knocked and came in. She took in the shared breakfast, the glow that surrounded them. They both began to explain.

Carmen raised her hand to stop their stuttering. "Well, it is about time. You two have been pussyfooting around each other for long enough. Welcome home, Hugo."

She gave them both a bear hug, delight all over her face.

It had distressed her to see both her favourite people, after her own family, so sad and isolated.

She was just reaching for glasses and brandy when Sarah heard the camels making a lot of noise at the door of the stable and a car pulling up at the front of the house.

"We'll celebrate later," Carmen said, waving them out to start a new day and hopefully a new life.

"It is quite late now. I expect that will be the forensic people just arrived. They said it would be about now. I'll go and sort out Sweetpea and Daisy, if would you go and help them, Hugo, show them where to go," said Sarah.

She set off for the stable and busied herself making a fuss of her two favourite animals, grooming them, cleaning out the stable and putting in fresh water and food. She was heading out of the doors with a wheelbarrow of old bedding to take to the compost heap. She could see the visiting car clearly. It wasn't a Guardia car; it was a red, open top sporty looking number! Posing against it talking to Hugo was an elegant woman.

Sarah looked at Hugo. From his expression she knew who this glamorous woman was - his ex-fiancée, Lucia, the one who had walked out on him a week before their wedding day. Sarah was acutely aware of her own appearance – T-shirt, old jeans, working boots and probably bits of camel hair and hay sticking to her as usual.

"… farmer's boy" then "… camel-herding boss," floated up to her. The tone was so disparaging and mocking. Her heart and confidence sank to the floor. The glow of breakfast shrivelled up and was gone, leaving a deep ache and anxiety in her heart. She shrank back into the shadows of the stable, hoping the visitor would not stay long.

That hope went the way of her heart when this beautiful woman in fashionable clothes, long painted nails, carefully styled hair walked around the car towards Hugo, arms held out in inviting and seductive gesture. Sarah knew Hugo had hardly recovered from the hurt and anger he felt after he was abandoned almost at the altar just over two years ago. She wondered how she would react if her ex-husband turned up unexpectedly, looking gorgeous. Would she be bowled over and hopeful of rekindling the passion she had once felt for him? Her life was so different now; she was really happy here on the farm with all its problems. Would he join her here? Would she go back to London with him? She knew immediately that she would not/could not do that. Her life was here. But would it be the same if Hugo left or worse, stayed but married to that woman? What did last night mean to him? Was it just a rebound reaction after the tension of the day for him? Relief after all the drama for her? Was there any depth to their relationship?

She decided to garner what confidence she could and walk down to say hello, thinking it would be better to confront the situation than hide away as she was. She was halfway there when another car pulled up behind the sports car. This time it was the Guardia. With his hand at her elbow, Hugo almost pushed Lucia back to her car, ignoring the angry words and body language. Her plan had obviously turned out rather differently than she had anticipated. He opened the door for her to get in, indicating that he needed to speak to the new visitors. Before she got in, she gave him a proprietorial kiss on the lips, tossed her head in the direction of Sarah, who now stood halfway between the stable and the car and drove off with a roar, spraying gravel and dust everywhere.

Hugo stood for a moment with his hand to his mouth. Sarah had no idea what was going on in his head or his heart. Then he shook his head, squared his shoulders and walked to meet the policeman and a woman who was dressed in a protective all-over suit, overshoes and gloves.

Sarah took a deep, steadying breath and went out to meet the three of them as they walked past the stable to the Bodega.

Hugo introduced her as '*Signora* Jones,' the owner of the farm. He didn't smile, his face carefully expressionless.

"*Buenos dias*," said the policeman, shaking her hand. The woman smiled in greeting, indicating her gloved hands and shaking her head.

"*Gracias. Y a usted,* (and to you)," replied Sarah. "This is the Vineyard manager, Hugo. He will show where José fell. Thank you, Hugo." So formal, so cold. "*Disculpe.* (excuse me)."

She turned quickly and went back to the stable to finish her work there. She was shaking. After emptying the wheelbarrow onto the compost heap, which was steaming gently she noticed, she went quickly to the kitchen. She needed a moment to gather herself and she remembered she still needed to clear away the breakfast things.

However, her moment was not to be. Carmen was still there finishing the clearing up.

"Oh, thank you, Carmen. That was very kind; there was no need…"

Her good friend looked up then, taking in Sarah's pale and tense face.

"Would you like some coffee?" Sarah nodded, afraid that if she said anything more, she would cry.

After presenting her with a mug of steaming, frothy coffee, Carmen patted Sarah's shoulder and left to go back to her own home, planning to return later to make sure Sarah was alright.

Sarah took a sip of coffee but could hardly swallow. The woman in the red car looked so glamorous, so immaculate, so seductive. How much did Hugo still miss his almost-wife? How acute was the hurt and anger, even though it was over two years since she had left to return to Spain? Sarah couldn't imagine what he might be thinking now or feeling. She wondered if he was feeling as confused and as conflicted as herself.

Would he welcome her back, forgive her and be willing to try again? Would he always be afraid that she would run back to Madrid again? It seemed to have given her what she wanted – the more fashionable and affluent way of life she obviously enjoyed. Sarah found it hard to imagine she would want to be a farm manager's wife. Sarah couldn't imagine that he would leave the farm to go to Madrid with her. The thought sliced through her heart like a frozen ice blade. The pain, the shock of thinking he could leave after the wonderful night they had had together, after he had said he didn't want to leave the farm. It all got too much. Sarah broke down in sobs; huge, gulping, breath-robbing sobs. They could not be contained.

After what seemed an age, but was probably only a few

minutes, the racking sobs subsided. She took a deep breath, blew her nose, wiped her face dry. The coffee tasted better now. She sat cradling the mug between her hands, arms resting on the table, staring out at the yard and the vineyard beyond, her mind refusing to think anything.

Hugo was in much the same shocked state. There seemed to be two of him in the winery; one was answering the forensic officer as precisely as he could, though there was not so much he could say. The saw, ladder and wrench would reveal the most reliable answers, once they revealed the fingerprints on them. Max had more or less confessed his role in José's fall by talking about the ladder when no-one had mentioned the accident or how it had happened.

The other part of him was in turmoil. Why had Lucia come back? To show him how good life was in Spain? To rekindle their relationship? Her attitude had been part intimate, part mocking, disdainful even. He had been so sure he loved Sarah; so sure, that he wanted to stay at the farm, but as soon as he saw Lucia, his treacherous heart had leapt. She had come back! Perhaps she wanted to marry him after all? Even as he thought it, he recoiled from the idea. He wouldn't be able to trust her; he'd be always be trying to please her, making her want to stay. He would be held ransom by her. Always giving her what she wanted, but it never being enough. He would always feel he was lacking in something she wanted. That could never work. He remembered Sarah's pale and stricken face as she walked out of the stable. He could see she was trying to compose herself. He wanted to run to her, to reassure her, but the Police arrived. He needed that wretched woman to go. She was very frustrated he could tell, but it couldn't be helped. She vented her anger with the parting shot referring to Sarah as his 'camel-herding bastard boss.' Why had she come to the farm now? Just to torment him, belittle him; show him what he had not been able to provide for her when they were together – the fast car, the expensive clothes, the high maintenance life style? He was so angry. Regardless of the initial lurch of his heart, he knew he could never go back to her. He was tense with locked up emotion. He had to contain it to deal with the police investigation. He had been able to do nothing more than introduce Sarah in a tight formal voice that sounded harsh even to his own ears. He saw the questioning, bewilderment in her eyes but had no chance to reassure her.

A shadow fell across the doorway. Hugo turned hoping it was Sarah, but it wasn't. It was Daisy! It was as if she had sensed his confusion and anguish. She approached slowly making her low grumbly noises and laid her head on his shoulder. In spite of himself, he gave a big sigh and leaned back against her soft shoulder, putting his arm under and around her neck. All the tension and confusion just drained out of him. He felt completely empty.

"Signor Hugo! Signor!" The sharp tones of the scientist brought him back to the work in hand.

"Oh, yes. *Desculpe*. It has been a difficult time I hadn't realised how tired I was. What was it you wanted to know?"

The woman smiled. She had realised they had arrived at a difficult time. The woman in the red car had some connection to this man leaning for support on his camel, but not much respect for him and certainly none for the owner of the farm, Signora Jones.

Luckily her work in the winery was complete. Max had obviously not expected to be discovered as his fingerprints were everywhere, on the tools, on the tank where he has steadied himself when sawing part through the rungs of the ladder or decided which valve to open in order to let all the grape juice flow away.

'At least now, the vintners in the area can at last relax knowing that their vines and cellars are no longer under threat of sabotage. It is not often I have such a satisfactory ending in my forensic work,' the officer thought.

Some of them had suffered from his jealous actions and lost a whole year's vintage. Many suspected him, but without proof or catching him red-handed, there had been nothing they could do.

"Thank you, Signor. You have been very helpful. I can see that the whole episode has been very difficult for you." She smiled," So this is one of the famous camels of *finca Los Palmas*? The tales get more embellished with the telling. They are even saying that one of them lay down by the injured man to keep him warm and still!"

"There is no embellishment, Ma'am. This is the camel, Daisy. That is exactly what she did. Yesterday it was her mother, Sweetpea, who heard Max was here and alerted us by the noise she was making. She kept the intruder in here until the police came."

The woman turned to her colleague, "You were here yesterday. Is that what happened?"

The man laughed. "Yes. This one even dashed out knocking Max to the floor as he tried to make a break for it. It was quite a sight. It never looked as if they intended him any damage, just to keep him here. Very clever!"

"Thank you. You have been most co-operative and helpful. I know it has been a difficult day, but would you follow us to the station now. We will need you to sign a few papers to tidy things up. Please give my regards to Signora Jones.

With that she picked up her case and together with her colleague returned to their car, laughing as they went.

Chapter Twenty-Nine

Hugo felt exhausted. He was overwhelmed with extremes of emotion; anger at Lucia for arriving as she did in a flashy red sports car, surely not hers, and with such a haughty disdain laced with mockery for him and dismissal of Sarah as if she were a backward, uneducated peasant. He was in agony as the image of Sarah's bewildered face filled his mind. He knew he should go to see her, to reassure her of his true reaction to his ex-fiancée's visit, but he couldn't trust himself to contain his anger and he didn't want to be angry in her presence. If he did, would he rage against the woman who had just sailed into his day, flaunting her expensive car and designer clothes. The woman who had left him only a few years ago, just before their wedding day. It was if she was telling him – 'Ha! See! I wouldn't be enjoying this luxury if I had stayed here with you."

Hugo's self-confidence was shaky at the best of times but the undoubted truth of that unspoken assertion shattered it to bits about his feet. He needed to secure the bodega door; he needed to see Sarah; he needed to go home to change his clothes; most importantly he had to go to the police station to sign some papers, hopefully to tie the whole incident up. Still in an agony of indecision, he knew really that he should go with the last instruction and go to the police station. It had to be done and once completed he knew he could relax then as the matter would be completely in the hands of the police. Hopefully by the time he returned in fresh clothes he would feel more himself. Looking neither right nor left he marched to his car, avoiding looking towards Sarah and set off to Arrecife. En route he pulled over and sent her a quick text explaining where he was going and why, then having changed, he would be back at the farm to be with her.

Sarah was still sitting, immobile, at the kitchen table, clutching her now cold mug of coffee. There was no doubt who that woman was or the attitude with which she had looked sneeringly over at her as she walked towards the red car. The joy in her new relationship with Hugo that she had felt when they had breakfast together had withered to dust with that triumphant look. She had no idea how Hugo felt. All she could see now, looking out of the window, was a man who bore no resemblance to the loving, laughing man she had gazed at over the table only an hour ago. This man was rigid, pale and trembling a little. What emotion was he holding in with such a stance? Anger? If so, anger at whom? The woman in the red car or Sarah? Had he thought she had just been using him; a little light relief after some anxious few weeks? No surely not! Surely, the time she had been at the farm had been long enough for him to realise that she was not that sort of person? Had the feelings he had had for his ex-fiancée returned? She did look very glamorous; 'Unlike me,' thought Sarah. She had never given any thought about how she might appear to other people when she was working. She couldn't do what she did everyday wearing a tight skirt and stilettos. The thought of herself tottering around the stable sorting out the camels dressed like that brought a faint smile to her lips.

She saw Hugo look as if he were coming to see her to explain what had been going on and she began to get up from her chair, but he just got into his car and drove away. The knife in her heart turned a few more times and she groaned with the physical sensation of the despair she was feeling at that moment. She was not used to this degree of emotion; it had not been this bad when her husband had said he was leaving her. She was now convinced Hugo had left to follow the woman. Then a flame of anger burst through the tears. How dare that woman swan in here throwing their new feelings for each other up in the air? How could Hugo just drive off like that? How sincere had he been last night? Was he just using her? Even as she thought it, she knew that couldn't be true. Hugo didn't have an insincere bone in his body. Actually, she had no idea where he had gone or why; all her anxious thoughts were just conjecture.

Lifted by the anger and her previous common-sense thought, she got up, had a drink of water while more coffee was brewing. When it was ready, she took her hot drink out to the stable to finish her work with the camels.

Sarah couldn't settle to anything. She was back in the kitchen having sorted out Sweetpea and Daisy, but was pacing about the room, picking things up and putting them back again where they were, her mind in too much turmoil to decide on any action. Suddenly she knew she had to get out. She phoned Inés, on the off-chance it was her day off and she could meet her. Even if she were working, maybe there would be time for a coffee.

Inés was pleased to hear from her. Yes, she was working but she had just had some good news and wanted to share it with her friend.

By the time Sarah got to the coffee shop, she was feeling a bit more settled. She had had a shower, put on her red dress, some make up and her favourite perfume. She was ready to go out. Both women were delighted to see each other. They hadn't met since the "Thank you" celebrations, which seemed ages ago now.

She could tell Inés was bubbling with excitement and was bursting to share her news. Once the coffee and cakes had been ordered, Sarah invited her to tell her what it was that was making her so excited. She was expecting Inés to say she had found, finally, the love of her life. She was not prepared for the news that followed.

"Oh, Sarah! It is wonderful news. It all started really when I came over to help with the preparations and cooking for your pickers and then for the Harvest Supper. I hadn't enjoyed myself so much for ages. I thought about it afterwards and realised that, although I enjoyed the work I was doing at the hotel, what I really wanted to do was to go into catering. I approached my manager and asked if the Hotel would sponsor me to do a six-month cookery course. After a few moments thought he said yes and that they would be able to send me to the school in Barcelona. There is a very famous school there. It has such a brilliant reputation. Many famous chefs have been trained there. However, I would have to agree to continue working at the Hotel afterwards full time for six months on my return and half-time for another year. I contacted the school immediately. They are usually fully booked for at least a year in advance so I wasn't expecting anything to happen straight away."

"Gracious!" said Sarah, "I had no idea you had such plans, though I did think you had created some delicious dishes for the days of harvesting and for the supper. You looked so at home and even gently organised everyone in the kitchen without them really noticing. It all ran so smoothly. What is happening now, do you know?"

"This is why I am so excited. If you hadn't phoned me, I would be calling you, even driving over to the farm to tell you the news. As I said, they are usually booked up a year in advance, but when I phoned, the Maître d' explained that just 5 minutes earlier she had had a call from a student who was booked to go on the next course. She had to cancel her booking at the last minute. Her mother had become very ill and she needed to be with her as she was not expected to live for much longer. As it was so last minute, she lost her deposit."

Inés paused for a few sips of coffee and a nibble of her cake, to gather her thoughts and calm her excitement. Sarah thought she was trying not to cry with the heightened emotion that swirled around her. After a deep breath, she continued.

"That lost deposit equals half the total fee for the

twelve-month course. If my sponsor would cover the other 50%, I could do a full year! I discussed it with the Hotel immediately. They said yes, as it would carry considerable prestige for the company. However, I would have to return to a year's full time work there and part time for six months. All this happened this morning. I am so excited." A few tears escaped in spite of her efforts at control.

"Wow! That's wonderful. When does the course start?" Sarah asked, expecting the answer to be in six months' time.

"Oh Sarah, this is why I am so excited and a little overwhelmed. It starts in two weeks' time. I will be leaving for Barcelona next Friday in order to find somewhere to live and find my way around before term starts. I have so much to do. This may be the last time we can meet up before I go, though I will phone you from Spain obviously."

"So soon! No wonder you were bursting to tell me. How wonderful for you."

Before Sarah could say any more, Inés looked at her watch.

"Mama mia! Look at the time! Sorry it is a flying visit; I have to get back to work. I want to keep in the good books now for sure."

With a quick kiss on each cheek, she was gone.

Sarah hardly knew how she got back to the car and began the journey home. Her sense of loss in 'losing' Hugo, as she thought, was now compounded 100% by knowing Inés would be in Barcelona for a year. She would miss her dreadfully. Working on the farm had occupied so much of her time and attention she had made little time available to get out to meet other people and make some more friends.

Carmen and José were the only other people she knew to speak to, apart from Hugo. Sarah was delighted for her friend; it was such a brilliant opportunity. She had heard of the school, the Culinary Institute of Barcelona. It was indeed highly sought after for the wide range of skills one learned there. With that at the top of her CV, Inés would be offered whatever position she applied for.

For herself, she felt desolate and already lonelier than she had felt for many years. She had to pull the car over after a few miles; she could hardly see where she was going for the tears.

In the quiet of the car, she sobbed her heart dry, leaning her head on her arms on the steering wheel. In the exhausted calm that followed, Sarah drew a deep breath and was about to sit up and continue her journey home, when there was an urgent knock on her side window and an anxious voice calling, "Sarah! Are you alright? What is the matter?"

Sarah groaned knowing that she was required to speak to whomever it was calling, sat up and peered blearily at the person outside. She had half expected it to be the Guardia.

Chapter Thirty

"Hugo! Hugo!" Hugo opened the door and Sarah tumbled out into his arms.

"Oh Sarah," murmured Hugo into her beautiful black hair. He wrapped his arms around her as she sank gratefully against his broad chest.

"Whatever has happened? Why are you out here? I have been calling and calling your phone, sending texts, getting more and more worried that you didn't want to speak to me or that something awful had happened to you."

He leaned back to look keenly at this wonderful woman's face and very quickly held her closer than ever. Sarah's sobs of relief calmed a little.

"Oh Hugo! I am so glad to see you. My phone had gone dead, so I left it at home to recharge."

Hugo sighed with relief. "Thank goodness that was why you didn't reply. Come. I want to get you home to *Los Palmas*. You don't look in a fit state to drive. I'll pull the car over to the side a bit more and lock everything up. I'll drive you back, then Carmen can bring me back to collect your car. It will be safe till then. I can tell you what has been going on, en route."

Sarah contented herself with leaning back in the car, so glad to have the lift home; very delighted to be talking to Hugo when she thought she may never have the chance again. However, she did delay his account of events by asking, "How come you were out here on the Arrecife road in time to find me?"

"Serendipity, I think. Let me start at the beginning. I was so angry with Lucia for coming back to the farm just to insult us. She was awful. I was not attracted to her again at all. That must be what she is really like. A lucky escape for me I think, even if it was painful for a long time afterwards. Then the forensic people arrived which helped move her on. They were very thorough, then as they were leaving, they asked me to follow them to the station to sign some papers in order to get things sorted as soon as possible. I was exhausted and confused; torn in all sorts of directions – go with them, see you, go home for a change of clothes... In the end, I decided to go to Arrecife. At least the journey gave me a chance to calm myself down. I wasn't there long and that is how I came to be travelling on that road, and to find you collapsed over the steering wheel, half, if not completely dead. You have no idea how relieved I was when you sat up, looking very sad, but alive." He pulled up outside the house at the *finca*. He turned to look at her with such a warm and tender smile. They leaned towards each other and exchanged a long and passionate kiss.

"I didn't come out to see you when you were standing so rigidly in the yard, after the police left. I thought you were angry with me, thinking I had taken advantage of you last night. I was frozen with foolish doubts and indecision. Any confidence I had just left. When you didn't come in but drove off suddenly, I thought you were racing off after that woman. I couldn't settle here so I arranged to meet Inés in town. Her news, plus the thought that you had left for good was too much. Hence folding up half dead on the steering wheel."

"And I still haven't got back to my flat for a change of clothes," laughed Hugo.

Reluctantly, they left the intimate space of the car and went indoors.

Sometime later, they were enjoying coffee, fortified with a slug of brandy at the kitchen table. Sarah sighed, "I'm so glad you found me at the side of the road. Now I understand how you felt and why you left so suddenly. It has been a turbulent morning for all of us for sure."

"Now I know why you weren't answering my calls or texts. So obvious when you know, isn't it? But so difficult to think that clearly when you are all upset, in a muddle," replied Hugo.

He was just about to kiss Sarah again, when there was a knock on the door and Carmen and José walked in.

"Thank goodness you are both home and well. I was getting concerned," said Carmen, ignoring the glow surrounding them both. 'Very well if I'm not mistaken,' she thought to herself.

Hugo got up to greet them both. "I was just coming over

to ask a favour of you, Carmen, I would ask you, José, but I know you have not been cleared to drive just yet." José shrugged to show it was all out of his control.

Carmen was so eager to share her news she plunged straight in without waiting to hear what the favour was.

"We have come over with news from Inés," said Carmen. "In 10 days, she is leaving for Barcelona to study cooking. Why she has to go there I don't know. I could teach her all she needs to know right here." Her enacted indignation softened into delighted smiles.

"Of course, I couldn't. She will learn so much more about everything over there. I have heard of the school. It is very famous and very expensive. It is so marvellous that the hotel is paying for her to go. I would like to have gone when I was younger, but had no one to sponsor me. I have taught myself a lot from books though," she said proudly.

She paused, looking wistful, "I will miss her dreadfully. However, she will be renting out her flat in Arrecife for the year so will be staying with us during her holidays." She smiled in anticipation.

"That's wonderful news, Carmen," said Sarah.

"Yes. Inés said she had met you briefly in town for coffee. Did she tell you about it?"

"She said she had exciting news and that she would be leaving for Spain soon, but had to return to work quite quickly so there wasn't too much time for details," said Sarah, glossing over the full conversation to allow her dear friend the full glory of bringing such good news.

"What was the favour you wanted to ask, Hugo," José, speaking in his preferred Spanish, cut in, in case Carmen set off on even more details.

"¡Ah *sí*!" replied Hugo. "I was returning from the main Guardia station in Arrecife - they wanted me there soon after their visit here this morning in order to sign some papers – when I came across Sarah, half," he hesitated a brief moment to think what to say, "asleep on the steering wheel. She looked too exhausted to drive any further, so I said I would bring her home and ask Carmen if she would drive me back to collect the car. If you would drive Sarah's car back here, I can drive back to my flat. There are a few things I need to do there today."

"Well, come back here afterwards, Hugo," said Carmen. "Come to our house for supper. Sarah, will you join us? We can celebrate Inés good news and also having that awful man, Max, locked away at last. At least now we can relax a bit, knowing this year's vintage will be safe from his jealous actions."

"Yes, he certainly was a wolf in sheep's clothing. No wonder you were all so mystified by me inviting him to join us for the Harvest Supper. He seemed so friendly and he said his daughter would be here. All calculated lies of course." Sarah shivered with distaste. "Thank heavens for Sweetpea's sharp hearing."

With that, Carmen and Hugo left to collect Sarah's car, before leaving she rang her daughter to invite her for supper as well. She knew her daughter would help with any preparations she hadn't been able to do. Though secretly, she knew she would get it all done in time. Sarah, hoping they would have some of Carmen's amazing paella, left to check on the two camels.

In the quiet of the stable as she fed and watered them and while she was giving each of them their brush down at the end of the day, her mind wandered back to the day she went for the extra wine for her Thanksgiving Supper. She remembered how friendly and chatty the two women, who worked there, had been and how smoothly they managed the surge of tourists as they poured in by the bus load to hastily taste and buy lots of bottles.

A new thought struck her. 'Oh my!' she said to herself, 'Now Max is in prison and will be for some time, apparently, he had confessed to many other times when he had sabotaged vineyards around the area if he thought they would be better than him – I wonder what will happen to the Bodega. I'll go over in a day or two to meet them again and to ask what is happening there. They looked as if they could manage the selling part if the supply of wine was still there.'

Feeling pleased at the prospect of meeting the two women soon and maybe developing a friendship with them, Sarah went to check on her Bodega doors, say a last goodnight to the camels and went indoors to get ready to go to Carmen's for supper with them – and with Hugo. "How fantastic is that?" she asked Sweetpea, who replied with a low rumbling purr. Sarah was going to wear a dress she hadn't worn since the London days – how far back did they seem now? However, here on the farm, it seemed fussy and out of place. She no longer felt at all like the woman who had worn it not that long ago really. Instead, she chose some black velvet leggings, flat sandals decorated with beads and an ivory tunic. It was simple in style in a soft cotton overlaid with lace. The pale colour sat well on her tanned skin. With a touch of make-up and lipstick she felt ready to celebrate Inés' good news. Now Hugo was back and all the confusion cleared up, Sarah knew she would be able to manage life without her friend for a while. She very much hoped that Inés would return to the island after her time in the "big city."

Sarah had got used to seeing Hugo in his working clothes, generally jeans or shorts and a T-shirt, so it was a surprise when he arrived wearing smart stone-coloured chinos and a white short-sleeved shirt.

They met by the door of Carmen's house. He beamed, "You look beautiful Sarah."

"You scrub up pretty well yourself," grinned Sarah. "You look wonderfully handsome when you dress up," she explained, seeing Hugo's puzzled expression at the very English phrase.

"¡Sarah! Hugo! *Hola!* Wait a moment!" It was Inés who had just parked up in the yard. "Wait a moment and we can go in together."

Carmen and José were so pleased to have their three favourite people coming to supper at their house. Meals they may have had together in the past seemed to have been impromptu affairs at the farmhouse. Carmen was nervous and excited in equal measure for them to be all meeting at her house.

Much to Sarah's delight, Carmen had made paella, full of spicy sausages, prawns, scallops, garlic, peppers, saffron, chicken. It was loaded with so many tasty things. There were lots of salads and tapas dishes to go with it. Then there was a chocolate and rum mousse, with churros and thick creamy hot chocolate.

"Oh Carmen! That was absolutely delicious," said everyone at once.

"Yes, Mama you are such a wonderful cook, but when I get back, I will teach you all of the things I learn in Barcelona – if you would like me to, of course!"

Conversation moved on through what details Inés knew about the course. It sounded very demanding.

"Eventually I would like to open a small café on Haria. It is an idea I have held in my mind since helping out here. I really enjoyed it. I loved to see the delighted faces of the people when they had eaten what I had prepared."

A sudden thought came to Sarah.

"To get established and build yourself a reputation with low output and expenses, would you like to have a restaurant here on the farm? It is a spur of the moment thought. Might there be a suitable building here?" She put the question to the other three around the table. She suddenly felt a shiver run down her back and an image of what she thought of as her great aunt appeared to her. She was smiling and nodding, both arms extended as if to embrace them all.

"What do you think Sarah? Sarah!" Carmen looked concerned. Sarah had gone silent and distant and had obviously not heard what was being said.

"Hmm? Oh sorry. I was distracted for a moment." The vision faded as Sarah's consciousness returned to the room. "Sorry, what were you saying Carmen?"

"José and I were just remembering that years ago, when she was younger, Signora Clara did just that. It was a long time ago now, but was very popular at the time. However, things got much busier on the farm, with all the things we had started to do here, so there was little time for cooking. Someone from the town came to take over, but numbers gradually dropped away and eventually she closed down here and opened a place in Haria. I don't know if it is still there."

"Whoa! Whoa!" said Inés, laughing. "Wait a moment. Let me get to Barcelona first. And see if I can complete the course. It will be very challenging. The courses there are advanced. Also, I will be working at the hotel for at least two years on my return, to repay them for sponsoring me.

"That is true," said her mother, "but I am sure you will do well."

"It will be exciting to be in Barcelona," said Sarah. "Life will be very different there. Perhaps you will fall in love with the bustle and opportunities of the big city and not want to come back."

Hugo shuddered, thinking of how his now "sophisticated" ex-fiancée and behaved on her visit earlier that day. "Oh, please come back, Inés. *Manten los pies en el suelo.* (Keep your feet on the ground)."

"Oh goodness, yes!" said Carmen, but as she said it, she knew that many islanders had been seduced by the big city life of Spain and had not come back.

"The first thing for me is to find somewhere to live. I only need a small place and I don't want to share with a stranger. I have been in my flat here on my own for too long now to do that. I had better start searching this week. Ooh! That makes it all seems very real."

The clock in the sideboard struck midnight. "Gracious!

It is late. The time has gone very quickly. I am on early shift in the morning. I must go."

"Me too," said Sarah, suddenly feeling very weary. It had been an eventful day.

They all helped clear up as far as they were able. Then Carmen sent them on their way. "I can do the rest in the morning. Thank you. Off you go, all of you." The party broke up with many exclamations and expressions of thanks to Carmen for the meal and congratulations to Inés for getting a place at the Culinary Institute.

Outside the kitchen, Sarah asked if Hugo would like to come in, in spite of feeling very weary.

"I would love to, *mi amor, mi querida,* (my love, my darling) but I can't work in these clothes, so I had better go home."

He bent to kiss Sarah goodnight, ending up going indoors anyway. It was sometime later when he drove home.

Chapter Thirty-One

The next morning Sarah had just showered, dressed, come down to the kitchen and was putting some coffee on when she heard a car pull upon the drive.

"I wonder who that is? It is still early. Oh! it's Hugo!"

She unlocked the door just as he arrived.

"I've brought breakfast," he said, putting a baguette, two pain au chocolat and a couple of danish pastries on the table.

"Oh wow! This is very European. Where did you find these on the island? They look delicious!"

"Not as delicious as you," replied Hugo, leaning close to kiss her. The kiss got very passionate. Sarah stepped back, laughing and breathless, locked the door, turned off the coffee machine, took Hugo by the hand and led him upstairs.

Making love with Hugo was like no other experience she had had – not even in the early days with David, when hormones and lust were the driving force. Then it had been rushed and over very quickly. Now, this felt like love, not lust. It was tender, respectful, relaxed and deliciously sensuous.

"This is so wonderful," she whispered.

"Hmm mm," was the murmured reply.

Sarah was lost to the sensations. At last, she stretched and caught sight of the clock. "Hugo, it is long after 9.00. We'd better go down, have breakfast and get the day on the road."

"I suppose so. Come on then, you sexy thing."

They quickly showered and got dressed. They had just come downstairs, with Hugo preparing the coffee, when they saw Carmen and José heading their way. Sarah hastily unlocked the door as she opened it, stepping out to greet them.

"Hola! Bueno dias. We are making coffee and have plenty of treats Are you coming in?"

"*Gracias*! Just briefly. We are on our way to the hospital for José's next check-up. We are hoping he will be able to leave the wheelchair and crutches, maybe just have sticks, though they won't be much easier, I fear."

Carmen sighed. It was difficult as it was to make her husband take care and avoid putting weight on his injured leg with him in the wheelchair. It would be worse with him using sticks. She said a little prayer under her breath for his safety and for more patience on her part.

"I think we have time for a coffee. Thank you."

"It was such an enjoyable evening with you two and Inés. The meal was so delicious. Will you show me how to make that hot chocolate we had with the little donut things? The whole thing was so delicious and comforting."

Carmen looked puzzled for a moment. "Donut things? Oh Churros! Of course. Very easy; maybe tomorrow. We are meeting Inés in her lunch hour." She glanced at her watch. "We had better go! Come on, José!"

José had been busy eating a pain au chocolat, so quickly blotted up the flaky bits of pastry with a licked finger, gave Sarah and Hugo a conspiratorial wink, set off carefully after Carmen.

As she settled down with a large mug of hot frothy coffee and a warm croissant with unsalted butter and strawberry conserve, Sarah became more business-like.

"Hugo, where are we in the farming year now. It is a relief to get the grapes in and the juice safely fermenting, thanks to you. What has to be done next?"

"The vines will need some attention, but perhaps we should consult Señora's books about that? The figs are almost ripe and ready to pick but that is not such a big job, though will probably best be done on favourable days."

"Oh yes! The biodynamic stuff! I'll get the boxes," said Sarah. "I put them back upstairs."

As Sarah put some of the boxes on the big table in the dining room, she said, "I would like my mother to come over to stay fairly soon. If she can come, I would like to do up the bedroom where all these boxes are kept at the moment. This evening after supper, would you help me go through them box by box. Some of the things are in Spanish and I still don't understand it very well."

"*Si*, of course! Shall we bring everything down out of the room, then I can start sorting out some of the papers? You can then assess the room to judge what needs to be done."

They both went up to the room in question.

"This room would be great," continued Sarah. "I know

the other bedroom is already empty, but this one has a wonderful view onto the vineyards and onto Haria in the distance."

"Ah yes!" said Hugo, looking out of the window. "It is a good view. Your mother will like it."

"I will ring her later, when she gets home from work. Oh! I just remembered. I said I would write to Mr Selby to, hopefully, discover more about my great aunt. I'd better go and sort out Sweetpea and Daisy. They will be feeling hungry and wondering where I am. Are you okay here for a while?"

"Of course. I will check on the wine first. I will have to wait for José to return to know what to do next, but I can check nothing is leaking."

Once all the boxes were downstairs, they began the work of finding out what was in them all.

Hugo patiently sorted out the papers relating to the farm into what looked useful, some that were no longer required and could be burned and some to discuss with Sarah.

Sarah began unpacking some other boxes that had been very heavy.

"My goodness! Look at all this beautiful china and table ware! There is a complete dinner service for – one, two, three… twelve people and beautiful glasses of many different kinds. They are hardly used. Some are still wrapped up as if just from the shop. I wonder if she bought some of these things for when they would be married and a few presents from friends? I wonder if her husband/fiancé ever saw them?"

She displayed the china and glasses on the shelves of the sideboard and in a glass fronted cabinet. The room seemed to come to life. It had appeared cold and empty until now. As a result, Sarah didn't like the room much and hardly ever went in there, nor into the sitting room next door, spending her waking hours outside or in the kitchen. Now she could almost hear happy conversation, clatter of knives and forks on plates, bottles of wine being opened, wine poured into the elegant glasses and laughter. It all seemed so real for a moment, she had to look around at the table and was a bit startled to see only Hugo standing there, and not Clara being a wonderful hostess to a table full of friends. She decided that she would love to have a table full of friends for a meal. At the moment they would need a very big table.

"Are you alright, Sarah? You've gone pale and distant. Am I wearing you out?" said Hugo with a tender smile. He walked over to her to look more keenly at her, concerned.

"Hmm…? It is just bringing out all this china and so on has really changed the room. Um. It is as if I was seeing it as it was in Clara's day, full of friends here for a happy meal together, everyone laughing and chatting. For a moment it was very real." She laughed, a little embarrassed.

Hugo nodded as if he understood.

"Actually, it happens to me from time to time. It is as if Clara is here," Sarah continued. "She smiles at me, encourages me. She even warned me about Max's intentions so I wouldn't be misled by his 'friendly' attentions. That is how I knew what to say to Sweetpea when she first arrived. Clara was there showing me what to do and what to say.

Oh dear! You are going to think I am completely mad and not want to speak to me again," she finished, feeling rather embarrassed.

"No, no! I understand. I have had similar experiences, though maybe not so vivid. It is as if Señora Clara is very much wanting us to succeed here."

Sarah rejoiced inwardly at that little word - 'us'; this was now a real partnership for both of them.

Chapter Thirty-Two

A couple of weeks went by. José's leg still needed more time to get stronger, so was now moving about on crutches, under Carmen's watchful eye. Once he had got the hang of the crutches and his arms had strengthened, it was easier for him to get around. He insisted on checking on the fermentation process each day. He was so relieved to be able to take an active part in the winery again. It was very much his domain on the farm and it had saddened him to have to take more of a 'back seat' in the proceedings until his leg was sufficiently mended.

Meanwhile, Sarah and Hugo had sorted out all the Biodynamic papers and files, as well as Clara's own notes and observations.

"*¡Qué!* What a mess," exclaimed Hugo. "There is so much information here. It all needs to be filed under different headings. Do you have a filing system here? A cabinet? Folders?"

"No, nothing," admitted Sarah. "An oversight on my part, I think. We could really do with an office, couldn't we?

Especially if we are going to expand, which is what we have spoken about from time to time."

"*Si*, of course." Let me see what and when I need to do with the vines, then I will see about setting one up."

"That would be fantastic! I wonder where…?" Sarah's eyes were drawn to the large and never used sitting room.

There followed some very busy days and weeks. The relationship between Sarah and Hugo blossomed, bringing them both a deep joy neither had experienced before. Sarah sometimes wondered how it was that their relationship had gone from a rather distant hesitant one to the intimate level they both enjoyed now. She supposed it was because, actually, they had loved each other long before they confessed their feelings, that the relief, tenderness and friendship already existing between them, made a closer relationship the most natural and most desired by them both.

Hugo had found all the information he needed to do with the next phase of work in the vineyards in the manner to which Clara had used to such good effect. Daisy was a great help, carrying a lot more things than Hugo could possibly do, saving him a lot of time. One big move forward, Hugo reasoned, was applying, to the vineyards and other areas designated for crops, a special spray which somehow 'enlivened' the soil. A kind of homeopathy for soil, Hugo saw it as. He was glad they could buy the preparation ready to use. Daisy came into her own, carrying the containers holding the spray in special panniers, so Hugo could finish the process very quickly.

The compost heap, now rather large, was turned and set to a tidy heap, covered in soil and then according to the instructions, various specific preparations were inserted into the heap through small holes. The final one, Valerian, was watered in liquid form over the whole heap. These special preparations speeded up the rotting process and made the resulting compost full of nutrients and energy to enrich the soil and encourage excellent crops. This was the method Clara had used to such good effect – the Biodynamic method.

The farm office had fitted well into the sitting room. It was at the end of the L-shape towards the back of the room, which meant that a large part of the room could still be used as a sitting room. It had a beautiful fireplace, so would be perfect in the winter when the cold north winds blew more strongly. Sarah had imagined all her friends gathered round the big table for a delicious meal then retiring to the sitting room, golden in the firelight, for coffees and brandy. The office was screened off from the rest of the room and had its own window looking out over the steep walls of the old volcano behind the farm. All Clara's notes, books and papers were filed and clearly labelled, thanks to Hugo's patient work. It would be quick and easy to find information they needed on just about everything they could want to try on the farm, from growing avocadoes to zinnias, taking in vegetables, vines and figs along the way. Hugo confided to Sarah, that Clara kept appearing briefly to his mind's eye all the time he was doing it, sometimes even indicating which file a particular paper would best go into. Hugo agreed with all these suggestions and was often pleased to get such direction. It was very complicated in the early days, with so much to sort out. He was very satisfied with his work when it was finished. Sarah was impressed and delighted.

Sarah's mum had a date set to arrive and work had continued apace to prepare a pretty bedroom for her. It was now light and airy in the simple Spanish style. It was welcoming and serene, with a chair by the window so the view could be enjoyed in comfort.

Meanwhile, Inés had left for Barcelona, nervous but bursting with excitement at the same time. Carmen really missed her and looked forward to receiving the letters she received on a regular basis. Her daughter had found a small apartment near to the school at a very good price, which had been another great stroke of luck. Carmen was very proud that Inés had this opportunity, which helped with the emptiness she felt. There was plenty to do though to fill in any spaces in her time. Sarah found a recipe for fig jam amongst the papers, so she and Carmen decided to pick all the figs, with the help of Sweetpea, and make some fig jam. It was delicious! They sold what they didn't want to keep at the market in Haria, dividing the proceeds between them. It went very well with warm croissants, Sarah thought.

The dress designer and dressmaker were working hard to create enough garments for the Fashion Show for later in the year. A friend of theirs had set up such shows on the island many times and knew what to do and had agreed to set this one up for them. There was a lot to consider, from venue to lights, music, advertising… It was agreed between everyone that a theme of a Fiesta would be prefect.

The demand for lots of fabric kept Carmen extra busy

dyeing various types of materials for them. With some experimentation, she discovered she could produce a range of shades from palest shell pink to vibrant fuchsia and scarlet. Set against other colours of ivory, white, taupe or turquoise, with some orange scattered in, the clothes promised to be every bit as colourful and exciting as a Spanish Fiesta.

José went from wheelchair and occasionally crutches to walking with a stick. Now he was more mobile, he became a lot more active in the winery. (Carmen had an urgent word with Hugo to make sure he didn't do anything foolish).

He and Hugo cleaned out the cellar, repairing sections of the wall where necessary, cleaned and repaired barrels ready for the new vintage.

There were still three barrels down there from Clara's last vintage. They decided to keep two of them but bottle the third. José still judged it to be excellent.

Finca los Palmas hummed with activity as people and camels worked hard to move it all to the next level after the problems and delays of the earlier summer.

Everyone went to the court when Max was brought to trial. They were relived to witness a much-deflated Max sentenced to ten years in prison for all the damage and distress he had caused amongst the vineyards of the island over many years. The vintners heaved a sigh of relief and were full of thanks to Sarah, Hugo and the camels for bringing him to justice. Of course, the news of the part the animals had played in his arrest went round the island like wild fire. They were quite the celebrities.

Chapter Thirty-Three

Elizabeth, Sarah's mother was due to arrive the next day just after lunch. Sarah was excited and nervous in equal part. She so wanted her mother to like the house and farm, her friends and island life. The following day, she was waiting impatiently for her appearance at the Arrivals gate, well before the ETA.

"Mum! Mum! Over here!" Sarah shouted and waved enthusiastically so her mother would notice her amongst all the other people meeting their own friends and family off the flight. She felt a wave of emotion flood though her. It seemed ages since she had last seen her mother.

"Sarah!" said Elizabeth, giving her a big hug. "It is so good to see you. It has been a long time. I hardly recognised you for a moment. You are so tanned and with your long black hair, I thought you were someone local." She laughed to show there was no hard feelings only admiration for how changed and beautiful Sarah was now. So different to the pale, tense, young woman who had worked in London.

Partly to hide the tears of joy that were gathering in her

eyes, Sarah began to gather up Elizabeth's bags, turning to go to her truck.

"Oh, wait a moment," said Elizabeth. "I have been so excited to see you and see where you are living – this mysterious farm - I nearly forgot… Ah here he is. I have a surprise for you. There was a delay at luggage collection otherwise we would have come out together."

"Mr. Selby! This is a surprise!" It was the first time she had seen him in something other than the dark grey tweed suit and waistcoat he habitually wore when working. He was wearing a cream linen trousers and jacket with a pale blue shirt and a panama hat. It was such a dramatic change. It made him seem more approachable, thankfully. Sarah had had a moment of dismay when she heard her mother say who had arrived with her. He was always so formal.

"Hello, Miss Jones."

"Please call me Sarah. You've known me a long time – all my life in fact!"

Mr. Selby smiled apologetically, "Old school die-hard habits I'm afraid. When I heard your mother was visiting, I thought I would come out at the same time. I haven't been here before and, to be honest, I am curious to see the farm as well."

"Well, I'd better get you both to *finca Los Palmas* pronto," said Sarah. "The truck is over here. We are all eager for you to see it. It has been tough at times, especially at first, and I often questioned the wisdom of my decision to come here, but now I love it and would hate to go back to London."

The visitors spent the journey frequently exclaiming about the houses, the barren landscape, the large cacti in the gardens, the colourful bougainvillea and the many tall palm trees until Sarah cut in with "here we are!" as she turned into the drive.

Elizabeth leaned forward to get a better look. "Goodness Sarah! It is rather out of the way and on its own. Aren't you worried about being out here by yourself?"

Sarah laughed. "I'm not out here on my own. Carmen and José live here as well. Their house is just near mine… and here they are."

Her friends were on the drive to welcome them.

"Let me introduce you. We can sort out the luggage later. Um… Mr. Selby…?"

"Don't worry about me, mmm… Sarah." He smiled at his hard-wired reticence to call clients by their first names. "I am booked into a hotel in Arrecife. I didn't want to trouble you for any hospitality."

'Oh, thank you," replied Sarah, relieved, "Making provision for visitors extends just to one person at the moment," she glanced queryingly between her mother and the older man "or one couple."

They both laughed and shook their heads.

"Mum, this is Carmen and José, my good friends and advisors. They live just there," she added, pointing to their pretty house. "I don't know what I would have done without their advice and support."

"Carmen, José, my mother, Elizabeth and an," she hesitated, "an old friend of the family, Mr. Selby, who is curious about the farm."

While the four exchanged pleasantries, Sarah began to wonder if Mr. Selby's unexpected visit was connected

265

to the letter she had sent, asking about the rumours that her mother and herself were illegitimate. Concern and excitement landed in her heart at the same time. "I wonder what he has discovered – if anything?"

A sudden realisation caused her to cut into the conversation, "Where's Hugo? Is he out in the vineyard?"

As if on cue, there was a clatter and a jangle from the stable and Hugo came out leading Sweetpea and Daisy. They were dresses in their celebration finery and walked towards them with all the pride and self-conscious care of children knowing they were in their best clothes and this was an important meeting.

"Oh, my goodness!" exclaimed Elizabeth taking a few steps backwards, "They look so big – and amazing."

When they were closer, Hugo said softly, "*Jmell bayohav*," and sedately, the two camels sat down, bells and harnesses jingling.

Sarah laughed in delight. "Hugo! That's clever. You've been busy!"

Still smiling, she turned to her mother, drawing her nearer, "Mum, meet my friend Hugo. He is in charge of the vineyards and helps his Uncle José with everything else as well. He is also a '*mudarib al jamal*,' a camel trainer now I see." She beamed at Hugo, who smiled back. "And this is Sweetpea and her daughter Daisy."

The two camels gave a throaty, grumbly purr in the visitors' direction, then turned to look elsewhere.

"'*Abqaa*,' stay there" said Hugo and stepped forward to meet the two visitors. "*Buenos dias,*" he said, shaking their hands. He gave Sarah a shy smile, obviously pleased with the camels' entrance and behaviour.

Sarah broke away from Hugo's smile, lost for a moment in the love she felt for this handsome islander. The pause didn't escape her mother's sharp eyes.

'Hmm… that is interesting. I will keep quiet for now though,' she thought.

"Well, I don't know about you," Sarah said, turning to her mum and Mr Selby with a wide smile, "but I could do with some coffee. Come on in."

Sarah led the way to the kitchen as Hugo took the camels back to the stable where they would be cooler.

"I have made a special Spanish cake for you," said Carmen as they settled around the large kitchen table, '*Tarta San Marcos*.'"

"That looks wonderful," said Elizabeth. Everyone agreed. The conversation paused for a while as they all enjoyed the delicious cake and savoured the much-needed coffee.

"Look at the time!" said Sara. "Mum, let me show you your room. I hope you like it. You look out over a lot of the farm. Will you stay and join us for dinner, Mr. Selby? We can take you back to your hotel afterwards."

"That will be very nice, thank you." Mr. Selby gave a small bow as acceptance.

"Meanwhile, I can show you around," offered Hugo.

"Wait for me," said Elizabeth, as she followed her daughter upstairs. "We won't be long, will we?"

"Well, a few moments. You start with the stable, Hugo, and we will catch you up."

"*Por supuesto.* Of course," said Hugo, lifting his arm to Mr Selby in invitation to walk outside.

The evening meal was ready soon after they returned, thanks to Carmen's bustling about and earlier preparations. They all gathered around the table in the dining room. It looked beautiful, with a tumble of bougainvillea in a large vase on the sideboard, candles on the table with all the place settings and glasses now unpacked from their boxes. José had lit the fire as well. The evenings could feel chilly after the warmth of the day, especially when the wind blew down from the north.

Hugo served up chilled Cava, as Carmen and Sarah put the finishing touches to the meal.

The time passed quickly, with lots of questions from Elizabeth and Mr. Selby; some of his questions seemed very detailed to Sarah and aroused her curiosity. She began to speculate on what he may have discovered about the farm and Clara.

"Thank you, that was delicious," said Mr. Selby, "but I think I had better check into my hotel before they release my room, thinking I am not coming."

"I can take you, Signor. I am familiar with the hotel." He turned to the others, "Goodnight, *tia y tio*, see you tomorrow. Goodnight, Sarah," he smiled mischievously, "see you in the morning."

"It has been a delightful evening, thank you. Very kind of you to draw me into your family circle. I would really like all of you to join me for lunch at the Hotel tomorrow. My visit isn't purely because of curiosity; there are a few things I would like to share with you. I'll see you in the foyer at 12.00. Thank you." With that he followed Hugo to his car. Hugo had remembered to put the older man's luggage in his own car from Sarah's truck and the two men set off for Arrecife and Mr. Selby's hotel.

He left behind a buzz of conversation as Carmen, Sarah and José wondered what it might be that he wanted to share.

"The dining room looked wonderful, Carmen. Wasn't it lovely to have the room used and full of chatter and laughter? The fire really brings it all together. Thank you for thinking of that, José."

The couple beamed at her, José even going a bit pink that his lighting a fire had been appreciated.

Chapter Thirty-Four

The following day, Sarah, Hugo, Carmen and José all arrived at the hotel at 12.00 on the dot; all of them curious about the purpose behind the invitation and excited about having lunch in a very lovely hotel.

"Ah Splendid! Good morning to all," Mr. Selby shook hands with everyone, smiling broadly.

'It doesn't look as if he has bad news to give us – even if it is news at all?' thought Sarah. An image of her great aunt appeared very clearly in front of her; she was waving, smiling – and she was dancing! 'Definitely not bad news then.' Sarah smiled to herself. This unusual communication from Clara was getting more frequent. Something must be building up somewhere.

"Come this way to the Privilege lounge where we can have a drink on the house. There is an outside terrace and it is pleasantly warm today."

He turned and walked off to the right, put the code in the door and stood to one side to allow the party to walk in. He settled everyone down on the terrace around a square table in the warm sunshine, went back inside and soon re-appeared with glasses and two bottles of chilled Cava.

"Here we are! I have to remember that in Italy the sparkling wine is Prosecco but in Spanish countries the drink is definitely Cava. It is rather refreshing."

He poured generous glasses of the wine, then reaching down for a briefcase at the side of his chair, he looked round at the party, their faces a mixture of curiosity and enjoyment.

"You are wondering why I have invited you to what is beginning to look more like a meeting rather than just a luncheon." Mr Selby took a steadying breath, 'Well, following uh… Sarah's letter asking about recent allegations of Elizabeth and therefore Sarah being illegitimate, I retrieved all the files of Miss Clara Jones from the archives.

As we know, Miss Clara came to live here on the island to run the farm at *Los Palmas*. She fell in love with a young Spanish man whose parents had attained permanent residency of the Island and this had included him as well. Sarah and Hugo exchanged an intimate glance; one that didn't go unnoticed by her mother, who smiled to herself.

"What we had understood to happen later, was that Estoban left for Spain to fight against Franco. Tragically he was killed fairly soon afterwards. Distraught and homesick, overwhelmed with the challenge of living at the farm that had no water supply or electricity, she had a kind of breakdown. Her sister, the one who was still in contact with her, sent her the fare to sail home, leaving the farm under the watchful eye of kind neighbours and the two people who were working for her - Carmen and José." He gave the older couple a slight bow.

There were murmurs of agreement around the table.

"Perhaps that was why she was so generous with her teachings about the Biodynamic method for farming to those neighbours. Showing how they could improve the yield and taste of what they grew was a way of thanking them. I wonder how many took it up. It looks quite complicated, doesn't it, Hugo?" asked Sarah.

Hugo nodded his agreement. Again, the image of Clara appeared even more clearly to Sarah. She was smiling broadly.

'Mm, maybe," said Mr. Selby. "However, as I emptied the box, I discovered some more files and letters right at the bottom that hadn't been opened, I don't know why. What I found there when I opened them all is why I have visited the island and why I have invited you here today."

Much to the frustration of the others, he paused to top up their glasses and bring some plates with a selection of hors d'oevres and napkins. They looked delicious and such a treat, they helped themselves, while they waited for the older man to continue. He then pulled out a yellowing official-looking document and laid it out on the table for everyone to see.

They all leaned forward, intrigued. There was a suspenseful silence as everyone read the document and realised what it was. There were gasps of surprise, followed by astonished laughter. It was the marriage certificate for Clara Jones and Estoban Garcia!

"Oh, my goodness!" exclaimed Sarah. "That is a surprise but a really lovely one."

'Well, why the rumours?' was in the mind of Carmen,

José and Hugo. Sarah asked it out loud.

"It was a different time then; not so tolerant. Mr. and Mrs. Garcia, Estoban's parents, were devout Catholics. Clara was a lapsed Catholic so was never seen in their church. She was also a foreigner. A potent combination against her as a suitable wife for their son. When Estoban told his parents about Clara and his intention to marry her, they were very frosty. They told him that they did not want him to marry this non-Catholic foreigner. If he did, they would disinherit him and not want to see him again. This would be disastrous, not only from an emotional point of view, but also because some inheritance would be essential for most young men to get ahead. It would also mean he would be ostracised by the rest of his family. He would be completely alone, without any financial or moral support – a difficult situation at a time when it was difficult to earn a living in the rural parts of Lanzarote.

Also, Estoban didn't want to upset his parents. Family bonds were strong. However, now he would be going to Spain to fight and Clara had just discovered she was pregnant. Would he survive to return to get married before the baby was born?

His parents, immigrants from Spain, lived further south in Yaiza, while Clara lived in the north in Haria. In haste and after much discussion they decided the best thing would be to marry secretly to protect their good name as a family. They married a week later at the Nuestra Señora de la Encarnacion in Haria. It was one Wednesday in the afternoon with only two close friends, sworn to secrecy, as witnesses. There were no flowers, no celebrations; no one

273

would know that a wedding had taken place. The people involved would have seemed no more remarkable going to church in ones and twos in the afternoon than the many who did that on most days." Mr. Selby paused for a drink and to sample a few of the hors d'oevres. Excited conversation went back and forth, mostly expressing amazement and a sense of 'oh! that's why....'

"There's more,' Mr. Selby continued, speeding up the story as their lunch would soon be ready. "Sadly, only a week later Estoban received his army papers and only just eight days after his wedding, he left for Spain.

The sudden contrast between the joy of being married to the love of her life and having to say goodbye as he left for a dangerous and uncertain future, was great strain for Clara as you may imagine. She wrote at length to her sister about how sad she felt. More disaster followed as six weeks into the conflict, Estoban was killed by a landmine exploding under their vehicle as he was being transported to one of the main areas of fighting.

It was a few weeks' later that Clara received the dreaded telegram together with a small parcel of his belongings.

She was inconsolable. After a particularly anguished letter to her sister," he placed the old letter on the table," in which she expressed her heartbreak and concerns about how she was going to run a farm on her own, with a young baby. She was still very new at *Los Palmas* and was still learning about what needed to be done and how. Also, no-one knew she was married and soon it would show. She was concerned what the reaction would be and how she would let people know that she was already married. Estoban's parents would have been outraged by the deception if they found out the truth. As I said, it was a very different time then, almost Edwardian in attitudes. Illegitimacy was regarded as a sin of the parents, and by association, the child. The stigma would go through the generations. On receipt of this letter, fearing for her sister's mental stability, Gwen sent her the fare to sail home."

The others nodded. They knew about Clara's sudden departure for England. Now they understood why.

The story continued. The sisters decided to rent a small cottage in a rural part of the South Downs. With the loving ministrations of her sister and daily walks over the Downs, Clara gradually recovered her spirits and her health. The only thing the people in the area knew about the situation was that Clara was a war widow and was in the care of her sister.

As the date of the birth drew closer, the sisters discussed in earnest what would happen to the baby afterwards. They both understood the delicate situation in Lanzarote and the prejudices that prevailed there. This was all mixed up with Clara's love for Estoban and wanting to maintain his reputation as someone who gave his life for the freedom of his parents' country. With no-one wanting them to be married nor knowing that they had married before he left for Spain, if Clara returned with the baby, the gossips would have a field day and she would be ostracized from all directions. She knew she had to return to the farm. It was her life by then and was closely associated with her late husband. She couldn't, nor wanted to, remain in England. After much discussion and heart searching, they decided that her sister Gwen would adopt the baby at birth. She and her husband knew by then that they were unable to have children of their own, but both felt they had a lot to offer a child. When he was asked, Gwen's husband was pleased that Gwen would be adopting Clara's baby; it somehow felt different from adopting a stranger's child. The baby was already part of the family anyway. This would be a solution to both problems. The relevant papers were drawn up and very soon after the baby girl, Elizabeth, was born she was given to Gwen so they would bond together. Who can guess the agony of that moment that Clara must have felt; torn between the natural instinct to keep the baby and knowing that it would be impossible?

Once Clara had recovered from the birth, she left England for her farm on the island. She never saw the baby again. She knew that if she had been to say goodbye to her sister and to Elizabeth, she would never be able to leave her. If she stayed in England she would be shunned here as well. It would be difficult for her to make her own living honourably as a single mother.

From then on, Gwen regularly sent photographs of Elizabeth.

"It must have been bitter sweet moments for her when the photos arrived," said Mr Selby, "but I think it gave her energy to carry on developing the farm, so she could send money back to Gwen for her daughter's care."

"To continue the story," said Mr. Selby, "With a heart heavy with grief for the two beings she had loved most but were no longer with her, Clara plunged into making a success of the neglected farm.

Sarah this means that not only are you, nor your mother not illegitimate, but that Clara is not your great aunt, but your grandmother!"

Someone drew in a big breath, someone else sighed an "Ah" of understanding. Hugo gave Sarah a big hug. Sarah hugged her mother. There were tears in everyone's eyes. There was huge sympathy for the difficult decision Clara had to make; her love that was so great she didn't want to harm Estoban's reputation in the eyes of his parents.

Elizabeth said, "Gosh! I don't think I could have had you adopted, Sarah, for anything or anyone. But that was then, we live in such a different world now, thank goodness."

The waitress came to Mr. Selby's side and quietly told him that lunch was served and invited the party to come inside to a table that was all set for them.

Once the party were settled in the dining room, they were all beginning to recover from this life-altering news, and finding their voices after the stunned reaction to Mr. Selby's announcement.

Sarah expressed concerned about how her mother had received the news of her adoption as a baby. Their lives suddenly looked very different. Elizabeth reached out to hold her daughter's hand.

'To give me time to adjust to this news, Mr. Selby called me to his office a few weeks' ago to tell me what he had discovered. It has been really difficult not to tell you, but we wanted to let you all know as it affects all of us equally. It was a shock as you can imagine, but as I thought about it the news made more sense of my life at a deep level, without me quite being able to say how exactly. It is hard to explain.

Now I feel even more loved by Gwen than before and very loved by Clara, who loved me so much she gave me to her sister so I would have a more settled life, free from any of the narrow-minded prejudices that plagued so many women at that time. I feel very relaxed about the shift sideways as it were.

Sarah was very quiet. Carmen thought she would speak to give her friend time to process what they had all just heard.

"This is good news. It makes sense of Señora Clara's sudden and prolonged absence. I had not long started work here before she left but I did the best I could with the goats and the cheese. What I made always sold well in the market. I am very glad she was able to get married even if it wasn't quite a usual ceremony. It was a different time with all the fighting in Spain then the War. We didn't know what to make of the Germans at that time. Their ships were coming and going to and from the island all through the war. We all had to be very careful what we said. As things developed, I can see now that Clara would have been in serious danger if she had brought Elizabeth back here because she had married a Spaniard and the baby was of "mixed blood." It was a strange time here."

"Oh, my goodness!" gasped Sarah, as the realisation sank in of the implications that had existed in a country over-run by Germans. Mother and baby wouldn't have lived for long. A shiver ran down her back. What a time it was then! The world had gone crazy in a very bad way.

"Yes," agreed José, continuing in Spanish, with a nod to Hugo to translate for the visitors. "I was taken on at the farm a short time before the Señora left, to take care of the vines and keep an eye on the wine. We did the best we could. We kept it up together. The Señora was very pleased to be back on the farm, though she looked pale and a bit more withdrawn. We put it down to her being in the cold English weather, didn't we, my dear?" José said, turning to Carmen.

"Si," said Carmen. "There were a few rumours, of course. There always is here when something unusual happens. These died down when the Señora returned alone. She soon recovered her colour and her energy, then we could hardly keep up with her. José and I had become very close by then. He asked my family if he could marry me. Of course, they said 'yes' – and I did!"

Everyone laughed and congratulated them. Hugo raised his glass in a toast to both of them. He was fascinated by this new development, but was also concerned for Sarah, who had been very quiet all this time.

"Sarah, are you alright? This must be quite a shock?"

Sarah shook her head to lift herself out of the reverie into which she had fallen. She had seen once again the woman who had just been revealed as her grandmother. She had held her arms wide in welcome, then put both hands over her heart, then extended them to her daughter, Elizabeth and her granddaughter Sarah, obviously full of joy that her family was here in Lanzarote and the real story revealed. Tears filled Sarah's eyes yet again. She blew her nose loudly to distract her emotions. Also, she didn't want her mascara to run down her cheeks while they were here at the hotel!

"Hmm? Oh yes, sorry Hugo. I was lost in thought for a moment. Gosh! That was a surprise, wasn't it? A lovely one though. It explains a lot – like why I was so drawn to come to Lanzarote in the first place, then deciding almost immediately that I would stay regardless of my complete lack of experience in any form of farming. I feel very at home here, more so than in London. It also explains my black hair, even though your hair, Mum, is light brown. The Spanish genes must have skipped a generation! What an extraordinary woman!"

Sarah fell back into her own thoughts as plates were cleared and dessert menus brought. General chatter about which one to choose and more comments on the story they had just heard flowed around her and faded. Part of Sarah was back on the farm, actually walking there. She went to the winery and then to the stables to see the camels. Sweetpea rumbled and grumbled a greeting as did Daisy. Sarah felt drawn to the far right of the building - a place she didn't really go to. There was a pile of tarpaulins and old sacks. She couldn't move them, but knew that she must look there on her return to the farm. She took a deep breath and 'returned' to the hotel, expecting to find the others just finishing their desserts. However, they were still deciding what to have. Her 'visit' had taken only seconds, even though she thought she had been away at least 20 if not 30 minutes.

'Curious!' thought Sarah. 'Someone must have sprinkled fairy dust over me or something… as if!'

She chose *Tarta de Santiago* -almond tart – with vanilla ice cream for her dessert, as did José. Mr. Selby and Elizabeth said they would try the churros and hot chocolate. Carmen and Hugo had *Crema Catalana*. Sarah ordered a bottle of Cava to celebrate the revelations. She was so uplifted, delighted to discover she was at her grandmother's farm. It all fitted around her like a warm duvet.

The staff quickly caught on that this was an unplanned but special celebration and gave them the final coffee, chocolates and brandy on the house.

"Goodness!" said Elizabeth. "This is fantastic! I thought you would all be dismayed and upset with Clara, my birth mother" She smiled to herself, hugging this new situation to her heart, "for her secret wedding, but here you all are celebrating like it is the best news ever."

"Yes," said Carmen. "The true story squashes, once and for all, the vicious gossip that has been circulating in the area about Sarah's and your legitimacy, which is why Sarah asked Signor Selby to look into the matter more closely. It puts Sarah, and the farm, on solid ground now in the view of some of the locals, even though most people in the area were supportive of Clara. She gave a lot back to the community."

"Well, I never," replied Elizabeth, "That must have been difficult for you Sarah. I knew nothing of all this, of course, and never thought to question the status quo. It feels wonderful though, to know my mother cared so much for my future she was prepared for her sister in England to bring me up. I don't feel I was 'abandoned' or anything. The whole thing had been very carefully thought out."

As the truth of the situation sank in, Sarah and Elizabeth got a bit emotional and their eyes filled with tears all over again. The others were concerned but were soon reassured that they were tears of relief and joy. The coffee and chocolates quickly restored their good humour. Now they were the only ones left in the dining room, but one waiter stayed on to supply more coffee, brandy, even more desserts if anyone wanted some.

Much later Sarah reached for her purse to pay for the lunch. However, Mr. Selby insisted that the meal was his treat. Secretly he was relieved his revelations had been received so joyfully; a reaction he had definitely not anticipated.

Sarah had a sudden thought, "Will this news change anything about the conditions for me to stay here?"

She knew now more than ever, that the farm was where her future lay. She had been concerned that Hugo would be reluctant to stay with her if it had been found that she was illegitimate. She looked across at her friend and lover but saw only delight and love as he smiled back at her.

"I don't think so," said Mr. Selby carefully. "To tell you the truth I was a little nervous about bringing this news to you all. I had no way of guessing what your individual responses would be. I am very pleased it has been received so positively. There are a few more papers which I can bring over to the farm before I return home, if I may? Perhaps in a couple of days' time? I have arranged a few excursions from the hotel, including a tour of the Timanfaya."

"That is a great tour," said Sarah. "It takes you to places that the general public can't go to. It is such a carefully protected area. Very interesting. Keep your eyes open as you go around the tops of a range of some old volcanoes, I think at one of the highest points of the range. You will go around a u-shaped valley and far below, tucked in there is *finca Los Palmas*. Please make time to visit us at the farm before you leave. Um... Mum, you travelled here with Mr. Selby. Will you be going back together?"

Mr. Selby smiled. "I thought Elizabeth would like to

spend longer here than I, so we have booked separate return flights."

"Oh excellent! If you would give me your phone number, we can arrange a day for you to come over."

Time, conversation, coffee and chocolate had sobered everyone up enough to drive safely back to the farm. Profuse thank you's for a delicious lunch and the wonderful news followed. Goodbyes were said and soon Mr. Selby was able to return to the quiet terrace and enjoy some warm sunshine, maybe just one more glass of their excellent brandy and a relaxing sleep.

Chapter Thirty-Five

Back at the farm, Carmen, José and Hugo went straight to the kitchen to talk some more about what they had all just learned, while Sarah went to check on Sweetpea and Daisy. The camels had been patiently waiting for her return and were pleased to see her. She took them out to the area at the back of the buildings. The camels rumbled and grumbled, rolled in the grass, browsed on the leaves of some shrubs, pleased to be outside after so long in the stable. Sarah watched them fondly. They were very big but had become so much part of her life at the farm. As well as being very useful, for all their disdainful demeanour, they were an emotional support. She felt a genuine connection with them, especially since she knew she could communicate with them in Arabic and in telepathic pictures. This train of thought led her to her strange 'visit' back to the farm when they were at the hotel, a little earlier in the day. She needed to check something out.

Calling the camels to her, she led the way back to the stables. After cleaning their stalls, putting down fresh bedding, food and water, she went over to see what was in the corner that she had been drawn to in her dream-state. The camels, as curious as cats, followed her as far as they could.

Gingerly, Sarah lifted a corner of the tarp, feeling a bit uncertain what would be underneath. When neither snakes, scorpions nor bats came out, she took heart and heaved the whole thing to one side.

"Sarah! Are you alright? You've been out here ages. We've made some coffee; yours has gone cold."

"Hello Hugo. I've been cleaning out the stalls and took the camels out so they could stretch their legs. They haven't had much to do lately."

The camels were making so much noise greeting Hugo, he could hardly hear Sarah, but he could see she was all right and was beckoning him over to look at something in the corner. He squeezed past the camels, giving them a friendly pat as he did so.

"What is this, Hugo? Do you recognise it?"

"No, but Carmen or José may know. I'll go and get them. Sweetpea! Daisy! Go back, back; now go over there a minute."

Soon all four people were gathered tightly into the end of the stable, looking at what Sarah had uncovered. It looked like a jumble of old leather straps, now rather dry and some of which were broken plus what looked to be a heap of old metal. It hadn't gone rusty, because it was so dry in that part of the island.

"Do you recognise anything any of this, José?

José moved closer, shuffling some of the pieces around. "Ah! I have wondered where these were. I was thinking of them last week." Hugo translated as he talked.

"…and…?" prompted Sarah.

"*Si*, these are camel ploughs; two, maybe three. Hah! *Perfecto*! Now we can prepare the ground quickly for new plantings."

"Camel ploughs! Will our two know what to do with them? Will we? asked Sarah.

"Sounds quaint and old fashioned to me," said Hugo, full of doubt. "A tractor would be better?"

"Ah! replied José. "*Si, 'Ciertamente'* (certainly) old fashioned, but gentler on the soil than a tractor. We have camels, but the old tractor is not good. I will ask my son to look at it. Perhaps it can be revived and then it may be useful."

As José moved the pieces of the ploughs around to get a better idea of what was there, they could see the corner of a large chest, most of it still under the covers. Hugo pulled the heavy tarpaulin further back to reveal a sea chest.

"I wonder what this is," said Hugo.

Sarah knew then, that whatever was in the chest, was the reason she had been drawn/sent to that hitherto undisturbed corner of the stables during her 'visit' earlier in the day.

They had been at the hotel over lunch for so long, it was getting dark in the stable now, so they managed to get the chest out of the corner, past the ploughs and half drag, half carry it to the kitchen door. Carmen fussed about brushing off dust and a few cobwebs before allowing it in.

Once inside, they stood a moment looking at it, then Hugo eased up the stiff catches, then slowly opened the lid. All of them held their breath, in nervous and excited anticipation about what they would find; all hoping it would contain something and not be just empty.

They breathed out together, it was almost full, but the contents were covered in layers of tissue paper. By unspoken agreement, they indicated that Elizabeth should be the one to 'draw back the curtain' as it were.

"Phew! Lots of mothballs anyway," she said, as she pulled back the covering.

While Sarah and Hugo cleared the table, Elizabeth and Carmen gently and respectfully pulled out the top layer. It comprised neat bundles of letters, postmarked UK. Carmen handed the nearest one to Elizabeth. They were from Gwen. In this bundle they were about Elizabeth's wedding. Gwen had done a brilliant job of bringing the occasion alive for Clara. Elizabeth smiled and nodded as she read one of them, while the others waited patiently.

"Goodness! I think Mum, or should I say 'Auntie'?" said Elizabeth.

"No, 'mum' is right for you," interrupted Sarah. Elizabeth smiled in acknowledgement. "My mum in England was writing to my biological mum over here to tell her all about my life. Isn't that beautiful? Even after all the years, she was keeping to their agreement to do that." Elizabeth felt enveloped by the care and love of these two exceptional women. Her eyes became blurred with tears. This palpable love more than compensated for whatever her initial reaction was to the information that she was adopted.

Sarah began comparing dates on the postmarks and saw that each bundle consisted of a long letter for each month of every year. "That is some commitment," she said when she shared what she had noticed.

The bundles were removed and placed in chronological order, then put in boxes to keep them organised.

Hugo made some fresh coffee. This was going to be a long job. Care was taken to put their mugs well away from the chest and its precious contents. It was poignant and sad to notice that the envelopes relating to Elizabeth's life as a baby and toddler were discoloured; Clara hadn't been able to wait to wash her hands before opening the letter. Some envelopes had the ink of the address blurred by drops of water.

Sarah looked at her mother. "Tears?" Elizabeth nodded, not wanting to speak for the emotion caught in her throat.

The dates and years on the postmarks added up. They were about Sarah as a baby and her escapades as a toddler and as she got older.

Once all the letters had been removed, they weren't even half way down the chest.

"Shall we put the letters in the office for now?" suggested Sarah. "It will take a long time to read all these. I expect you want to mum, the same as me?"

"Yes. There is a lot to see still," said Elizabeth.

The next layer was of bundles of photos. Elizabeth and Sarah resisted the temptation to look through all of them. They would be there for hours, otherwise.

There were baby and children's clothes, all wrapped in tissue with reverential care, the layers thick with mothballs. Elizabeth smiled as she wrinkled her nose at the pungent smell. "No moths, or anything else, were going to get to these. Oh, Sarah! I remember you wearing this. You looked so sweet - for about five minutes before you rushed out into the garden." She laughed at the memory. "No wonder I couldn't find these. They were here! How kind of mum." Gwen would always be 'mum' for her after so long.

There was a break from the unpacking for more coffee with a splash of brandy in it, together with some of the cake from yesterday. No-one wanted to stop. It was as if they were meeting Clara personally for the first time, even for Carmen and José who knew nothing of this side of her life. It was fascinating and moving at the same time.

"¡Ay! Ay! Ay!" said José when he saw the next layer. "These were Estoban's belongings!"

There were some medals, his Army ID book and passport, some uniform buttons. Not much at all. It was a pitiful sight. Poor compensation for the widow. So painful to see, even now. Then there were a few men's working clothes and a nice suit, not particularly fashionable. In the next layer down was a woman's costume in blue cotton, such as Clara may have worn to go shopping. Both outfits were very carefully wrapped and had obviously been laid in the chest with great care.

"Oh, my goodness!" said Sarah, realising why this should be so. "This must be what they both wore when they got married. Their clothes needed to be unremarkable. Neither of them could look like they were going to a wedding, or draw attention to themselves. Clara couldn't look like a bride!"

Sarah paused, caught in the emotion of this realisation. She remembered her own wedding and how she had felt when she put on her dress. It was wonderful. Clara may not have ever felt that thrill.

"There's still more here!" said Carmen. There at the bottom of the chest was more tissue paper and obviously something wrapped inside. The next item to come out was a very smart man's suit in many layers of tissue paper. This one had been very fashionable at that time; "A Zoot suit," said Sarah smiling. "Estoban wanted to be very trendy. Some special occasion obviously."

The next layer revealed a beautiful long white gown in silk crepe, draped over the waist and body. It had a high neck and long narrow sleeves. It was meant for someone very slim. There was a long veil with a stiffened cap that would have been fitted to the head and held in place with a spray of artificial flowers. Everyone was quiet as they considered the story these unworn gorgeous clothes told, packed underneath the plainer outfits.

"Of course!" said Elizabeth in hushed tones. "They had to get married in haste before Estoban went to Spain and no-one could know because of the resistance of Estoban's parents. These plainer ones were the clothes they eventually got married in, whereas these other beautiful outfits were what they had bought before the call-up papers arrived and put an end to any plans they may have made for a more tolerant future. Their real wedding clothes were never worn. How sad."

Some photos they looked at the following day, agreed with what she had said. They were taken of their wedding in the church. Estoban was in the ordinary suit and Clara in her simple blue costume. She didn't even have any flowers. It spoke volumes.

Then Carmen gasped. "That woman there, one of the two witnesses; she is my mother! I never knew. She never said a word about this, not even after Clara died." For once Carmen was lost for words. Here was another secret that would remain as such because her mother had died a few years ago.

It was late now. The clothes were moved, with great care, to the big table in the dining room, covered in tissue paper, to be carefully wrapped the next day. A box was found to put the photographs in so they could be easily accessed over the next days and weeks. They carried the now empty trunk into the dining room and shut the door. Everyone let out an emotion-laden sigh.

Carmen got some glasses out and put a generous slug of brandy in each.

"To Signora Clara and Signor Estoban," she said raising her glass. "To Signora Clara and Signor Estoban," responded the others.

Finding this chest and its contents made Clara very much more real to Sarah; someone she could get to know rather than some shadowy figure she hadn't known existed less than a year ago.

Chapter Thirty-Six

The following morning, Sarah, Hugo, Elizabeth, Carmen and José had a meeting in Sarah's kitchen. They all felt the need to talk about what they had discovered and seen the day before and to work out if this would affect any future work on the farm. It was an emotional and lengthy discussion, but in the end, there was a consensus that this new knowledge made any work done on the farm more meaningful and the future more secure.

By "populating" the past, it gave a more solid foundation upon which to build the future. Such was the positive energy generated, that even Elizabeth got very excited about it and was even turning over in her mind the possibility of moving to Lanzarote to work on the farm alongside the others. She decided she would keep quiet about this idea; wait to see what it looked like once back in UK.

They brought forward ideas that had been discussed earlier but had got side tracked by Max's behaviour and preparing for Elizabeth's visit. Between them they began to formulate concrete plans to bring those ideas into reality.

Hugo resolved to understand much more clearly the Biodynamic Principles when it came to caring for the vines and the wine making. They no doubt made a difference to the quality of everything. He was pleased he had taken the time to catalogue Clara's books and notes, so now he knew where to go to get any information he needed at any time. José was eager to teach his nephew what he knew about the winemaking process and to work together with him on developing and improving the vineyards and the quantity of wine produced.

The prickly pears were still producing ripe fruit so the women decided they would make as much jam as they could while the fruit was in season then sell it gradually through the year. Elizabeth was intrigued by this and said she would love to help. They decided they would start making jam the next day. They could pick the fruit and get the ingredients needed this afternoon.

Sarah wanted to check on the progress on the fashion show. An idea was forming in her mind about how she could use the show to pay homage to her grandmother and grandfather (it gave her a thrill to think of Estoban as such) and to lay the ghost of her and Elizabeth's supposed illegitimacy. Maybe a hint of 1930s fashion but certainly using the white wedding dress they had found at the bottom of the chest in a collection to end the show. She arranged a date the following week to discuss progress with Valeria and Bella. She would also be able to use the meeting to get more fabric for Carmen to dye.

Elizabeth was fascinated hearing about everything that went on at the farm and what they were planning for the future. They arranged for the two older women to gather ripe prickly pear fruits that afternoon and maybe collect some cochineal beetles to make more dye. Sarah said she would catch up with them later and bring Sweetpea with her panniers fitted to carry everything back to the house.

Then they all 'came up for air,' looking around to come out of the intensity of their plans. They looked at each other and all burst out laughing at their seriousness. They had plenty of time to get all these plans going. They would be able to space activities out over the days in order to allow time to attend to the day to day running of the farm.

In the middle of all these plans, Sarah remembered that her mother was actually on holiday and had never been to the island before. To make the most of Elizabeth's time with her, Sarah arranged for the two of them to explore Lanzarote.

With the help of the concierge at the hotel where Sarah had stayed when she first arrived, they booked a coach tour of the Island, which took them through the Timanfaya volcanic Park taking in the Jameos del Agua – the underground lava tunnels and lake that had been developed as a theatre, restaurant, café and shop. It was such a strange place. They went down a tunnel that led out to the Atlantic Ocean. Elizabeth was intrigued but was glad when they emerged from the other side of the complex on to the surface. They also went along the volcanic ridge above the farm and were able to look down to see the house and buildings nestling in the arms of the u-shaped valley surrounded by the very steep sides of the volcano, some of which had been terraced. Sarah made a mental note to learn how Clara did that and see if it was possible to grow more things in that way. The concierge had also suggested a few places for them to go that were away from the main tourist areas for real shopping and good places for lunch out. Sarah was delighted he remembered her from those months ago. He really wanted to know how she was getting on, how the farm was doing and congratulated her on how she had settled in and got on with the job in spite of her inexperience. He hoped she would call again and update him on any further progress. Sarah was delighted to promise to do that.

On the tour they stopped at Max's Bodega. Sarah was pleased it had continued operating in the owner's absence. It had a more relaxed atmosphere than before and the women certainly looked happier. Sarah wondered how much he harassed them on a daily basis. She was very happy to meet up with the two women again. They had been very helpful and friendly on her first visit there. They remembered her; *la dama de los camellos* they called her. There wasn't much time to talk as the two women were busy serving the other members of the tour, but during the conversation, Sarah got the idea that they were relieved Max had been caught. They experienced the Bodega as definitely much happier and more profitable without him. While they were chatting, Elizabeth sauntered round looking at all the different red and white wines for sale. She eventually chose a bottle of white and a bottle of red to take home with her to UK as they were already wrapped up.

Much to Sarah's delight the two women arranged to meet up with her for coffee after her mother had returned home. It was something she had hoped would happen. It made her feel more as is she belonged, rather than just an unusual, if not eccentric, island visitor.

On the Sunday, the two women went to Teguise to the Market there. Carmen had told them that the food was all locally produced and a lot of it was organic. Sarah hadn't been there before so enjoyed exploring all the speciality food stalls and craft shops. Elizabeth bought some small gifts to take home to her friends. "A bit like the ornaments made of shells with 'A Present from Margate' or somewhere that you used to bring back from a day at the seaside," she laughed. This led to them talking about the many happy memories they had from holidays and days out. They arrived back at the farm with bags of goodies for several meals.

Mr. Selby came to the farm for lunch as promised the day before he left, he had enjoyed his stay on the island, but had also continued with more research into Clara and Estoban while he was there. What no-one knew about this very staid English solicitor was that he also operated as a private detective. Over the years, he had exposed several shady, even illegal business deals, infidelity and in one case even murder. There was more behind the facade of benign country gentleman than anyone could imagine. As no-one had even suspected he did such clandestine work, even part time, he obviously did his job very well.

They had an enjoyable lunch at the farm, catching up on what he had seen and done and what Elizabeth had been doing since her arrival. He was just leaving, when he stopped at the doorway, and feigning an 'almost forgot moment,' he handed Sarah a very fat envelope, smiled and left. Elizabeth remarked that he had reminded her of the TV detective Colombo, for whom such a ruse was very much part of his investigative procedure. Full of curiosity, she and Sarah, opened the envelope. Secretly, Sarah had wondered if it would be a great big bill for services rendered. What a surprise when they saw that it contained details of Estoban's half of the family who were still living on the island. There were details of one of Estoban's brother's granddaughters. She would be Elizabeth's niece, maybe once removed or something!

This news was received by the two of them with a mixture of excitement and reservation. It was a thrill to know she and Elizabeth had relatives on the island, especially as they were both only children. It established them as 'Islanders,' rather than just a few foreign visitors or immigrants. It was also a concern about how this niece would react to the news of Clara and Estoban's secret wedding. Would it open old wounds and antagonisms. There was no outguessing that. It had been a different time then and attitudes had moved on; how much they had moved on would remain to be seen. Mr. Selby had given them the address of Isabella. She was living further south, still in Yaiza where her family had lived since the original family arrived from Spain. Hugo helped with the Spanish and with input from everyone else, Sarah composed a letter explaining Clara and Estoban's secret wedding, introducing Elizabeth as their legitimate daughter and Sarah as their granddaughter and telling her how Clara had left her the farm earlier that year.

Elizabeth was concerned that Isabella would claim that the farm should belong to her family as was the tradition in Spain. However, some research showed that Clara had bought the farm herself before she married Estoban –

something unusual for women at that time. It was registered in her name. Her cousins therefore had no legal claim on the land, even if they were interested in farming. Finally, curiosity and the thought that she had family on the island overcame Sarah's reservations and, with fingers crossed, she posted the letter.

Chapter Thirty-Seven

Two days later, both Sarah and Carmen each received handwritten letters – would they contain nice surprises? They both hoped each letter carried good news rather than difficult ones.

Carmen's letter was from Inés, bringing everyone up to date on her experiences at the Cookery School, as Sarah would discover later.

Sarah's letter was from a Lanzarote address. With her heart beating too fast, Sarah opened it up. It was a long letter in Spanish from Isabella Garcia, Estoban's descendant.

Hugo translated:

"'Dear Sarah, your letter was a surprise, but exciting. I knew nothing of our connection to anything or anyone in Haria. My grandmother, Estoban's sister, is no longer alive so I asked my mother. She could remember something about an '*aspasionado.*'" Hugo looked up wondering what that would be in English.

"It sounds a bit like 'passionate?'" guessed Sarah.

"Ah! That would fit, thank you. I'll continue. 'passionate,

intense Uncle who lived in the north of the island and decided to go to Spain to fight against Franco. They never heard anything more from him. In the end, my grandmother accepted that he must have been killed. There had been some difficulty with some English woman he met, she remembered, but we heard nothing more about it or who the English woman was.

I am very pleased to read you are able to tell me more about my mystery great uncle. Please can we meet somewhere? There is a place in the north east end of Yaiza, '*La Bodega de Santiago.*' It is an interesting building and the food is very good. Shall we meet there on Saturday at 12.00? I will have my works name badge on display so you will know who to speak to.

Looking forward to meeting you.
Saludos cordiales, Isabella."

Hugo looked at Sarah as he was folding the letter. She was smiling but had tears in her eyes.

"Wow! I couldn't have hoped for a more friendly and inviting response. Will you come with me Hugo, for moral support and to translate?"

"Yes, of course, but should Elizabeth come too? She will be Isabella's aunty, won't she?"

"Of course! It takes some working out where we all belong in the family now it has suddenly got bigger," said Elizabeth. "I would love to be with you. It is so exciting to realise we have all this family over here that we never, in a million years, would have guessed we had. It is wonderful!"

They were just about to decide how to arrange Saturday,

who and what to take to the meeting, when Carmen tapped on the door and came in. Elizabeth had gone upstairs, but hearing voices and sensing some excitement, came down to see what was going on.

"*Buenos dias,*" said Carmen as she walked in, "I have had a letter from Inés. I was a bit worried. Apart from the odd text I hadn't heard from her for a while. I know now why. She has had some challenges and has been very busy. They have a lot of work to do in the kitchen, the classroom and then even at home! Her time is very full.

She had a difficult start sadly. She is already a good cook and understands a lot about it. As you know she is very hmm... '*notable.*'

"Noticeable?" said Sarah.

"Ah *si*! She is tall, slim with red hair. She was soon being bullied by a woman who kept calling her '*el perra*,' dog or '*judia*,' Jew.

"Why would they call her that?" asked Elizabeth

"It is from years ago, even from the Inquisition. Some Jews have red hair so anyone with red hair was assumed to be Jewish, even though some Spanish people have this colour hair. They would be arrested, tortured and killed. It is a very hurtful name. One or two others began to call her these names and um… '*risa disimulada.*'" Carmen looked at Hugo for a translation.

He had to think. 'Sneer, giggle but unkindly. Ah! snigger."

"Ooh nasty!" said Sarah.

Carmen continued. "In spite of all this, Inés tried to take no notice, but the bullying it got worse. The oven temperature would get changed when she wasn't looking, so her dishes got burned, or curdled or remained uncooked. Things would boil dry even though she would set the hob very low as instructed. In spite of explaining she had set the oven at the right temperature at the start, her teacher began to think she was no good and thinking she would have to leave."

"Oh no!" said Sarah. "But she can cook very well."

"*Si*, then her knives that she bought specially to take with her, began to 'disappear' one by one. Then one day, the bully was showing off one of her 'new' knives to her friends. Inés recognised it as one of her missing knives. She had marked them all. She asked if she could hold it as it looked very special. The woman was very uneasy and refused, saying that *el perra* would steal it. Inés said, "I cannot steal what is mine in the first place," and grabbing the woman's wrist flipped her onto her back on the floor. Unknown to anyone there, my daughter has a black belt in Karate" said Carmen proudly. "No-one would suspect such a smart and elegant person to be able to do those things. Leaving the woman on the floor Inés looked in her drawers and cupboards and found all her missing knives and a few pans as well. She suggested that the oven and hobs would remain as she had set them from now on. From that day her results improved immediately and was mostly the best in the class. She gets no more bullying now. That's my girl," said Carmen. "She is now left alone to concentrate on her training. However, she noticed that Jacinta, the main bully, actually had very little of any equipment left once Inés had taken her own things back. She began buying a few items now and then, getting to school early and putting them into Jacinta's cupboards, but saying nothing. She used to just smile to herself when her former persecutor discovered them. None of the other girls said they had done it. Nobody would think it would be Inés after all the things they had done to her."

"That is the nature of a true black belt," said Hugo. "You learn so much more than just throwing people about with ease. I did the training for a while, but finished when I left for Europe and never got back to it." Sarah looked at him in amazement. There was so much more to this hard-working, quietly spoken man that she had ever imagined. She loved him even more because of it.

Carmen pressed on, determined to tell them everything that Inés has told her.

"She goes onto say how she is learning quickly the *'pricipios de la Gestion'* ("management techniques'," translated Hugo) and is now adding her own ideas. She has always experienced the styles generally used to be aggressive and domineering. She knew that by changing them to be based more on *'cooperacion, and communications'* made for a better experience for everyone all round and people were more likely to work better. Even her trainers were learning this from her!"

"Yes" said Sarah "I saw some of her style when she was helping with feeding the grape pickers earlier in the year. It was very effective. No-one noticed they were being organised. Very clever."

"She can't wait to get back here," said Carmen smiling, obviously really looking forward to seeing her daughter again. She was missing her very much every day.

"*Ay! Lo siento*, I am sorry. I have talked for a long time.

I had so much I wanted to tell you. I am so proud of her. I miss her so much, even though I didn't see her every day before, she was close and I knew I could see her any time if I needed to."

"*De nada! De nada!* Carmen. It is lovely to hear how Inés is getting on. I miss her a lot too. I'm glad she sorted that awful woman out and in such style. Fantastic! No fuss. I didn't know she did karate. How splendid. She looks so elegant, as you said, you would never guess, would you?" said Sarah. "Well, we have news of our own, Carmen. You remember how Mr. Selby hastily gave me an envelope as he left, saying he almost forgot? Mum said that reminded her of what Colombo used to do." She smiled. "Inside was the name and address of Estoban's brother's granddaughter, Isabella, down in Yaiza. I wrote to her a couple of days ago telling her we had just had some interesting news about her great grandfather, Estoban, asking if we could perhaps meet up. We were just reading her reply now before you came in. She is very interested and excited to discover she has family up here and has invited us to meet her for lunch in Yaiza on Saturday. I think/hope Hugo, you will come with me for moral support and to help with any language problems should there be any?"

Hugo nodded and added, "and we thought that Elizabeth should come too, as she is Isabella's, um… aunt, I think! It has suddenly got a bit complicated."

The next day, Carmen took Elizabeth to Haria and the North coast. She wanted to show the island from a 'local's'

viewpoint, rather than the orchestrated, 'showcase' view of the visitor tours. This gave Sarah and Hugo some much needed time alone, and together with José, time to catch up on some farm work. Hugo had been returning to his own flat in Haria each night since Elizabeth's arrival, but now his and Sarah's need for each other had become so intense that Carmen's car had hardly left the yard before they'd locked the kitchen door and were upstairs urgently but tenderly undressing each other.

Much later, Sarah began to say, "Hugo, would you to like to m…" at the same time as Hugo said, "Would you mind if I mov…," "moved in here," they said together, then laughed, suddenly aware of how shy they had been to suggest it before.

By the time the two women returned from their trip with presents, wine, cheese, bread and even green volcanic beads, Hugo had moved what belongings he wanted to the *finca*, arranged for the flat to be cleaned and for a letting agent to visit the following week to set up a letting agreement.

Sweetpea and Daisy had had little to do for a while, but Sarah realised this was about to change, seeing the focus on the men's faces.

Chapter Thirty-Eight

Elizabeth's stay on the island was disappearing rapidly. Sarah was still concerned that her mother hadn't had the day trips she had hoped to give her. They talked about it over breakfast and Elizabeth, seeing that her daughter needed to have some time to work on the farm, wondered if Carmen would give her another local tour of places not on the 'tourist route'. They went to ask her. Carmen was delighted. As time was getting short, they agreed they would go that day. Carmen said she could be ready in about half an hour, so did an excited Elizabeth. Soon they were on their way chatting happily from the moment they set off.

Meanwhile, José went up to the winery to check on the progress of the fermentation. He decided it was almost ready to decant into barrels but not quite yet. He remembered about what they had uncovered in the stable.

'*Justo lo que necesitamos* (Just what we need)' he thought. With that, he went to the stables to bring out the ploughs. Sarah joined him and together they waxed and softened the leather straps, gluing soft but very strong patches behind

306

places where the straps were badly worn or torn.

"Where did you learn to do all this, José? You have so many hidden skills." The older man smiled.

"*¡Ay!* Señora Clara" he replied in Spanish, which Sarah could understand much better by now. "She taught me many things. I taught myself more when I needed to know something."

Sarah was very fond of José. She felt so grateful for the way he had accepted her, a complete stranger, as the new owner of the farm without question. He was such a solid, dependable support through all Sarah's times of discouragement, struggles and occasional successes. Without his and Carmen's unstinting guidance and knowledge she knew she would not be where she was with the farm and her neighbouring farming community. As they worked, she shared all these thoughts with him in part Spanish, part English. José was embarrassed by such talk, but pleased his work was appreciated. In a very short time Sarah had become almost another daughter to him.

Like Hugo, he had been relieved, if not a bit concerned because of her lack of experience, about Sarah's determination to live at the farm and make it a going concern again. He had been worried that he and Carmen would have to leave if the farm was made into a holiday village. By mutual agreement, he was more of a partner in the management of the farm than just an employee. When they finished reviving the harness, they turned their attention to the plough shares themselves. They brushed off what little bits of dust that had gathered, oiled it all and sharpened the edges. By lunch time, the camel plough was all set to be used, after lying idle in the stable for a few years.

While Sarah and José were busy with their renovating, Carmen and Elizabeth had a wonderful day together. When they returned, they were full of enthusiastic descriptions of what they had been doing on their day out. Carmen shared how thrilled she had been to hear about the real reason for Clara's long stay in England all those years ago and felt a direct link to her original and only employer, Clara, through her recently 'discovered' daughter. Elizabeth was equally pleased to get to know Carmen, because she was such an interesting woman and because she knew so much about her birth mother, Clara, and who was such a support to Sarah. She still had moments of joy and amazement when she thought about how she came into the world and was then loved by two strong, determined women. It was so special to know who her real mother was and that so much love had surrounded her all her life.

Their day out had started with a visit to Mirador del Rio, a 400m high building, designed by César Manrique, high up on the Risco de Famara and been amazed by how high up it was.

"A fantastic view," enthused Elizabeth, "right out over the Atlantic. There was even another island out there!"

It was rather windy, so they had admired the view through some spectacular curved windows.

Then they had gone on to Orzola and found a windy beach to walk along for a while, keeping a wary eye on the incoming tide.

There were a few hardy people windsurfing there. "Gracious! It looked hard work, but very skilled. We had lunch – where was it, Carmen?"

"Restaurante la Merasia," said Carmen, "the fish there is very good. You and Hugo should go there sometime, Sarah. It doesn't take long to get there."

They had a brief tour of the lava caves and café at Jameos de Agua before coming back to Haria for coffee and to buy some food for supper.

"I'm cooking for us all this evening," announced Elizabeth. "I got some lovely things."

Supper was a happy occasion with everyone having tales of their day, during which it was just dropped in casually that Hugo had moved into the farm.

Apart from Carmen, muttering, "It is about time too," the news went unremarked. It was if they had assumed that he lived there already. Without quite knowing why, Sarah was relieved for reasons she didn't want to delve too deeply into.

Chapter Thirty-Nine

On Saturday, Sarah, Hugo and Elizabeth set off to Yaiza to meet one of their newly discovered family. The restaurant looked inviting. It was one storey high, white with panels of sky blue at intervals along the front. The car park was large and still fairly empty thankfully. There was a spacious outside area, under the shade of the biggest tree Sarah had seen on the island, separated from the car park by a low, white wall. The tree cast dappled shade over tables set for two, four or six people with plenty of room between them, unlike some cafes that pushed so many tables into a small space one could hardly move. The tables were set with striped cloths and terracotta or blue plates. It looked very pretty and Mediterranean.

"I wonder if Isabella is here already," said Sarah. "We are a few minutes early."

Even before they were close enough to read the name badge, Elizabeth said, "That's her, there. Goodness, Sarah, she could be your sister!"

Isabella stood up and walked towards them, looking as

amazed as they felt.

"*Buenos dias!* You have to be Sarah; we look so much alike!"

She kissed everyone on each cheek, then stood back to have another look, grinning.

"*Buenos dias,* Isabella. *Si,* I am Sarah and this is Elizabeth my mother, Estoban's daughter, and this is my good friend Hugo."

Isabella remembered she would be the 'hostess' of the meeting as she was familiar with the restaurant.

"¡*Venir! Venir!* (Come! Come!) We have a table booked. First some Cava to celebrate our meeting then coffee, *si*? Please call me Issie; Isabella is such a mouthful."

They all agreed. The table was just at the edge of the palazio, just enough in the shade, but near enough to the sun as the wind did still feel a bit cool.

There was a shy silence once they were all seated. Issie and Sarah both started talking at the same time – twice, then burst out laughing. The other two couldn't help but join in. The thin veneer of ice had been shattered.

"How did you find out about us?" asked Issie.

Sarah explained as briefly as she could about Max's intentional insult, which caused the start of the research.

"*Que susto!* How awful!" interrupted Issie, a raised eyebrow querying if this were true.

Sarah shook her head, then with the help of Hugo and Elizabeth, together with the photos and marriage certificate they had brought with them, told the story of Clara moving to the island, meeting Estoban and their secret marriage.

Sarah apologised for the secrecy and for deceiving Issie's

grandmother.

"*De nada, de nada*" said Issie. "I understand it was a different time then. We are more tolerant now," she said smiling at Hugo and Sarah. "*¡Ay! Ay! Que romantico. Por favor, continua,* (Oh! Very romantic. Please, continue)." She continued rolling her hands to encourage them to carry on with the story.

They spent some time studying the small sepia photos. The cava had all been drunk and the coffee replenished.

The tone of the story became more subdued when Sarah came to the time Estoban was called to Spain much earlier than expected. He was torn between staying with his pregnant wife or following his heart to go to defend his parents' homeland from the dictator Franco. Clara could see the passion burning in his eyes and urged him to go, knowing he would never be fully with her if he stayed.

"I will be back very soon; you'll see," were the last words he said to Clara. There was a sombre silence following the news of his death, the return of a pitiful few of his belongings and Clara's sudden departure for England.

At this point in the narrative, the waiter came to take their orders for lunch. The need to choose between so many delicious sounding dishes raised everyone's spirits again.

Once the order had been given, Elizabeth continued with the story of her adoption by Clara's sister Gwen. There was more eager studying of photos and settling Issie's concern for Elizabeth discovering she was adopted after all this time.

"Obviously it was a shock," said Elizabeth, "but I couldn't help but feel the love the two sisters had for each other and for me. I had two loving mothers, even though I only knew one of them then. I am very happy with the discovery and it solves a few mysteries like where all the photos went that Mum and Dad took of me. They took loads almost every day, so there should have been bags of them. Mum sent most of them here so my birth mother could follow my progress."

Sarah continued the story, "Our Solicitor came over to visit, bringing with him all the letters he had, with the details of the wedding and so on. Just as he was leaving, he said he had been doing some more research and gave me this envelope," she pushed it over to Issie. "And that is when I contacted you last week."

Issie sighed, regarding her newly discovered family with pleasure. "¡Ah! The truth is so much kinder than the um… *especulacion and los chismes.*"

"Speculation and gossip," said Hugo quietly.

"*Si,*" said Issie.

Over lunch the conversation was more general; where everyone lived, Yaiza, the farm, the camels…

"Oh! You are '*la dama de los camellos*'? A friend was telling me about when she went grape picking at this farm near Haria, and for three days, these camels carried the grapes back to the winery to be pressed. Then they came to the thanksgiving supper all dressed up."

Sarah laughed. "Yes, that's me at the *finca Los Palmas.* Hugo here is the one who made the garlands and dressed Sweetpea and Daisy in all their finery. They seemed to enjoy being dressed up and also the company. Daisy went looking for everyone when we had finished and the people had all gone home. She seemed disappointed we weren't going to have those many visitors every day. She is quite a madam and loves the attention."

"Sweetpea and Daisy! What lovely names!" said Issie.

"Thank you," said Sarah. "Sweetpea arrived out of the blue. She had run away from a cruel camel breeder. She was badly injured and beaten poor thing. She made herself at home as soon as she arrived. Her arrival made such a difference to me. I was about to give up at that point. I had no idea what I was doing or what I had to do and what I did was exhausting me and not moving things forward at all. She became my friend and helped to keep me going."

"I had no idea you had got so low. You never mentioned anything in your letters," said Elizabeth.

"Nor I," said Hugo, looking at Sarah with renewed respect.

Sarah shrugged with an apologetic smile. "I didn't want you to think I couldn't cope, I suppose. Sweetpea was so much help with the heavy work and things moved on more quickly. I loved having her around. Then some weeks later she disappeared overnight – I never shut her into the stable it would be too hot. Oh dear! I was distraught - *deconsolado* – for so long. I had decided she had died somewhere in the volcanic lands. Then she came back one morning, with her baby Daisy. What a joyful day that was. Sweet pea is definitely my camel, but now Daisy is definitely Hugo's"

Issie then explained that her great grandparents had both died as had Estoban's brother. His wife Ana, was not so old but her memory was not good. She could vaguely remember the news of her future brother-in-law's sudden departure to fight in Spain. No more was heard of him she said, so they all gradually accepted that he had been killed, but they did wonder why they weren't told.

"Of course, that news would have gone to his wife, that no-one knew he had," remarked Sarah.

Issie nodded in agreement and continued with her story. "Grandma remembered there had been a fuss when her parents-in-law heard that their son wanted to marry a non-Catholic English woman who farmed in the North of the island; a long way away in those days and farming as a profession for women was not well regarded." She finished with a shrug indicating she didn't understand such an attitude.

To save embarrassment, it was decided that everyone would pay for their own meal but Issie insisted the Cava and coffee were her treat.

"*Gracias*! said Sarah. She looked at Hugo and Elizabeth as if to get their agreement, then asked Issie if she would like to come to the farm to see what it was like. Elizabeth was due to leave for London the next Sunday so would Issie be able to come on Saturday for lunch? Hugo said he would message directions.

Issie was delighted and asked if they would mind if her sister came as well.

"Not at all," said Sarah.

On that note, photos, letters and papers were gathered up carefully; goodbyes were said with lots of hugs and kisses and the meeting broke up.

The hurt, disappointment and grief of the past were thus healed and the two families were finally united, after three generations not knowing of the existence of the other.

Chapter Forty

A couple of days after the family reunion, with the newly renovated ploughs, Hugo and José decided to give it a go. José's leg was still not strong enough to withstand the various physical stresses that would be involved, so Hugo, with instructions from José standing nearby, began work on the smaller patch of land near the house, where they wanted to grow some vegetables that season.

Sweetpea was curious about the new harness and strange machine behind her. She was confused by Hugo walking behind her, when usually people were in front or at her side. She kept wanting to turn around to go and stand behind him. Also, Daisy, always eager to help Hugo in any task, bounced over and around man and plough. After half an hour nothing had been achieved at all. José and Hugo were about to give up and see about getting the tractor repaired and use that to plough the fields even if it did destroy the picon mulch.

Sarah, looking on from the kitchen, was laughing so much tears were rolling down her cheeks. She wanted the camel plough to work as much as the men. The camels needed to feel useful, to be used. She had an idea.

Wiping her eyes, Sarah made coffee for the two men struggling outside, then with two large mugs of hot coffee and a big packet of their favourite biscuits, went out to share her idea. Half an hour later they made another attempt. This time Sarah walked at Sweetpea's head to keep her going forward. Daisy was rigged up with her specially sized panniers. In one side, there were bottles of water for the humans, with some cake in a tin. In the other side were a few odds and ends to even up the weight. As a result, Daisy knew she had a role to play as well and calmed down. They all set off, with Sarah leading both camels and José giving Hugo instructions. Even with Sweetpea pulling hard, it was not easy for Hugo to keep the plough going in a straight line. However, after a few lines, he got better at it and soon was ploughing a good straight furrow.

Although the pace seemed slow, the first small field was ploughed by lunch time, much to everyone's surprise.

"Phew! That was a good plan, Sarah. I was about to give up," confessed Hugo. "Now Sweetpea and Daisy understand what is expected of them and will remember what to do when we do it again."

"*Muy bien*! Good," said José, full of smiles.

"*Aleamal alsaalih! Aleamal alsaalih alfatiat!* Good work girls," said Sarah, dismantling the harness, ploughs and panniers and leading the camels back to the stable for a drink, some food and a rest, fussed them and stroked them.

Just then Carmen and Elizabeth emerged carrying a tray laden with a big dish of thick Spanish frittata, crusty bread and dishes of salad, together with cans of cold San Miguel. They had both been busy in Carmen's kitchen.

"Fantastic! Thank you, Carmen," chorused the three workers. Everyone sat around the table on the terrace, chatted, laughed, admired Hugo's new skill as a camel ploughman and generally relaxed together. Elizabeth couldn't have been happier. She enjoyed being with Carmen, being surrounded by everyone's optimistic happy energy and the calm supportive atmosphere of the farm itself. She was not able to see the hazy figure of her birth mother standing near her, so happy to see her daughter after all these years even if she was in a different dimension now. Sarah, once again, expressed concern that her mother wasn't having much of a holiday during her stay at the farm.

"Actually," said Elizabeth, "I would rather be involved in the farm. I like to be busy and Carmen and I are like life-long friends, which is wonderful. I'm not a great one for window shopping or buying lots of stuff. I've had some great days out in between, especially going to Yaiza to meet Issie and going round the north coast and Haria with Carmen and the coach tour. I know you all have a lot to do on the farm and can't afford to take too many days off. I'm enjoying myself more than I have for ages. Thank you."

Sarah noticed Carmen looked wistful when the trip to Yaiza was mentioned and thought that she would really have liked to be there, even though she understood it was better for Sarah and Elizabeth to go on their own, with Hugo as translator if needed.

"Carmen, Issie and Elena are coming here on Saturday. Would you join us for lunch? You would be able to tell them about Clara when she was younger and what you remember about Estoban. They will be eager to hear as much as possible. We have so much more to share with them than we were able to when we had lunch with them."

Carmen nodded, pleased to be involved. She had spent so many years with Señora Clara.

There was a break for a siesta, then camels and the ploughing team set about working the second larger paddock. Hugo could see the advantage of using a camel as opposed to a tractor. It was more manoeuvrable and had less negative impact on the soil. He was working out how this system could be used in the European style vineyard where the vines were all in straight rows.

Now that everyone knew what to do, even Daisy, who was there with her panniers if anyone wanted a drink or a biscuit. The field was finished smoothly and quickly.

Sarah had read that it was counterproductive to "treat train" camels. They are very focussed on food, unlike dogs. They don't associate the action they are being trained to do with the treat. They understand the food part and will be inclined to skip the action part and barge their owner out of the way to get at the food more quickly. 'They are too smart for their own good,' thought Sarah.

Once out of the plough share, Sarah made a fuss of Sweetpea and brushed her down – a nightly ritual they both enjoyed. Hugo took off Daisy's panniers and groomed her with similar mutual enjoyment. The camels grumbled and purred, had their usual evening meal of hay and a drink, then lay down for the night.

A great sense of progress and satisfaction hung over

everyone at the shared supper. Talk turned to what they would be able to plant and when. It all felt very positive.

Chapter Forty-One

Sarah was looking forward to showing her two cousins, Issie and Elena, around *finca Los Palmas*. She walked out to meet them and was expecting to see Issie smiling, as she had been when they left Yaiza just a few days before. However, both Issie and Elena looked like they'd been having a row, their faces were thunderous.

Sarah smiled anyway and said, "Hi, you both look upset. You'd better come inside. I'll make some coffee and you can tell me what has happened."

They'd hardly got inside before Elena turned on her and almost shouted, "I'll tell you what has happened. You come along out of nowhere, all smiles, then tell us our great grandparents forced two people into having a secret marriage and because of that your mother, that must be you," she rounded on Elizabeth, "had to be adopted and brought up by someone else. Neither you nor Sarah knew who your 'real' mother was. You breeze in here saying the farm was left to you in someone's will whom you didn't know, never heard of. Well, how do we know you haven't made all this up. Now we are deprived of a farm that should be ours; not belong to some English foreigner trying to hide her illegitimacy!"

Sarah was shocked and distressed by the vehemence of this tirade. She indicated to her mother to sit down and keep quiet, then served the coffee and put a plate of little cakes on the table. Issie was looking very uncomfortable but could find no way of calming her sister down.

From her time in London, Sarah had learned how to deal with over-heated angry clients who had completely misunderstood a particular situation.

She sat down and calmly drank some coffee and had a nibble of her cake, looking expectantly directly at Elena, as if waiting for her to continue. She carried on for a while about being cheated out of her inheritance and how it wasn't right and why should she believe anything that Sarah said.

In a very calm and steady voice, Sarah set out to tell Elena the facts, not allowing her to interrupt, and to present her with any supporting documents.

"I'm sorry you should feel so distressed by this news. It does sound rather far-fetched I admit. If Estoban, your grandfather's brother had indeed bought this farm, I would agree with you. Wait!" She raised her hand to silence Elena who looked ready to launch into another monologue. "However, he didn't buy it; he never bought it. He wasn't interested in it. Clara Powell bought it with her own money before she met Estoban, so was the legal owner. Here are the deeds, signed by a solicitor in England and by one here in Lanzarote, thus ensuring the agreement complied with the Island's laws.

"We didn't say your great grandparents forced Clara and

Estoban into a secret wedding. It was a very different time then to what it is now. It may look like that to you on the surface, but I'm sure you know how religious and social beliefs were like, way back then. It was also a very turbulent time, with the war in Spain. If anything, the two young people brought it on themselves."

"Well, that's alright for you to say," blustered Elena, beginning to calm down but still not willing to give up her ideas. "Where's the proof of all this?"

"Right here!" said Sarah placing the deeds of the farm on the table in front of the young women. "To put your mind at rest, I will fetch the rest of the information you need."

By the time Sarah returned, her arms full of files and photograph albums, Elena had read the deeds and rather grumpily conceded the farm could not be theirs, unless bequeathed in Clara's Will.

"Remember," said Sarah, as she put everything down with a thud in front of Elena, "Clara had never met Estoban's parents, so she never knew anything about his family, only that they didn't want her to marry their son. He was called to Spain very much sooner than he had anticipated. By this time Clara had discovered she was pregnant." Again, Sarah held up her hand to calm Elena's outburst. "I'm sure theirs' wasn't the only marriage ceremony held with the bride already expecting a child, whatever their religion. Estoban didn't want to leave without marrying the woman he loved. He knew there was a real risk he could be killed. There was no time to discuss the matter with his parents, but he didn't want them to be hurt by hearing rumours of his marriage to an English stranger. Hence the hasty secret wedding. It must have been very difficult for him, torn between loyalty to his parents, his fierce and deep love for Clara and being very aware of his sense of duty to return to his parents' homeland to fight for its freedom. Here is a copy of the wedding certificate and a photo of them on their wedding day."

Still reluctant to let go of her version of events, Elena grumbled, "They don't look like they were at a wedding to me. Where are their fine clothes? They look as if they have just rolled into the church as an afterthought, after going to a market!"

"Exactly," said Issie, speaking for the first time since their arrival. "If they had turned up with Clara in a long wedding gown and veil and Estoban obviously in his new suit, it wouldn't have been a secret, would it? They had to look like villagers just dropping in at church to light a candle and say a prayer."

"Hmm! I suppose you're right," said Elena. "What's in here?"

"That is all they could recover from Estoban's remains after the vehicle he was in was blown up by a big landmine. Clara kept them close to her until she died."

The tragedy of the situation finally hit home to Elena. Tears began to form in the corner of her eyes.

"Oh! that is so sad. How awful, and this is all? A few uniform buttons, the Army ID book and a posthumous medal?"

"I'm sorry to be so graphic but it was a powerful mine. It exploded right underneath the personnel carrier. There were bits of body everywhere, with no way of identifying any of it. I don't know if the buttons were from his own uniform or from the Army stores. The ID book would have had a copy in HQ. Apparently, there was enough left of the one he carried to identify him as one of the men who had been killed – hence the medals. Of course, they had Clara's address so they could notify her of his death but not necessarily that of his parents. They had no idea what had happened to him as I have said.

Elena put her hand to her mouth. "War is so brutal!" She shook her head and drank some now cold coffee to stop herself from crying.

"It was a desperate and confused time, Elena. People here were afraid they would be taken over by the Nazis. There were already a lot of Germans here and many German ships were anchored at different ports around the island. It must have been awful. It was a dangerous time for anyone suspected of having parents of different nationalities. They would not have survived."

Elena let out a long sigh. She looked at Sarah. "I'm sorry Sarah. I seem to have got completely the wrong end of the stick and was looking at the situation as it would be now."

Sarah walked to Elena's side of the table.

"Come! Let me give you a hug. I understand how that could happen."

The two women embraced for a long time. When they both stepped apart, they each had to dry their eyes, which made them both laugh.

"I think something stronger than coffee is called for here. Mum will you make some fresh coffee and I'll get the brandy and glasses. Spanish tradition, Mum," she added, seeing Elizabeth's shocked expression at them drinking brandy in the morning.

The tension drained away from everyone and from the kitchen. Soon they were chatting as the cousins examined some of the letters Sarah had brought in; the ones Clara's sister wrote to her every week to tell her about Elizabeth's progress. Sarah phoned Carmen to come round to meet the sisters. In the end everyone had an enjoyable day. They all went to Carmen's house, where the young women were introduced to José and Hugo. They had heard the shouting and decided to keep out of the way for a while.

Soon they were all enjoying Carmen's delicious paella and chocolate cake, both dishes guaranteed to lift the mood of any gathering. Back at the *finca*, the girls were delighted to look around the house and see the china and glassware Clara had carefully packed away.

"I think she had gathered these things together for her 'bottom drawer' – to bring to her marriage. Would you like a few pieces to keep as a link to a great aunt you didn't know you had?" They each chose a beautiful vase, agreeing they would display flowers in it all the time.

Sarah and Hugo took the cousins to meet the camels. They weren't too sure about them, but loved the story. They visited the winery and the vineyards close to the house and some of the nearer parts of the farm. The vines growing in the specially made hollows interested them. They hadn't seen them close up before. Once they had heard about the condensation rolling down to the bottom of the hollow, thereby sustaining the vines, they were impressed by the ingenuity of people who had lived on the Island long before them. They could see how much land was terraced on the steep sides of the volcano and how much the prickly pear had invaded that part of the farm.

"Oh!" said Issie, "That's what they make prickly pear jam out of. I have never tasted it because the plants look so spiny. I couldn't think what the jam could be made out of."

"You must take a jar back for each of you," said Sarah. "Carmen and I have made quite a lot between us. The fruit lose their spines when they are ripe."

"Thank you. That would be interesting. Knowing you have made them will give us confidence to taste it!" Issie and Elena both laughed.

When they heard about the beetles that lived on the cactus, which provided a dye that could produce so many shades, they remarked that perhaps that was why there so many of the cacti everywhere.

"They do grow like weeds," said Carmen. "If one of the pads gets knocked off, onto the ground, it quickly sets root and grows to a large plant. They are difficult to get rid of. We thought we would try to make the most out of them seeing as there are so many of them here."

Everyone nodded in agreement.

This led on to mention of the upcoming Fashion Show. When Sarah asked them if they would like to be involved, maybe as models, Issie and Elena were very eager and willing to be a part of it; they wanted to know all the details, dates, times…

"Does this mean we can have some couture clothes?" asked Issie. "Made to measure?"

"Absolutely, part of the perks I'd say," added Sarah.

By this time all disagreement had been put to one side,

making room for them all to explore the feelings aroused by meeting a whole new part of the family.

"Now I come to think about it," said Elena, laughing and looking hard at Sarah, "You could so easily be taken for our sister!"

"Brilliant!" said Sarah. "I'm an only child and would have loved some sisters, and now, here you are. Fantastic!"

Chapter Forty-Two

Elizabeth returned to UK with cases full off various jams, volcanic green beads and wine from *Los Palmas*. She said she would return later on for a week to see the Show.

The weeks leading up to the Show were manic. Hugo and José wanted to press on with the ploughing in order to plant more vegetables when the time was right. Further rummaging in the stable uncovered a harrow for a camel to pull.

"*Perfecto*," said José, "Now we can prepare the ground very quickly so we can plant the seeds for tomatoes, peppers, squash, peas and beans. We will be growing so many vegetables soon. The harrowing makes the soil finer and easier to plant the seeds and easier for the seeds to germinate and grow." He beamed at Hugo at the thought of finally growing something to eat on the farm, apart from figs. The wine grapes were not suitable to be eaten, only to produce juice for the wine.

"We could even try a few 'exotics' like chickpeas and chillies," said Hugo, inspired by the potential of this new direction. It is warm enough here in the summer. It is worth a try."

José agreed. Neither of them had felt so enthused about the farm for ages. Both agreed it was a good feeling.

The camels had quickly learned what was expected of them with the ploughing, so Hugo and José expected the harrowing to go as smoothly and quickly, which it did. Hugo marvelled yet again at the quick intelligence of these beasts and their excellent memories.

While the men were occupied with the planting, Sarah, Carmen, Valeria and Bella were gathering all the elements needed for the Show. They were very pleased to welcome Issie and Elena into the plans. The girls very much wanted to be involved in the preparations as well as being models.

The rest of the models were chosen to represent a wide range of age and sizes and both men and women. Valeria was pleased with the variety and was busy with the minor alterations for the clothes to fit everyone perfectly. Sarah could see how much work was involved in getting the Show up and running in time. She could see Valeria was getting very stressed. She paid a visit to the college in Arrecife to speak to the Head of the Fashion and Design department. Sarah's idea was to ask if some students could help with the alterations and final bits of dressmaking involved. Once the Head understood what was being planned and the charity that would benefit from the ticket sales and the end of Show collection, she was fully on board with the idea. Sarah emphasised how it would be good experience for any of the students who helped out. There was enough to do at all levels of the Show to occupy a number of students.

Later that afternoon, the Head of Department rang Sarah saying they had ten students to help with the sewing, preparations and backroom part of the show to give them real life experience of what was involved. Soon the ten young men and women arrived at Valeria's studio with sewing machines and a high level of competence - to Valeria's relief – and excitement at being involved in a fashion show outside of college.

Bella phoned Sarah the following day. "Sarah, you are known throughout the Island as "*La dama de los camellos.*" Sarah laughed at that title. "It would be a great attraction if you came here with the two of them in the harnesses that they wore for the thanksgiving supper. If you agreed, I could arrange it with the police."

"Wow! They would certainly attract a lot of interest and curiosity!" said Sarah. "They are not easily distracted by noise and seem to enjoy the attention and being around people. How would we get there? We don't have the camel equivalent of a 'horse box'."

"It's not far to Haria from the farm, is it? About 4k? Could they walk that far?"

"Not on the road, no. Their feet are too soft. I'll ask José. Perhaps he will know of someone who has suitable transport. I'll get back to you."

José did know of someone who would be happy to provide the truck and he would leave it at the farm a week or so before the show to give the camels time to get used to being inside a much smaller space. Sarah and Hugo agreed that Clara must be nudging events along, as so many things were just falling into place. She had appeared to each of them several times, smiling, looking very happy.

Sweetpea and Daisy were gradually introduced to the 'camel box,' as Sarah called it. They did a few trial runs after they got used to being inside it. Hugo drove while Sarah stayed in the back soothing and encouraging the big creatures to keep calm. There was little need. They seemed to enjoy the experience and were curious about what they could see through the ventilation spaces.

Hugo oiled the harnesses to keep them soft and pliable and Carmen made a few additions in bright red to put on them.

It was very quiet on the farm, which Sarah had found soothing after the constant noise of London. To get the camels used to louder noises, Sarah played CDs of people talking and shouting, with the noise of cars and so on. Would it help? Sarah didn't know but was encouraged that neither animal seemed disturbed by the loud noises, though Daisy did wander about looking for all the people she could hear!

The day of the Show arrived. Everyone arranged to meet at the church. The priest was as excited as any of them. It was good PR for the church and the fee would make a lot of difference to it.

Chairs were put out on the Plaza. There were lights on the trees along the catwalk already and the music all set up. The café had been reserved for an hour before the show to provide cava and nibbles for the invited guests. Elizabeth had already arrived on the island.

Satisfied they could do no more, Sarah, Carmen, Elizabeth and their cousins went back to the farm to change and to fetch the camels. The women were wearing dresses in all shades of red; the men in red shirts. The camels were soon in their festive harnesses. They looked magnificent and knew it. They looked even more regal than usual.

They were all gathered in the kitchen having a fortifying coffee, with brandy and some chocolate cake, when they heard a car pull up on the drive. They all looked at each other concerned. The memory of the untimely arrival of Hugo's ex-fiancée came to Sarah and Hugo at the same time. They nodded to each other and together went out to greet whatever or whoever awaited in the yard. They had hardly got outside when they let out whoops of joy and quickly returned to the kitchen bringing with them Inés, who had just returned to Lanzarote.

"Inés, Inés! *Mi querida hiya*! (My darling daughter!)" Carmen rushed over to her daughter, giving her a big hug and many kisses, closely followed by José.

"I wanted to be here for the Show so left a few days before the end of term. My goodness! Don't you all look amazing," said Inés.

"It is amazing to see you Inés, but we were just leaving. What would you like to do? Stay to freshen up and follow us later or come with us now?"

"Give me a few minutes to use the bathroom and I will come with you. I have a jacket in the car that Valeria made for me with some material that Mama had dyed. I will wear that."

"Perfect!" said Carmen.

333

Chapter Forty-Three

It was the day of the Show. Hugo and Sarah took the camels in the truck; Sarah took her show clothes in a bag to change into when she got there. She didn't want camel wee or worse splashing on her during the journey. The people involved in the show parked behind the church. Sarah got the camels out of the 'camel box' then went into the church to change into her red outfit. Hugo stayed with the animals to make sure they didn't set off after Sarah and tidied up their harnesses. Everyone in the church was all set to go. With her heart beating as if to burst from her chest with excitement and nerves, Sarah re-joined Hugo and the camels out of sight at the side of the church.

The Plaza was packed with people, the lights were on, music was playing, the guests were seated with a programme and order form. Bella was at her MC's desk.

On the dot of 4.40pm as the light was already dimming, the music went quiet. An expectant hush fell over the crowd. A spotlight lit up the space at the side of the church. Into the space stepped Sarah leading Sweetpea, closely followed by

Hugo with Daisy resplendent in their colourful harnesses. The camels looked amazing, matched only by Sarah and Hugo, both looking distinguished and very different in their red outfits; such a beautiful couple. It was a very dramatic tableau.

The whole crowd gasped in astonishment, then erupted into cheers and applause.

"Ladies and gentlemen," announced Bella. "*La dam et el hombre de los camellos*!'

More enthusiastic cheers and whistles.

Sarah, Hugo and the camels walked regally down through the crowd to the end of the runway, the camels loving the attention. Then they turned and walked back to the church.

The music, that had accompanied this short parade, stopped; the lights went out. Then in a burst of sound and light, Issie and Elena stood in the illuminated doorway of the church in the most gorgeous richly coloured dresses. With a reassuring smile to each other and holding hands, the two sisters walked down past the seated guests, did a couple of very professional turns and walked back.

More models emerged in quick succession, two young women, two more mature women, teenage boys, 30- year-old and 60-year-old men, everyone in '*Los Palmas* red' in some way, varying shades from deep rich red to palest pink, all highlighted and off-set by ivory, cream and taupe with bright orange here and there to add to the festive air of the show. Cameras flashed everywhere. People cheered and applauded.

Then there was a silent pause… an air of expectation hung over the crowd. It looked as if something extra was about to happen.

The music changed again, this time to popular tunes of the 1930s by Cab Calloway, Artie Shaw and Tommy Dorsey. The infectious beat was hard to resist and people were just about to get up to dance when the spot light blazed onto the church door once again.

There was a puzzled silence as a couple appeared in the doorway wearing Clara's plain blue suit and Estoban's old working clothes. A disappointed murmur began to spread through the crowd.

A puzzled silence fell over the crowd; what was going on? Where were all the brightly coloured outfits they had just seen?

The microphone crackled into life. Bella began to explain what these outfits were.

"Ladies and gentlemen, by special request, this is what Clara Powell of *finca Los Palmas* and Estoban Garcia wore to their hasty, secret wedding, just days before Estoban had to leave for Spain to fight against Franco," said Bella. "The family were not pleased with Estoban's choice of bride, so the ceremony could not be made public. Estoban knew he would be in danger in Spain and wanted to get married before he left. The plain clothes were to make them look like people going to church in the afternoon for a few moments silent prayer, as people did in those days."

A gasp went around the Plaza followed by excited conversation. Whispered comments of "so they were married after all" and "so that's why such dowdy outfits…"

"Now, to conclude our show, and to honour Sarah's grandmother, Clara Garcia, the clothes they had hoped to wear if events had unfolded differently. Sadly, Estoban never returned to wear his suit; he was killed very soon after he arrived in Spain. This pair, so much in love, were never together on the earth again."

An awed hush fell over the crowd. Many knew of the rumours that had circulated about Sarah and were intrigued by her unexpected appearance. The truth was so much more satisfying than anyone could have speculated.

Once more the spotlight shone on the dark church door. A young woman walked out to the centre of the doorway. She was wearing the wedding gown that had been found at the bottom of the trunk. It fitted the model perfectly. She looked gorgeous in the closely fitting, swathed ivory silk. She was joined by a young man dressed in Estoban's stylish 1930s suit. The music changed to the big band sound of Tommy Dorsey as the couple walked down the catwalk. Cheers, whistles and applause broke out with a buzz of conversation.

In between the cameras flashing and cheers, were sounds of noses being blown, signs of tears being surreptitiously wiped, then all the models came out together. They looked fantastic. The whole collection was so varied, so attractive, so special, so wearable. The camels came out once more but just to the space at the side of the Church.

Bella spoke to the crowd, which had grown steadily bigger throughout the show as word got out about how good and different it was.

"Thank you for your wonderful reception. If you have enjoyed the Show, please make a contribution in the buckets being brought around. The Show was held for the

'*Asociación Tinguafaya*' that provides much needed respite care for families with children with terminal illness or serious learning difficulties. Thank you for your generosity. Myself, Valeria, Issie and Elena will be here for a while to receive your orders. Thank you very much."

Photographers and Journalists gathered round the camels, the models - everyone involved in the show, even the Priest. This was great copy. Great for Haria; good for the Lanzarotean fashion industry and good for the island in general. The copy would no doubt spread around the world. Every paper likes a 'good news' story. The café sent a complimentary hamper of Cava and tapas to the church; they had had such a profitable afternoon from the crowds who came to see the Show. Adverts sent out days before had hinted that the camels may be present, which drew a lot of people.

Issie and Elena were overjoyed to have been part of such an exciting and successful Show. They returned home full of plans to tell their friends about their terrific day and encourage them to order some of the clothes they had seen and worn. They said a fond goodbye to Sarah and Elizabeth, now securely embraced into their Lanzarote family.

Eventually people dispersed, the music console packed up, lights taken down, chairs returned to the Ayuntamiento and clothes carefully packed to go back to Valeria's workshop/studio. Each model had an outfit of their choice to take home – with 80% discount, much to their delight.

It was late by the time camels and people returned to the farm. The camels were relieved to be back in the familiar calm of their stable. Sarah and Hugo removed their jangly harnesses, brushed them down, refreshed their food and water and after giving them a lot of fuss and telling them how wonderful they had been, left them to rest after their exciting day.

Back in the kitchen, the exhausted but elated friends celebrated with large glasses of Cava. Sarah produced a hamper with dinner and dessert for everyone. They were all so tired it was wonderful to have a delicious meal there ready to eat.

Once the meal was finished, people said weary goodnights; Sarah, Hugo and Elizabeth went to bed. Carmen and José left for their house and to finally catch up with Inés, who had surprised and delighted everyone by arriving home earlier than expected.

Chapter Forty-Four

Elizabeth had arranged for a working week off which gave her ten days in Lanzarote. The Show was on her second day. 'In at the deep end' was how she experienced it. The day after the Show, everyone was very pleased with how it had gone, but were very weary. After a leisurely breakfast of coffee, crusty baguette with unsalted butter and strawberry jam and warm crumbly pastries, all thanks to Hugo's now daily early morning trip to the bakery, it was decided they would all go for a 'farm walk' and take the camels with them. Sarah and Hugo wanted to see how they could further develop the farm to increase its income and realise its potential.

Sarah went to sort out the camels.

"You were brilliant," she told them, as she cleaned the stable and put in fresh hay and water. They each had a piece of alfalfa cake as thanks. "I think you enjoyed the colour and attention. You looked very noble; quite magnificent." She smiled as she groomed them. She loved the calm routine; her 'daily relaxation meditation' she called it. As she brushed, memories of the fashion show reeled across her mind's eye.

Then the images got all broken up; Sarah was aware that now she was looking down the catwalk from about 2.00m up. She turned to look at Sweetpea; her white camel was looking intently at her. Then she aware of moving down through the crowd, seeing all the cameras flashing, the laughing faces, people looking out of their upstairs windows, pouring out of cafes and shops. She could feel her heart expand with a wonderful feeling of exhilaration. Sweetpea rumbled and grumbled. If camels ever had a 'laughing face,' Sarah was looking at it now.

"Is this how you felt, Sweetpea? This is you remembering your entrance at the beginning of the Show, isn't it?" The image faded from her mind. Sweetpea nodded her head.

"Oh, Sweetpea! I'm so glad you enjoyed it. You were wonderful. I think, because of you, we have had loads of donations." She gave the camel's neck a big hug. Daisy joined in for a cuddle too.

"Sorry to disturb your camel love-in," said Hugo, grinning, regarding the love of his life surrounded by camels. "Come on. You'll stink. Elizabeth and I are all ready for the farm safari."

"Gosh, yes! Love-in indeed. Actually, it was I suppose. Sweetpea was showing me how much she enjoyed the Show and what she felt like during her dramatic entrance and first journey down the catwalk. She loved it."

Hugo had got used to these telepathic communications between Sarah and her camel. It was really special. And happened fairly frequently. He often wondered what it would be like to have such a connection with Daisy. To his surprise he had got very fond of her. Then he became aware of a strange feeling in his head. It was as if he was standing inside the stable looking out at himself in the doorway and he was filled with what he could only describe as love. Then he seemed to be looking down the catwalk from above his head. He wanted to skip and jump with excitement but had a sense that he shouldn't. The feeling went and he came back to looking inside the stable from the doorway. He looked at Daisy and she was looking intently at him. He burst out laughing dispersing any remaining images and emotions.

"Wow! Sarah! Daisy has just showed me her experience of standing at the side entrance in the spotlight. Do you remember she started to skip and buck? I was worried that she was frightened by the noise and bright lights. No, she loved it and was so excited, she couldn't keep still, until a rumble from her mum and calm words from me reminded her of her role, so she settled down and we all set off down the catwalk. How special was that? He walked over to Daisy and gave her a big hug.

"Now who's having a camel love-in?" said Sarah. "Come on. Mum will be waiting."

Both laughing and followed by the camels, they gathered up Elizabeth and set off for a gentle walk around the farm.

When they got back, Carmen came to the door. "Hola! Put the camels in the stable and come in for coffee. Inés wants to see you and meet Elizabeth. She was very excited to hear the true story about Clara and Estoban."

They went over to Carmen's house and enjoyed a happy hour, reminiscing over coffee all the events of the previous day.

As time was going on, Sarah, Hugo and Elizabeth

returned to the farmhouse kitchen for a late lunch of bread, cheese, tomatoes and olives. While they were eating, Sarah began to outline an idea that had been going round in her head since their walk, especially after hearing all about Inés's time at the cookery school.

"Wasn't it fantastic yesterday? she said. "Everyone worked so hard to get it organised. I don't know how much we raised but the collection buckets looked full when they came back. I've been thinking it would be nice to have another 'Thank You' supper like we had after the grape harvest. I know it was tainted at the end by that awful man, Max. However, it was great until then, and even afterwards, some good came of it, because he was caught trying to do to us what he had been doing to other vintners in the area for years and is now in prison.

It would be good to have a totally joyful party to thank everyone for their hard work – even the Priest!" Sarah laughed, "he seemed to enjoy it as much as everyone else. He was really pleased to have the church used for something other than religious services. It may have given him food for thought. It is Monday today. When are you going back, Mum?"

"On Sunday afternoon," replied Elizabeth.

"Shall we have the party on Saturday, 5.30 for 6.00? I'll go and get Carmen and Inés so we can have a chat about it."

Hugo went to help José in the winery. It would be about time to move the fermented juice to barrels. He's checked Clara's notes and it was important to do it when the wine was ready rather than wait for some 'favourable time.'

'That makes it simpler,' he thought.

Carmen and Inés arrived with chocolate cake and Sarah made some fresh coffee.

"Do you make several of these cakes every week, Carmen?" asked Sarah. "You seem to have an endless supply – thank goodness for me!" They all laughed.

"Do you think we can get a party together for Saturday?"

"Yes!" said the other three women together.

"I will be here," said Inés. "I am on extended Christmas break. I have worked so hard I have finished all the work. I have nothing to do till next term. A party will be great fun and very much appreciated by everyone I'm sure."

"Okay!" said Sarah, "how shall we do this?"

Carmen said she would invite Valeria and Bella, and ask them to contact all the people who helped them before and on the day.

"I'm not sure about the priest, though. He may put a damper on everyone's spirits," said Inés.

"Yes," said Elizabeth. "People may feel they have to "behave,"" she made quotation marks in the air. "Perhaps we could send him a bottle of the *Los Palmas* wine – very special, I believe, and a cake?"

"That is a good idea. He will feel appreciated for his part in the show," said Carmen.

"The variety of food we made for the Thanksgiving Supper went down well," said Inés. "Shall we do similar? I would love to make some of the dishes I have learned to make in Barcelona as well, perhaps some with a hint of Christmas? It is not so far away now."

"I have a few dishes I can make," said Elizabeth. "I have made them so often I can remember the ingredients."

"Fantastic!" said Sarah, getting her notebook. "If you give me a list of the ingredients you need, I can get them. I've missed the market in Haria though; it was at the weekend."

"Never mind," said Carmen, "there is the farmer's market, Mercola Agricola in Teguise, on a Wednesday and Thursday. You can get organic fruit and veg there, honey, cheese, all sorts."

"It can be rather touristy, there with tourist prices," said Inés. "Mama, Sarah, do you know the suppliers who bring their goods to Haria market?"

"Yes, I often go directly to them if I can't get to the market," said Carmen. "I have a list of the addresses of most of them. I will bring you a copy, Sarah. It is useful. We could go tomorrow and collect what we need from the producers. It will be more economical that way."

"Perfect!" said Sarah

It was Friday evening. All the preparations had been done that could be done. All the invitations had been sent; only a few said they were unable to come. Bella's brother said he would love to come, but only if he could bring his turntables and provide the music. "That would be great," said Sarah.

Elizabeth had gone to bed early. It had been a busy day full of conversation, laughter and the occasional moment of potential disaster averted at the last moment.

Sarah and Hugo were having a quiet drink on the terrace. They found, bought or borrowed several chimeneas and big fire bowls which they had put around the terrace. It could get chilly at night in December. Hugo lit one nearest to them. It was soon throwing out some welcome heat. The two of them sat in companionable silence appreciating the calm after all the activity of the last few weeks.

Sarah turned to Hugo, "You know? I have never met a man quite like you."

Hugo laughed softly, not quite sure where this was going. "What do you mean?"

"Well, you are always there for me and have been right from the start. If I don't know about something or what to do, you never laugh at me for not knowing. You explain carefully or stop what you are doing to show me."

"*Claro*! Of course!" Why not?"

"My ex-husband always laughed at me for not knowing things. If I got upset, he didn't know what to do so walked away. You never do that. You are always there for me in some way."

Hugo pulled Sarah closer to him. Sarah continued, "You can fix things if they are broken; you built our office and put all of Clara's papers and books in order. You are so kind."

Hugo kissed her so tenderly and lovingly, she almost cried. Checking the fire was safe to leave, they too went to bed.

Sarah fell asleep in his arms. Hugo lay awake, studying this woman, her face lit by the moon shining through the window. He realised he had loved her right from the first day she arrived. Although he had been angry and hurting from when Lucia left him and determined not to love anyone again, after a while he could no longer deny it. He had to own up to himself how lovely she was, especially on the day she left to meet Inés in Haria wearing the red dress. He smiled to himself. He knew now what he would do tomorrow. He didn't think Sarah would mind. Still smiling, he drifted off to sleep.

Chapter Forty-Five

Saturday was a clear blue-sky day. The clouds and cool wind of the last few days had gone. José and Hugo strung out fairy lights around the terrace and *finca* and got enough wood nearby to keep all the fires burning for days. Francisco, Bella's brother arrived early to set up his decks and sound system. Finishing touches were put to bowls, platters and cakes. Tables were laid. Flowers arranged. Extra tables were brought to hold more food, wine, beer and glasses. The cava was on ice.

Those who needed to, went home to put on their party clothes. Issie and Elena, who had been there all day, had brought theirs with them.

"Oh my!" said Sarah, clapping her hands as the two sisters came out of the other guest room where they had changed. "Don't you look fabulous!" She made a circular movement with her hands. "Give us a twirl. *Dan os un giro.*"

Laughing they turned around as they had done at the show. Elizabeth came out to see what the merriment was all about.

"Gorgeous!" she said.

"*Gracias*. We wore these at the show and liked them so much, we bought them."

By 5.00 everyone was ready. As if by some unspoken agreement, they were all wearing something in various shades of *Los Palmas* red.

"This calls for a celebration," said Carmen. She disappeared for a moment and reappeared with two bottles of cava and a plate of dark chocolate pastries.

"Palmero de chocolat. This will fortify us and keep us going till dawn," she said.

No-one needed any encouragement and the pastries had soon all disappeared.

By the time the first guests arrived, the music was playing, lights sparkled in the twilight, the fires were all lit. The hosts were well into the party spirit.

Hugo went to dress the camels in their festive harnesses, bells and blankets. He even wove some LED lights along the some of the harnesses. They were in the yard ready to greet the guests. They certainly set the scene. All the guests arrived promptly. It was the first time many of them had met since the Show, even since the Harvest Supper. They were so happy to meet up again. Eventually, Sarah and Hugo got everyone sitting down, ready to enjoy their meal.

Inés was elected as the Maître de for the evening.

"To practice what you have learned," Sarah encouraged her, smiling.

Inés rose to the occasion. She looked immaculate in a red tunic and slim, taupe jeans.

Bowls and plates were refilled or replaced;

Glasses topped up; salads seemed to appear from nowhere. No-one got flustered or left out.

'She could do it naturally, before,' thought Sarah. 'Now she has perfected this talent. Amazing to watch. I would never be able to say quite what she did, but everything all works so smoothly.'

After quite a while, the first course was replaced with desserts, chocolates and sweet treats. Sarah stood and tapped her glass with a spoon, to attract people's attention.

"Thank you, to all of you, for coming here this evening. It is my chance to give you my heartfelt thanks for all the hard work you put into the preparations before the show and on the day. Let's give a toast to Valeria and Bella and their teams. Without them there would have been no clothes; no Show." Everyone stood and cheered.

Valeria said thank you to all the team.

"As a result of the Show," she said, "Myself and Bella are setting up our own couture salon in Haria. It will bring more people to the town; put Haria on the map as a place to go. We have finally collected in all the donations and I am very pleased to say we raised €1,000 for the respite centre – their biggest contribution this year." There were loud cheers and whistles, then lots of women asking for details of where and when their salon would be open.

"A toast to Francisco for the fabulous music and lights on the day and tonight," continued Sarah.

"To Francisco," chorused the guests. He bowed in acknowledgement.

"A toast and a special thanks to all those who made such delicious food and the local farmers who produced the ingredients." Cheers echoed round the valley.

Sarah took a sip of wine to steady her nerves.

"To Issie and Elena and their family, my newly discovered relatives, all descendants of Clara and Estoban Garcia and his family."

More loud applause, cheers and whistles, as they all remembered the dramatic and moving revelations that concluded the Show.

"To Carmen, José and Inés and their families for your friendship and support you have given me since my arrival." She had to swallow hard to clear the emotion that was welling up from her heart and choking her voice. "And finally, to Hugo for everything. He is the most wonderful man I have ever met."

Applause, foot stomps and cheers showed everyone agreed with her. Elizabeth quietly wiped away some tears, so happy her daughter had found a good man after all she had been through. It was such a lovely evening.

Hugo then stood and held up his hand for quiet. An expectant air hung over the tables. "Thank you for all your help," he began. "Mostly, I want to thank Sarah for all she has done since she arrived. She was pale, tense, knowing nothing about farming, vineyards or Spanish. She has been so determined to make a success of the farm, one way or another, to honour the trust her grandmother placed in her. She has always been appreciative of any help shown her and has been ready to help others and to be a part of the farming community in the area. I have been amazed at the way she has included Sweetpea in everything we did and then welcomed Daisy, Sweetpea's daughter."

More cheers and glasses raised to the camels, who nodded and rumbled as if in response.

He took a deep breath and taking Sarah by the hand to help her stand, he said," Sarah, you are the most wonderful, beautiful, generous woman I have ever known." He knelt at her feet. "Will you honour me my becoming my wife?"

A gasp went round all the guests. There was a breathless pause as Sarah got Hugo to his feet. She smiled at him, at her mother, her friends and said "Yes! Yes! Yes!"

Then gave him a long kiss. Cheers, laughter, applause, foot stomping and whistles went on for ages. Francisco put on some upbeat dance music. The guests got up, chatting excitedly, refilling glasses. Soon the yard was full of music, dancing and laughter.

"I think we had better take the camels back to the stables and take off their finery, so they can settle for the night," said Sarah. "They look how I feel – tired and rather overwhelmed."

"Good idea," said Hugo.

Together they gathered up Sweetpea and Daisy, politely asking all the enthusiastic people gathered around the camels, to excuse them but they needed to go back to the stable to rest. Although the camels seemed reluctant to leave all the attention, they went to the stables and gave grunts of relief as the harnesses, blankets, bells and lights were taken off them. The two people settled into their night-time routine of grooming and putting down fresh bedding, food and water. Soon Sweetpea and Daisy were lying down side by side, falling asleep.

The party continued unabated outside, but inside the

stable, even with the door open, it was calm and peaceful. Sarah and Hugo stayed a while leaning against the wall by the door, enjoying the quiet.

"Did you really mean 'yes' just now?" said Hugo. "You weren't just saying it to save me any public embarrassment?"

Sarah smiled, "No, Hugo. I meant a very definite 'yes.' Why would I not want to marry the most wonderful man I know and my partner in the farm?"

"But you know nothing of my family, well, apart from the fact that I am José's nephew. Sadly, my parents were killed in a fishing accident some years ago. They had no family and I had no brothers and sisters. That's when I went to Europe, for a while. When I came back, Carmen and José took me in and made me part of their family, which was fantastic. I know there is only you in your English family. I was so pleased for you when you learned about the family you have here."

"I'm sure Carmen would have warned me off in no uncertain terms if you had been a ne'er do well," said Sarah. "The fact that they treat you as their son speaks volumes about you. It also makes more sense now I know about your parents. I'm so sorry. That must have been a very tough time."

"It happened a long time ago now," said Hugo. "You really meant 'yes'?"

"Of course!" laughed Sarah.

"In that case…" Hugo put his hand in his pocket and brought out a small blue box, "I'd like to give you this."

There, nestled in the red velvet lining was a most beautiful diamond ring. Sarah gave a quick intake of breath and hesitated. He seemed to understand.

"No, this wasn't Lucia's ring. I sold that one soon after she left, throwing the ring to the ground at my feet." He paused, shaking his head. That woman had really shown her true self then and since. He was well rid of her. "This was my mother's," he continued. "She never wore it. I found it tucked away in a bag with a few other pieces of jewellery I had kept after she died. I had it refashioned and remounted when I knew I wanted to marry you."

"It is so beautiful Hugo; thank you."

He slipped it onto her finger. It fitted perfectly. They sealed the gift with a long kiss.

"Come on, you two love-birds; that's enough of that!" It was Inés in the doorway. "Some of the older guests are leaving and want to congratulate you and say goodbye."

She caught sight of the ring. "Oh! That is so beautiful. I'm so happy for you both. Hugo, you are like a brother. Come on. Let's send these people home. They've eaten nearly all the food and there is only one bottle of wine left. Luckily, it is one of our own *Los Palmas* wines… I have hidden it!"

Laughing, all three joined the party. Eventually, everyone left, saying what a great time they had had, how delicious the food and the music was…

"I think Francisco will have a lot of bookings as a result of tonight" said Bella as she left. "He is very pleased he came."

Later, after everything was cleared away, Elizabeth had gone to bed and Carmen, José and Inés had gone to their house, Hugo re-stoked one of the fires and they both sat, sipping their hot chocolate, watching the eastern sky turn salmon, pink, orange then gold as the sun rose one side of the sky and the moon still shone low on the western horizon.

Sarah raised her mug in a toast, "Here's to us watching the sun rise, here, at *finca Los Palmas* together for the rest of our lives," said Sarah and together they went to bed.

About the Author

Wendy lives in the Forest of Dean, England, in an area of beauty, mystery and magic. She has always loved reading and writing stories, and has published two books based in locations in the Forest, called *The Stone Mirror* and *The Dragon Tree.*

Printed in Great Britain
by Amazon